# 'I beg you to take care, my lady.'

Charlotte turned sharply to see his face, wondering why he should take the trouble to warn her. Not that she needed it; she knew very well the precarious situation she was in.

'Stacey, it is taking you a devilish long time to find a couple of bottles of wine.' Cecil stopped suddenly and laughed. 'Oh, I see. Dallying with my sister-in-law, are you?'

Instead of releasing Charlotte, Stacey put his arms about her and drew her close. 'Trust you to come along and spoil things, Cousin,' he said.

'You'll get nowhere with her,' Cecil replied. 'Cold and still as a corpse, that one.'

'Oh, I don't know. She was thawing very nicely before you came and spoiled it.' He felt Charlotte squirm, trying to pull herself away, but he held her closer, and before she could protest had put one forefinger under her chin and tipped her face up to his, so that he could kiss her.

Sensations coursed through her and overcame her resistance. She leaned into him so that their bodies touched and seemed to fuse.

He lifted his head at last, but only to whisper in her ear, 'Do not act the outraged innocent, my lady. Remember what I said and take care.' And with that he kissed her soundly on the cheek and let her go.

Born in Singapore, **Mary Nichols** came to England when she was three, and has spent most of her life in different parts of East Anglia. She has been a radiographer, school secretary, information officer and industrial editor, as well as a writer. She has three grown-up children, and four grandchildren.

**Recent novels by the same author:**

# AN UNUSUAL
# BEQUEST

Mary Nichols

MILLS & BOON®

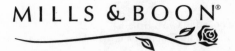

First published in Great Britain 2006
Large Print edition 2006
Harlequin Mills & Boon Limited,
Eton House, 18-24 Paradise Road, Richmond, Surrey TW9 1SR

© Mary Nichols 2006

ISBN-13: 978 0 263 18921 6
ISBN-10:    0 263 18921 X

KE 21. 12. 06
DBC  8. 12. 06

Set in Times Roman 15½ on 17¾ pt.
42-1206-88734

Printed and bound in Great Britain
by Antony Rowe Ltd, Chippenham, Wiltshire

# AN UNUSUAL
# BEQUEST

# Chapter One

*Early 1817*

Charlotte watched as the last of the mourners climbed into their carriages and were driven away. There had not been many of them because Lord Hobart had been old and had outlived most of his contemporaries and in the last four or five years had become something of a recluse, receiving few visitors and never going out beyond the boundaries of Easterley Manor grounds, which stretched from the tiny village of Parson's End in one direction and the lighthouse on the cliff in the other.

'My lady, a sad day.'

The parson's voice brought her back from the contemplation of the sodden garden and the last coach disappearing round the bend in the drive. 'Yes, Reverend, it is. I shall miss him.'

'What will you do?' The Reverend Peter Fuller
was a tall man, as thin as some of his half-starved
parishioners, and Charlotte often wondered how
much of his own food he gave away and how often
he waived the tithe from some farmer who had been
beset by disaster. He was a true Christian gentleman
and they often worked together to alleviate the
plight of the poor in the village and in trying to
bring a little schooling to the children.

'What do you mean?'

'Why, my lady, your father-in-law was a very old
man, you must have given a thought to what might
happen when he died. He has another son and he
will surely be coming back to take over.'

'He is in India where his father banished him, as
I am sure you know, Reverend. No one has secrets
in this village.' Cecil Hobart, younger son of his
lordship, was the proverbial black sheep of the
family. He had been an inveterate gambler in his
youth and his father had stood buff for him on so
many occasions, paying debts amounting to thou-
sands of guineas, that in the end he had said 'enough
is enough' and packed him off to India to make his
own way in the East India Company. At the time his
older half-brother, Charlotte's husband, had been
alive and the banishment had presented no problems
of succession. But Grenville had been killed in

Portugal in 1809, leaving Charlotte a widow and the mother of two daughters. There was no male heir but the absent Cecil.

Even after Grenville's death, Lord Hobart had not recalled his younger son and Charlotte and her two daughters continued to live in the family home, which Charlotte ran with commendable efficiency. In the last two years she had been nurse as well as daughter and housekeeper.

'He will come back just as soon as he hears the news that he is the new Lord Hobart,' the Reverend went on. 'And if he has not changed…' He paused, wondering how much he dare say. Cecil Hobart's reputation was such that he feared for any lady living under his roof. He did not know exactly how old she was, but guessed it was less than thirty, and she was still a very attractive woman with a tendency to believe the best of everyone in spite of evidence to the contrary. It would be easy for a ruthless man to pull the wool over her eyes.

Charlotte turned to face him, her soft aquamarine eyes betraying her sadness at the loss of the man who had been a second father to her and whom she had dearly loved. She knew that her calm, well-ordered life was about to change, that was inevitable, but she didn't want to think about it while grief filled her mind to the exclusion of everything but day-to-day tasks and shielding her two young daughters as far as possible. 'I wrote to Cecil several weeks ago when I realised the end could not be far off,' she said. 'In spite of the estrangement, I know his lordship wanted to see him again before he died. Alas, it was not to be, but perhaps he is on his way now. I must look after everything until he arrives. He may wish me to carry on as I have been doing.'

'And if he does not? Have you no family you can apply to?'

'None, except Lord Falconer, my mother's uncle, and I have never met him. He succeeded to the title when his brother, my grandfather, died, but he quarrelled with Mama when she wanted to marry Papa and said he washed his hands of her.' She smiled briefly. 'His dire warnings that she would regret marrying a nobody of an Irish sea captain were ill founded; my parents were blissfully happy until Papa was killed at Trafalgar. My mother died of a fever less than a year later. Great-uncle Joseph did not write and offer condolences and I assumed the rift was complete. By then I had married Sir Grenville…' She stopped, remembering how bereft she had felt on learning of her husband's death eight years before. Coming so soon after her parents' demise, it had been a terrible blow, but Lord Hobart had been a great comfort. And now, he too, had gone. She had never felt so alone.

'I understand, but, my lady, I strongly urge you to write to your relative. Time may have healed the rift and you may have need of him.'

She smiled wearily. 'I thank you for your concern, Reverend, but I will not go cap in hand to someone who has never even acknowledged my existence. Besides, I do not want to leave Parson's End. I have commitments here. I cannot leave the house and servants with no one in charge, or the village children who rely on me for their schooling.'

She had started the school after Grenville died to give her something to take her mind off her grief and what had begun as a kind of balm for her grieving heart had become a passion to see the education of the poor improved.

'That may be so,' he said, smiling indulgently. 'But that is not reason enough to stay if life becomes intolerable, is it?'

'There is no reason to suppose it will be intolerable and Fanny and Lizzie are upset enough over the death of their grandfather without dragging them away from the only home they have known.'

He had said his piece and there was nothing more he could do for her, except keep a fatherly eye on her. He took his leave and set off at a brisk walk down the drive, his gown flapping out behind him.

Charlotte watched until he was out of sight and then turned back indoors.

It was an ancient house, with irregular rooms, uneven floors, heavy old furniture that had been in its place for generations. Some rooms, like the late Lady Hobart's boudoir, and the drawing room, had been decorated in the modern fashion with light, stylish furniture and colourful drapes, but much of the rest predated the Civil War. But she loved it, old and new. She loved its huge fireplaces, commodious cupboards and chests, its long deep windows overlooking the gardens, impeccably kept and bordered by pine woods on one side and the cliffs and the North Sea on the other. She did not want to leave it.

Old Lord Hobart had been confined to his bedchamber for the past two years, but, even so, the house seemed empty without him. His presence had always filled it, even when he was not actively engaged in the running of it. He had been a big, much loved man, especially by Charlotte and her daughters, but the servants, too, had admired and respected him. He had been a stern employer, but a fair one, and because Charlotte had his unswerving confidence and support, they had obeyed her as if it were the master of the house himself who had issued the orders. Charlotte did not expect anything to change in that respect, not until the new master arrived and took over. After that, she did not know what would happen. The Reverend had not said anything that had not already crossed her mind.

Cecil Hobart was the son of his lordship's second marriage and several years younger than Grenville. She had met him once or twice when she and Grenville had first been married, but the brothers did not get on well together and Cecil spent most of his time in lodgings in London and only came to Easterley Manor when he needed funds. She had not been present in the room the last time he had visited, but she had heard the angry words even through thick closed doors. Afterwards Lord Hobart had sent his younger son not only from his house, but from the country.

'Ten thousand, he owed,' Grenville had told her later. 'And not a hope of recouping. Father threatened to let him stew in his own juice, but of course he could not do that. He has paid his debts and undertaken to make him a reasonable allowance, so long as he stays in India.'

'For the rest of his life?' she had asked.

'One must suppose so, unless he can produce evidence he is a reformed character, but I cannot see that happening.'

'What will happen when your father…when his lordship dies?'

'Then, my dear, the responsibility will rest with me. I shall do whatever my father asks me to do.'

Nothing more had been said, but how was he to know, how was anyone to know, that Grenville would decide to go off on that ill-fated mission to Spain in 1809 and get himself killed alongside General Moore at Corunna? Charlotte, mother of two daughters, Elizabeth, then three years old and Frances, fourteen months, had begged him not to go, that as his father's heir he need not, but Grenville had a strong sense of duty and adventure and seemed convinced of his indestructibility. 'General Moore needs experienced officers,' he had said. 'The Spaniards are brave men but ill disciplined and against Napoleon won't stand a chance without our help. I could not refuse to go. We shall be home again in no time.'

She could not dissuade him and he had set off full of hope and enthusiasm, never to return. Lord Hobart had taken the loss of his son and heir very badly and, though they had comforted each other, it had been the beginning of his downhill slide into senility.

The girls, hearing her mother's visitor leaving, had come along the hall from the kitchen where Cook had been trying to cheer them up with sugar plums. They came each side of her and put their arms about her waist.

'Come, girls, tea in the nursery, I think,' she told them. 'It is peaceful up there and will give the servants the opportunity to tidy up after our visitors. Then we will play a game of cross-questions before bedtime.'

'Will we never see Grandpapa again?' Fanny asked 'Never ever?'

Charlotte looked down at her, wondering how to answer. A blunt 'never' might be accurate, but would only add to the child's grief. While she paused, Lizzie answered for her. 'Course not, he's been put in the ground, but Miss Quinn says he won't stay there but go to heaven and we may see him again when we go there ourselves.' She gave a huge sigh. 'But she said it would be years and years and by then we will be old ourselves.'

Charlotte hugged them both, these daughters who were so dear to her and the only legacy her husband had left her. There was a tiny annuity that had been settled on her as part of the marriage contract, but as the late Lord Hobart had paid all her bills, most of that had been spent on helping the poor among the villagers. Unless the new Lord Hobart saw fit to give her and her daughters a home and continue as his father had done, they would be in dire straits.

Lord Hobart had not expected to lose his heir, nor his wits, and his will had been made years before when Grenville was alive and Cecil out of favour.

The house and estate would go to his elder son, who would tend it and care for it and make it pay just as he had done and his father before him. Cecil had, according to his lordship, already been given all that was due to him when his gambling debts were paid and his allowance fixed upon. The old man had been far more interested in his grandchildren, those already born and those yet to come and all unentailed funds had been left in trust for them, to be administered by trustees. It was an unusual bequest and Charlotte wondered how it would stand up in law, but she had no wish to try to overturn it. It provided for her daughters' dowries and that was all that concerned her. But Grenville had predeceased his half-brother and the Manor now belonged to Cecil.

Mother and daughters mounted the carved oak staircase which rose from the middle of the tiled hall and then up another set of stairs to the second-floor nursery suite and schoolroom where Joan Quinn held sway over her charges. She was waiting for them, her stern, upright bearing belying the loving feelings she had for the two little girls. 'Has everyone gone, my lady?' she asked Charlotte.

'Yes, Quinny, it is all over and now we must try to return to normal.'

'Of course. Tea has been brought up. Will you stay and have some with us?'

'Yes, and I promised the girls a game before bedtime. Tomorrow, we will do whatever we usually do on a Thursday.'

They sat round the nursery table and ate bread and butter, muffins and honey cakes, washed down with weak tea. After five days of being unable to eat properly, Charlotte suddenly found that she was hungry and the simple meal was exactly what she needed. She sipped her tea and surveyed her daughters. They had been broken-hearted by the death of their grandfather, who had always managed to talk to them on their own level and thought up interesting and informative games for them, who had taught them the names of the wild flowers that grew in the park and woods, took them scavenging on the beach and showed them the course of his military campaigns on a map. He had been a great soldier in his day, just as their father had been.

Lizzie was raven haired like her father, with brown eyes so like his that Charlotte was sometimes taken aback when she saw in them the intelligence and pride and refusal to be beaten that had been so characteristic of him. Fanny was softer, more rounded; her hair was paler than her sister's and her complexion pinker. She was the more sensitive of the two and found it hard to accept that Grandpa was not in his room dozing, as he had done so often of late.

'Do you think the new Lord Hobart will come?' Miss Quinn asked Charlotte. She had been Charlotte's governess when she was a child and, when she grew too old to need one, had stayed with her as her maid. Now she fulfilled both functions.

'New Lord Hobart?' queried Lizzie. 'What do you mean? Who is he?'

Miss Quinn looked at Charlotte without speaking. 'He is your Uncle Cecil,' Charlotte answered for her. 'I expect he will be coming soon to take Grandpapa's place…'

'No, no,' Lizzie cried. 'I don't want him to. I don't want anyone in Grandpa's place.'

'Nevertheless, he will come because he owns the house and the estate now and we will make him welcome.'

'Well, I shan't. I shall hate him.'

'Why? It is not his fault your grandfather died.' Even as she spoke she wondered how true that was. How much had sorrow over his younger son contributed to his slide downhill? The loss of Grenville had been the main factor, she was sure, but after that, the estrangement from his younger son had preyed upon his mind, though he was too stubborn to hold out the olive branch. Charlotte knew this, though his lordship rarely spoke of him. A second son, happily in the bosom of his family, prepared to work and take his proper place in the scheme of things might have mitigated his loss. Perhaps Cecil had changed, perhaps he was now ready to face up to his responsibilities…

She distracted the children from the conversation and they finished their tea and set about the game of cross-questions, which occupied them for an hour or so. After they had gone to bed, Charlotte went back downstairs, back to reality, and that set her wondering about the future again and whether her brother-in-law could be relied upon to give her a home. But even if he did, she would still need to find an income from somewhere in order to retain her independence. Whatever happened, she must protect and provide for her children.

The crowd in the card room at White's was noisier than usual. There were four men at one table who had imbibed too freely and were becoming boisterous. Viscount Stacey Darton sat a little way off, idly watching them and wondering how long it would be before they came to blows. One of them looked vaguely familiar and, though he racked his memory, he could not place him. He was thickset and his face was tanned to the colour of rusty hide, even more than Stacey's, which, after three years, still retained a trace of the sun he had caught in Spain. The man was dressed in a black frockcoat and calf-length grey pantaloons at least two years out of date. His neckcloth was drooping and his hair untidy. Though he did not look like one, Stacey assumed he was a gentleman or he would not have been admitted to the club.

His companions were better dressed, young bucks out to fleece someone they saw as a rustic; each had a pile of coins and vouchers at his elbow. The untidy one threw down his cards. 'That's me out, gentlemen. I assume you will take another voucher?'

'What, more post-obit bills, Cecil?' one of his companions enquired. He was tall and so thin his face was almost cadaverous, surrounded by lank dark hair. 'How do we know you will cough up when the time comes?'

Cecil laughed. 'Because the time has already come, Roly, my friend. My revered father was buried today.'

'Good Lord! Should you not have been at the funeral?'

'Why? He never wanted me when he was alive, why should I trouble with him now he's dead?'

'So, you've come into your inheritance at last,

have you?' another asked, looking at Cecil under beetle-black brows. He was shorter and broader than the first speaker, his complexion swarthy.

'Yes, but I'll thank you not to noise it abroad, Gus, or I'll have the dunners on my back before I can retreat.' He laughed harshly. 'Present company excepted, of course.'

'Oh, so you mean to repair into the country soon?'

'Naturally I do. I must take up my inheritance, though what state it is in, I do not know. From what I hear, my father had windmills in his head the last few years and didn't know what he was about.' He laughed again. 'It's all been in the hands of my sister-in-law.'

'What's she like?'

'Oh, she's comely enough, or she was, haven't seen her for years and she's had two bratlings since then, females, luckily for me. I'll soon rid myself of her.' He chuckled. 'Unless she's worth keeping. You never know…'

'Supposing she has married again?'

'Then she will most certainly be out on her ear and her husband along with her. I want no leeches on my back.'

'I think, my friend, you need some protection,' one of the others put in. 'What say we come with you?'

Stacey smiled, knowing the men were not wishing

to protect the man so much as the money he owed them and their debtor was well aware of it, but he shrugged as if it did not matter to him one way or the other. 'Please yourselves, but be warned—the estate is on the coast of Suffolk, miles from anywhere. A dead end.'

'Oh, we'll soon liven it up.'

Stacey was still racking his brain to remember where he had seen the one called Cecil, when he heard his name called. He swivelled round to see a huge man bearing down on him, his face split in a wide grin. 'Stacey Darton, by all that's wonderful!' he exclaimed, holding out his hand as Stacey rose to greet him, revealing himself to be almost as tall and broad as the newcomer.

Stacey had met Gerard Topham in Spain and they had fought alongside each other right to the end of the war, including the aftermath of Waterloo, and become great friends. 'Topham, my old friend, I did not know you were in town.'

'Nor I you. I thought you would be in the country with your family, or I would have let you know I was coming.'

'I needed a respite.'

Gerard laughed and folded his huge frame into the chair next to Stacey's, beckoning to a waiter to bring more wine. 'You've only been back six months and you need a respite? Civilian life not to your liking, my friend?'

Stacey resumed his seat, forgetting the noisy card players. 'Civilian life is fine, if a little dull; family is another matter. My father nags worse than an old woman and as for my daughter—' He stopped suddenly. 'Never mind that, tell me what you are up to.'

Gerard poured from the bottle the waiter had brought. 'I couldn't settle to civilian life either, so I offered my services to the Home Office…'

'Militia? A bit of a comedown after Spain, isn't it?'

'Not militia exactly. I've joined the Coast Blockade.'

Smuggling had fallen away after Pitt reduced the excise duty on tea, but it had received a boost when the wars with Napoleon began and a new line in merchandise offered itself: French prisoners of war going one way, spies coming the other. Later, when the French economy began to totter, English guineas fetched more than their face value. If reports Stacey read in the newspapers were accurate, it was still going on. The Coast Blockade had been formed to combat it. 'Catching free-traders. That must make you very unpopular. Most people accept them, accept what they bring too.'

'Maybe, but free-traders are far from the romantic figures those of us in our comfortable homes imagine them to be, bringing cheap luxuries, and doing no harm. Many of them are discharged soldiers with no work and a dangerous knowledge of firearms, explosives and tactics, learned in the service of their country, and they are putting their knowledge to good use. They are vicious and often murderous if someone stands in their way, and the damage they do to the economy of the country is enormous. Nabbing them is a challenge and I have never been able to resist a challenge. I came to town to report to the Home Office and tomorrow I'm off to ride along the coast, picking up what information I can along the way. Come with me, if you like.'

Stacey was tempted, but, remembering his responsibilities, smiled ruefully. 'I'm afraid I cannot. I must go home.'

'To be nagged?'

'Most likely.'

'What about?'

'Marrying again. My father thinks I have been widowed long enough and my daughter needs a mother, not to mention that he wants a male heir before he dies. Not that he is ailing, far from it. He is hale and hearty. Too hearty sometimes. As for my daughter, she has been thoroughly spoiled by her grandparents. I shall have to take her in hand.'

'And you are not relishing it?'

'She is like a stranger to me, treats me with polite indifference as if I were a visitor who has outstayed his welcome. Understandable, I suppose, considering I was with the army all her life and saw her very infrequently. Her mother was expecting her when I was posted out to India and would not come with me because of her condition and her fear of the climate. In the event she was proved right, because she died having Julia…'

Gerard had known that, but he hadn't known of the difficulties his friend faced on returning home. 'I'm sorry, old man. So, you are in town looking for a wife?'

'My father might wish it, but I don't. Anyway the Season is not yet begun and I am not in the market for a débutante; they are almost always too young and usually too silly. If I remarry, it would have to be someone of my own age or perhaps a little younger if I am to have an heir, with a modicum of intelligence and common sense, not to mention having some regard for me and me for her. I am unlikely to find someone like that in the drawing rooms of the *ton*. It won't be an easy task, considering whoever takes me on has to take my wayward daughter with me, and at this moment I do not feel inclined to inflict her upon anyone.'

'Oh, surely she is not as bad as that?'

'I wish I could say I was exaggerating, but she has become a hoyden of the first water, rides astride her black stallion all over the estate, shoots and fishes and hunts, just as if she were a boy. I wish she were a boy, I could be proud of a male child with those accomplishments. There isn't a feminine bone in her body and at thirteen that is to be deplored.'

'That will change, given the company of other young ladies of her age. Send her away to school.'

'I thought of that, but I can't find one to take her. She doesn't want to go, so, whenever I take her to view a school and meet the teachers, she behaves so badly they won't even consider her. And my father is no help. He humours her in whatever she wants and told me he likes to have her near him.' He stopped suddenly and laughed. 'I am sure you do not want to hear about our family squabbles. Let us have dinner together and talk of old times and free-traders and anything else but wives and children. I assume you have neither shackles.'

'No, and, if your experience is typical, I am glad of it.' He turned as the group of card players behind him tipped over their chairs as they rose drunkenly to go. 'I don't know what White's is coming to, allowing people like that through the doors. Who are they, do you know?'

'No idea,' Stacey murmured. 'That swarthy one with the scar on his cheek seems familiar, but I cannot place him. When you arrived he was telling the others he had just come into his inheritance. If it means a title and some blunt to go with it, I suppose that's why they were admitted.' He watched the men leave, lurching from side to side and grabbing hold of each other for support. 'He said the estate had been run by his sister-in-law of late and he was about to go to Suffolk to claim it from her. I pity her, whoever she is.'

They dismissed the men from their minds and did as Stacey had suggested and ordered dinner and enjoyed a convivial evening reminiscing about their time in Portugal and Spain and the horror that was Waterloo, the terrible state of the economy, the poverty and unrest in the country and the extravagance of the Regent, who must surely be the most unpopular ruler in England's history. And from there they went on to smugglers and lawbreakers generally, many of whom were driven to desperate measures by poverty and hunger, and what could be done to cure the country's ills. By the time they parted, they had set the world to rights and Stacey was feeling more cheerful, though none of his problems had been solved or were on the way to being solved.

* * *

His father had a town house in Duke Street and he
ambled back there at two in the morning, deciding
that he must do something about Julia, though he
freely admitted he knew nothing about bringing up
children, especially girl children fast approaching
womanhood. If only Anne-Marie had not died…

He reflected on his eighteen months of marriage,
eighteen months in which he had bitterly regretted
being talked into it by his parents. 'She will make
an admirable wife,' he had been told. 'She has the
right connections and a good dowry and she is more
than agreeable.' That had been true, but what they
had failed to point out and what he had been too
young to appreciate was that Anne-Marie was little
more than a schoolgirl with an empty head. She
wanted him for what he could provide: the status of
being addressed as 'my lady' and clothes and jewellery, piles and piles of clothes and boxes and boxes
of jewels. She was entirely ignorant of the duties of
a wife and, once he had got her with child, would
have nothing more to do with him and sat about all
day eating sweetmeats. Who could blame him for
purchasing his colours and going off to India to
serve with Sir Arthur Wellesley? Later, after a brief
sojourn at home, he had gone to Spain with him to
share in his setbacks and his victories. Sir Arthur

had been showered with honours and become first Viscount, then Marquis and now the Duke of Wellington, beloved of the people. Stacey came home to a problematic daughter and very little else.

Would Anne-Marie have matured if she had lived? Would their marriage have reached any kind of accommodation? He doubted it. But her legacy was Julia and their daughter was his responsibility, not his father's. He should not have left her so long that he had become a stranger to her. But he did not think returning with a new wife was the answer either. She would then have two strangers to contend with and, as she resented him, how much more would she hate a stepmother? He resolved to return home the next day and take her in hand.

The cold and rain of the last few weeks eased overnight and the sun was trying to shine, though it was hazy and the roads were still full of puddles that drenched pedestrians every time a carriage clattered by. He spent the morning at Gentleman Jackson's Emporium in Bond Street, honing his boxing skills, and the afternoon at Tattersalls, wondering whether to buy a mare to put to his stallion, Ivor. At six o'clock he went home, changed into a travelling coat, ate a solitary meal and took a cab to the Spread Eagle in Gracechurch Street to board the stage for Norwich.

He was only marginally surprised to find three of the card players of the previous evening were also travelling on it. After all, the man called Cecil had said something about going to Suffolk to claim his inheritance and it was roughly in the same direction.

The men were not as rowdy as they had been the night before; in fact, they looked very grey about the face with dull, red-rimmed eyes. Stacey was thankful they were disinclined to talk and, as soon as all the baggage had been stowed and the outside passengers had climbed to their perches, he settled in the corner of the coach and shut his eyes. They were out of town and well on their way before anyone spoke and then it was the man he had heard addressed as Cecil who uttered the first words. 'I know you, don't I?'

Stacey ignored him, but the man leaned forward and poked his knee, repeating his question. Forced to open his eyes, Stacey found the fellow close to him, breathing brandy fumes through blackened teeth, although Stacey noticed he had bought himself a new suit of clothes and was looking tolerably smart. 'I beg your pardon?'

'Don't need to beg my pardon, friend, I was merely passing a comment that we have met before.'

'Have we?'

'I believe so. Hobart's the name. Lord Hobart of Easterley Manor.'

'Your servant,' Stacey said without enthusiasm. He had taken an aversion to the man, though he could not have said why. It wasn't simply his looks, which he could not help, but his manner, which was rough and coarse. And the derogatory way he had spoken of his sister-in-law was not the way of a gentleman. He did not know the woman, but, whoever she was, she surely did not merit such disparagement, especially if she had been looking after his property for him.

'And you are…?' Cecil prompted.

'My name can be of no interest to you.'

'Indeed it is, if we are acquainted.' He suddenly banged his head and laughed. 'Malcomby, that's it! You are the Earl's son. I knew I recognised your physog.'

Stacey groaned inwardly. It seemed the man did know who he was. 'Stacey Darton,' he said.

'The Viscount. Well, well. After all these years.'

'I am afraid I do not recall…'

'No, you would not, I was only a young shaver at the time and you were a Captain of Hussars, very grand, I thought you. I might have taken up the sword to defend king and country myself if I had not had business on the sub-continent. Do you still not remember where we met?'

Stacey shook his head. In spite of his apparent indifference he was curious.

'It was at my mother's funeral. She was Madeleine Stacey, your father's cousin. You were named for her.'

'Cousin?' He remembered now. Madeleine was daughter to his father's aunt and as, at the time of her death, he had returned from India and was waiting to rejoin his regiment, he had gone with his father to the funeral. And this uncouth man was her son. He could hardly believe it, did not want to believe it.

'That makes us second cousins, does it not?' Cecil held out his hand. 'How d'you do, Cousin.'

Stacey, never an uncivil man, shook the hand and was then obliged to shake hands with his companions who were agog with curiosity. 'May I present my friends,' Cecil said, 'This is Mr Augustus Spike.' He indicated the beetle-browed man sitting beside him. 'And that spidershanks sitting beside you is Sir Roland Bentwater. We are off to Parson's End to claim my inheritance.' He evidently had not noticed Stacey at White's the night before. 'My dear father recently slipped his wind, but, though he sent for me, I sadly did not arrive in time to see him alive.'

'I am sorry to hear that,' Stacey said politely.

'And you, where is your journey taking you?'

'Home to Malcomby Hall.'

'Is it the first time you have been home? Since the war, I mean.'

'No. I returned six months ago.'

'And how is your delightful wife?'

'She died several years ago.'

'I am sorry for that.' The man did not seem to notice Stacey's perfunctory answers. 'And how are the Earl and Countess?'

'They are both well.'

'Good, good. I wonder you choose to travel by public coach when there must be horses and carriages to spare at Malcomby Hall.'

Stacey was beginning to wonder himself; his father would have allowed him to take the carriage, but he knew his mother used it all the time and he did not want to deprive her of it, especially as he did not know how long he would be gone. There was a gig and a phaeton, but they were not suitable for long journeys, nor would his parents use them when the weather was inclement, as it had been. The stage seemed the sensible choice, but now it looked as though he was going to have to spend several hours in the company of this unlikeable fellow.

He was saved having to answer when the coach pulled up at an inn for their first change of horses. He did not bother to go inside for refreshment, but waited in the coach. Half an hour later, they were off again, but, as more passengers had joined them and kept the conversation going, Stacey had only to put in an occasional remark. It grew dark and the countryside could no longer be seen except as a blur of trees and hedgerows; the talk became more desultory and many of the passengers dozed. It was easy for Stacey to pretend to do likewise.

It was gone three in the morning when the coach rumbled into the yard of the Great White Horse in Ipswich. 'This is where we part company, Cousin,' Cecil said. 'Parson's End is not on a regular coach route, so we must rack up here and make other arrangements to continue our journey. But we are in no hurry and who knows—we might find a snug little inn somewhere where the play is good.'

The coach pulled up in the yard of the inn and immediately the business of changing the horses was begun. Cecil Hobart and his friends tumbled out. Before shutting the door, Cecil turned back to Stacey. 'Give the Earl and Countess my greetings, won't you?' he said. 'You must bring them to Easterley Manor to visit when I have settled my affairs.'

'They do not travel far these days.'

'No? Well, neither did my father. But there is nothing to stop you coming, is there? Families should not lose touch, should they? But leave it a day or two, give me time to settle in.'

Stacey smiled and bowed his head politely in

response. That the man should turn out to be a relative was repugnant to him and he had no intention at all of visiting him, or even of thinking of him again. People were always claiming they knew him or were related to him, simply because of his title and wealth and whatever advantage they thought the connection might bring. Only in the army with people like Captain Gerard Topham was his title ignored and he was recognised by his rank of Major, which was the one he preferred.

The coach continued on its way with different passengers, taking the road to Norwich where it stopped at the Old Ram coaching inn where he had left his mount. Here he ate breakfast before setting off on horseback to complete his journey.

The sun was warm on his back as he rode and the birds were singing as if to tell him the winter was gone and spring was on its way. His spirits rose. Perhaps he would find Julia in a better frame of mind, ready to listen to him and behave in a more comely fashion. He was sorely disappointed within a few minutes of turning in the great iron gates of Malcomby Hall.

Deciding to take a short cut through the trees rather than ride along the gravelled drive that meandered on its way to the house, his attention was drawn to Julia's stallion, Ebony, tethered with another horse in a small clearing. He drew up and was wondering where Julia was and who owned the other animal, when he heard the sound of laughter coming from the direction of the lake. He dismounted and, leaving his horse with the others, trod softly towards the sound. Coming out of the trees at the side of the lake, he was stopped in his tracks by the sight that greeted him.

Cold as it was, Julia was bathing in the water and she was completely naked, her long blond hair loose and flowing out around her head; what was worse, there was a young lad with her, also completely naked. They were laughing and splashing each other like small children. But they were no longer children. She was thirteen, her body was that of a young woman. He was struck dumb for several seconds and then he roared. He roared loud and long. Startled, the boy and girl looked round and began a mad scramble to get out and retrieve their clothes, lying on the bank

'Julia, stay where you are,' Stacey shouted. 'You, whoever you are, get dressed and come here.'

The boy scrambled into his pantaloons, picked up his shirt and coat, but, instead of approaching Stacey, disappeared into the trees. Stacey let him go and turned his attention to his daughter. She was out of the water and standing with her back to him, pulling a chemise over her head. Even in his fury, he could appreciate her youthful curved figure, with its neat waist. 'When you are decently dressed, you may join me by the horses,' he said, and turned from her to retrace his steps. She came to him two minutes later, flashing defiance from her blue eyes. 'I don't know why you are making such a fuss,' she said as she scrambled into her saddle. 'We were doing no harm.'

He could not trust himself to speak, but mounted his own horse and, picking up her reins, led her horse back towards the house without saying a word. It was an indignity that infuriated her and she tugged once or twice on the reins to try and wrest them from him, but, when she failed, slumped in her saddle and completed the journey in smouldering silence.

'Go up to your room,' Stacey told her when they reached the side door of the house nearest the stables. 'Get dressed properly and, when you are fit to be seen, come down to the library. I wish to speak to you.'

After she had gone, he left the horses with the grooms and made his way slowly into the house, completely at a loss to know how to deal with the situation. He passed the drawing room on his way to the library. The door was open and his parents were sitting one on each side of the hearth; his mother was doing some embroidery and his father

was reading a newspaper. They looked so complacently content, he was incensed all over again. 'So
this is how you look after my daughter in my
absence, sir,' he said, stopping in the doorway to
glare at them. 'Reading and stitching while she is
running wild. Thanks to you, she is ruined beyond
redemption.'

'Oh, dear, what has she done now?' his mother
asked.

'You may well ask. I rode through the woods on my
way home and what did I find? My daughter, your
beloved granddaughter, swimming in the lake…'

'Oh, dear, it is so cold,' Lady Malcomby said.
'She will catch her death. I hope you have sent her
to Susan to be warmed.'

'If she were a boy I would warm her myself, I'd
dust her breeches so she could not sit down for a
week,' he said.

'Oh, come,' his father said. 'That's doing it too
brown.'

'You have not heard the worst of it. She was naked
as the day she was born—'

'Naked!' shrieked her ladyship, dropping her embroidery. 'You mean she had no clothes on?'

'Not even her chemise. Nor was she alone. There
was some yokel with her. They were laughing and
splashing each other…'

'Was he also… Oh, dear, was he…?'

He nodded. 'Not a stitch. Now perhaps you will tell me how to proceed, for I am sure I do not know what to do. I fear I shall thrash her as soon as look at her.'

'Won't help,' his father said. 'She is a child and I doubt she sees any wrong in what she has done and making a mountain out of it will only make her more wilful.'

'She is not a child.' He was almost shouting. 'She is nearly a woman. If you had seen her as I did, coming out of the water, you would know that. Children grow up, you know, they do not remain children just because you would like them to. Had you not noticed that?'

'Can't say I had,' his father said complacently. 'But I suppose you are right.'

'Then what am I to do?'

'Lock her in her room for a few hours, I find that usually does the trick.'

Stacey laughed harshly. 'Do you suppose locking her bedroom door will contain her? I'll wager she can get out of the window and down the ivy as easily as I once could.'

'Could you?' his mother asked, diverted. 'I didn't know that.'

'Who was the boy?' the Earl asked.

'I have no idea and tracking him down will serve

no purpose; she is too young to be married off. It is Julia I am concerned with. She will have to go away to be taught how a young lady should behave. Someone, somewhere, must be prepared to take her.' He turned from them and made for the library just as Julia descended the stairs. She looked demure in pale pink spotted muslin with a deep rose sash, and her hair tied back with a matching ribbon. She held her head high and was followed by Susan Handy, the stout, middle-aged woman who was her governess and who had been his nurse and governess. She had evidently come with her to make sure he did not carry out his threat to thrash her darling.

He smiled grimly. Miss Handy was quite unable to control her charge because she was too indulgent and too fat and breathless to run after her when she escaped. He ought to have done something about her when he first returned home two years before, but he hadn't had the heart to dismiss her, for where would she go? 'I do not need you, Miss Handy,' he said coldly. 'You may wait for Julia upstairs.'

'You will not be unkind to her, Master Stacey? I am sure she is very sorry for being naughty and will be good in future.'

'That we shall see,' he said coldly, ushering his daughter into the library ahead of him. His red-hot fury had abated and he was now icily calm.

'Papa…' she began.

'You will not speak, you will not say a word until I say you may. I am very angry with you and if I ever get my hands on that young man…'

'But it was not his fault. I found him bathing in the lake and it looked so inviting…'

'That's enough!' he roared. 'You will tell me honestly, did he touch you? Did he behave in any way…?' He did not know how to put into words what he was asking.

'Of course he did not,' she said haughtily. 'He would not dream of laying hands on the grand-daughter of an earl.'

He breathed a sigh of relief. 'Let us be thankful for that. You are going away to school, even if I have to scour the length and breadth of the country to find one that will take you, and nothing you can say or do will make me change my mind.'

She would not cry. He could see her herculean efforts to control her tears in the way she blinked and gulped and lifted her chin even higher and he admired her for it, but he would not weaken. 'Until I say you may, you will stay in your room, and Miss Handy will find some fitting study for you. A book on ladylike behaviour would be suitable if such a thing is to be found.'

'Yes, my lord.'

*My lord,* she called him, just as if they were mere acquaintances and not father and daughter. It cut him to the quick, but he made no comment and waved her away, too choked to speak. He watched her go, wanting to rush after her and hug her, to tell her everything would be all right and he understood, but he could not; she was too much like her dead mother. He had to find an establishment headed by an understanding woman who would make a lady of her without breaking her spirit. And where was such a one to be had?

## Chapter Two

Charlotte was chasing children along the beach when Stacey first saw her, running round and round and being caught and then setting off again, her arms wide, her bonnet askew, while the children squealed their delight. He reined in his horse to watch. His father had told him of a school in Ipswich that might take Julia and he had decided to ride along the coastal path rather than take the stage. He didn't know why, except that it might be quieter and more conducive to problem solving than being bumped about in a coach and having to listen to his fellow travellers trying to make conversation. And he could take his time. Why he wanted to delay, he did not know. He strongly suspected it was because he was not sure he was doing the right thing in trying to pack his daughter off to strangers. Wasn't that abrogating his responsibility? In the meantime she was safe enough at Malcomby Hall; his father had promised to keep a closer eye on her.

He had been deep in thought, clopping slowly along the cliff-top path when the sound of childish laughter brought him up short. How happy they sounded. He had ridden to the edge of the cliff and sat looking down at the beach. How many children were there? Ten, a dozen? Surely they could not all belong to the woman? She was how old? It was difficult to tell at that distance, but surely not old enough to have borne so many? And they were all different: some were dark, others fair, some warmly clad, others dressed in little more than rags. All but the woman were barefoot and a row of little boots and shoes stood sentinel on the side of the steep path that led down from the cliff top to the beach. The woman herself was dressed in a simple black gown and cape. Mourning, perhaps? But should a woman in mourning be laughing so joyfully?

Charlotte stopped suddenly, too out of breath to continue, and the children crowded round her, chattering excitedly. It was then she looked up and saw him. He was astride a big white stallion, dressed in a serviceable riding coat and a big cape. He doffed his tall riding hat and bowed to her. Discomforted, she looked away and began urging the children to gather up the seaweed and shells they had collected, while retying her bonnet, which had slipped down her back on its ribbons. Then she led them up the path towards him. He had not moved. Her first thought had been that it was Cecil who had come to claim his inheritance, but, as she drew nearer, she realised it was not. This man was a stranger and a very handsome one at that. Again, he doffed his hat, his brown eyes alight with amusement. 'Good day, ma'am.'

'Good day, sir.'

'You have a very large family, ma'am.' She was extraordinarily beautiful, he realised, with a clear unblemished complexion and eyes that were neither green nor blue, but something in between, and they looked him straight in the eye.

She smiled. 'Yes, haven't I? But I cannot claim them all for myself. These two are mine…' She drew Lizzie and Fanny to her. 'The others are my pupils.'

'Ah, you are a schoolteacher.'

She opened her mouth to correct him, then changed her mind. Today she *was* a schoolteacher and perhaps, if Cecil proved not to be amenable, that was all she ever would be. She would try out the role on a stranger.

She loved teaching the little ones of the village; they were so receptive and eager to learn. Their parents had been against the idea at first, demanding to know why they needed an education; they themselves had managed without one and so would their sons and daughters. Charlotte and the Reverend Fuller had persuaded them to agree to send the children to school, so long as they were not needed to help on the farms with which the countryside around was dotted. Picking stones off the fields, scaring crows, watching the sheep, and helping with the harvest would always take precedence, and some were expected to look after younger siblings, but as they were allowed to bring the little ones to the classes, they gathered each afternoon in an unused coach house at the Rectory, which had been converted into a classroom, and here they learned to read and count. The bright ones among them were learning to write and to compose little stories, with particular attention being paid to their spelling and grammar.

Nor was that all; she taught them a little history and geography and took them out in the lanes and on to the beach to study nature. Being country children, they knew as much of country lore on a practical level as she did, but they all enjoyed the outings. And that included Lizzie and Fanny, whom she took with her. Lord Hobart, before he became too ill to know what was going on around him, had remonstrated with her for allowing her daughters to associate with the lower orders, but she had persuaded him there was no harm in it and it might do the girls some good.

The other children had been wary of them to begin with; Lizzie and Fanny, clad in their warm clothes and stout shoes, were inclined to be a little haughty, aware of their superior status, but they had soon learned to unbend. It was surprising, or perhaps it was not, just how much they were able to teach the other children and how much they learned themselves. Not all of it desirable!

Today, with her mind full of the loss of her father-in-law and uncertainty about the future, she had been unable to concentrate on lessons and had decided to bring the children to the beach to study the life in the pools left behind by the tide. It was the first really mild day of the year; the turbulent winds and heavy rain that had drenched the countryside from the beginning of the year right up until the day of Lord Hobart's funeral had gone and now the air was clear. Down on the beach, the sea rippled gently over the sand, leaving behind little rock pools, teaming with microscopic life. It was so pleasant there and the children so excited, they had ended up playing a game of tag. She had been as energetic as the children, behaving like a child herself. Her hat had come off and the pins had come out of her hair, which could not be described as fair, but was not dark enough to be called auburn. To her it was a nothing colour, but to the observer on the cliff top it was delightfully unusual.

To have her behaviour witnessed by this rather superior horseman, who obviously found her conduct amusing, was disconcerting, but it was too late to revert to being the lady of the manor. She smiled. 'Yes, sir. Today we are having a little break from formal lessons to learn about the sea and the tides and the creatures who live in the rock pools.'

'So, I see.' Again that smile. 'I would that my school days had been as instructive.' He was bamming her, she knew.

'You did not like school?' The children had grouped themselves around her, staring up at the man in curiosity, almost as if protecting her. She turned to them. 'Put your shoes on, children.'

He watched idly as they obeyed, the older ones helping the smaller ones. One or two, he noticed, had no footwear at all. They were village children, being taught at a dame school, he supposed, but an unusual one. Dame schools usually confined themselves to teaching children their letters, and not even that sometimes. The teachers were often nearly as ignorant as their pupils, but this one was not like that. She was neat and well spoken and elegant, even in her plain black gown. 'I liked it well enough,' he answered her. 'A necessary evil.'

'How can you call it an evil? You undoubtedly had a privileged education, which is more than these little ones will have.' She did not know why she was being so defensive towards a stranger, but he had put her hackles up, sitting there on that very superior horse with his very superior air, criticising her. 'I can teach them little enough, but I do not think they see it as an evil.'

'No, I am sure they do not, considering they are allowed to disport themselves running about in bare feet and shouting at the top of their lungs. What is that teaching them?'

'It is teaching them to be happy, that there is more to life than hard work. It is teaching them to deal well with each other…'

'And you think such lessons are necessary?'

'Indeed, I do.'

'And what else do you teach them? When you are in the classroom, that is?'

Why was he quizzing her, why did he not simply ride away? she asked herself. What did he know of poverty? His clothes were plain, but they were made of good cloth and were well tailored. His riding cloak was warm and the horse he rode was a magnificent beast with powerful muscles and a proud head. Its glossy coat was almost pure white, except for a grey blaze on its nose. 'I teach them to read, write and count and a little of the world beyond their narrow horizon.'

'And polite behaviour?' He really did not need to ask; the children were lined up in pairs, holding each other's hands, waiting patiently to be told to move.

'Of course. But if you are referring to the affectations which go by the name of politeness in society, I am afraid that passes them by. Now, if you will excuse me, the wind is becoming a little chill and, unlike you, they do not have warm cloaks. Come, children.'

She picked up the smallest, a child of no more than two, and, taking another by the hand, led them away. The two girls she had claimed as her own were well clothed, but not extravagantly so. Did she have a husband? Or was the black dress a sign of widowhood? A gentlewoman come upon hard times, perhaps. She intrigued him.

He started his horse forward, moving slowly along the top of the cliff, thinking about schools and Julia and a handsome and intelligent woman who had managed to put him in his place. Out on the sea a few fishing boats rocked on the swell and ahead of him was a lighthouse, which reminded him of Gerry Topham. He supposed it was the kind of area he patrolled as an excise officer. He envied his friend his independence; not for him worries about a reprobate daughter and a father who insisted he ought to marry again. His experience of marriage did not incline him to repeat the experiment; as for children, they appeared to be more a bane than a blessing. But was that necessarily true? The school-teacher seemed perfectly at ease with them and they had been quiet and obedient when she had brought an end to their game and led them up the path towards him. If only he could find someone like her to tame Julia. His aimless thoughts were brought to an abrupt end when his horse stumbled. He dismounted to see what the trouble was and realised Ivor had cast a shoe.

'Damnation!' he exclaimed and looked about him for signs of habitation where a blacksmith might be found. There was nothing ahead of him, but, looking back, he could see a stand of pine trees and a curl of smoke that could only be the village to which the woman and the children were returning. Smiling a little, he turned the stallion and led him back to the spot where he had met them and from there followed a well-defined path that cut through the pines. He wondered if he might catch them up, but he did not do so before he found himself in the middle of the main street of the village.

There was a huddle of cottages, a church, an inn, some farm buildings and a smithy, to which he directed his steps. There were a few women on the street, who watched his progress with curiosity, but no sign of the schoolteacher and her charges. He surprised himself by feeling a little disappointed.

He found the blacksmith in his heavy leather apron hard at work beating a horseshoe into shape on his anvil, the ringing tones of his hammer and the flying sparks filling the air with a kind of eternal rhythm, at one with the days of the week and the recurring seasons. Beside him stood a sturdy Suffolk Punch, patiently waiting to receive the new shoe. Stacey stood and watched, knowing it would not do to interrupt in the middle of the task, but when it was done, the old blacksmith looked up. 'Yer need my services, stranger?'

'I do indeed. My horse has cast a shoe. Can you fix it for me?'

The old man followed him outside to where he had left the stallion with its reins thrown loosely over the hitching rail. After a cursory inspection all round the animal, he said, ''Tis a mighty fine animal yer have here.'

'Yes. His name's Ivor. I bought him off a Russian Count in Austria. He's seen me through many a battle.'

'Ridden him all the way from Austria, have yer?' It was said with a chuckle.

Stacey laughed. 'No, just from the other side of Norwich. Why do you ask?'

'All his shoes are worn. It i'n't no good replacing the one.'

'No, I realise that.'

'I've to take the horse back to the farm.' He nodded his head in the direction of the Suffolk Punch. 'It'll take me an hour or so.'

'It'll be growing dusk by then, too late to carry on tonight. Is there an inn where I can rack up?'

'There's the Dog and Fox. They'll give yer a bed. I'll have the horse ready by the time yer've had yar breakfast.'

'I'm in no hurry,' he said, and wondered why he said it. He turned to take his bag from the saddle. 'By the way, what is this village?'

'Parson's End, sir.'

Parson's End. What a strange name for a village. He had heard it before, he realised. And then he remembered Lord Hobart. Wasn't that his destination? What quirk of fate had brought him here? He could, he supposed, go the Manor and remind Hobart of his invitation, but then he remembered how unlikeable the man was and decided the Dog and Fox would suit him very well.

\* \* \*

Charlotte was in the garden the following morning when a footman came to tell her she had visitors. Gardening was one of her special pleasures and she would spend hours tending her flowers and consulting Harman, the head gardener, on which plants to place where and how to propagate and care for them. Clad in an old fustian coat, a floppy felt hat tied under her chin with a piece of ribbon and a pair of stout canvas gloves, she would dig and weed and clip to her heart's content. She had certainly not expected visitors today.

'Who is it, Foster?'

'Not one of your usual callers, my lady. Pushed past me and strode into the drawing room as if he owned the place…'

'Perhaps he does,' she murmured under her breath.

He looked startled, but went on as if he had not heard. 'And him with two companions that I never would have admitted if I could have stopped them. I am sorry, my lady.'

'Do not worry, Foster. I think I know who one of them is. Ask Cook to provide refreshment and tell them I will join them shortly.'

He left on his errand and she went in by a side door, along a narrow passage and up the back stairs to her room where she washed and changed hastily into a black silk mourning dress, a little more elegant than the one she had been wearing the day before, which had become stained with salt water, much to Joan Quinn's disgust. She brushed her hair, coiling it back and fastening it with combs before topping it with a black lace cap, then she took a deep breath and went down the front stairs to the drawing room.

There were three men there, two of whom were already lounging on the green brocade sofas, looking about them as if assessing the worth of everything in the room, the furniture, pictures and the small figurines which her mother-in-law had loved to collect. The third man stood by the hearth with his foot on the fender. His attitude was proprietorial and she had no difficulty in recognising her brother-in-law, though the scar on his face had not been there when she last saw him, and the slimness of youth had been replaced by fat that strained at his coat and pantaloons.

'Cecil?' she said.

He made her a mock bow. 'At your service, sister. May I present my good friends, Sir Roland Bentwater and Mr Augustus Spike?'

The two men, one tall and thin as a pole, the other thickset and swarthy, rose and sketched her a bow to which she replied with a slight movement of her head. 'Gentlemen.' Then, addressing Cecil, 'I did not know you would be coming today. If you had let me know, I would have been better prepared to receive you…'

'We don't need receiving. This is my house, I come and go as I please.'

'Of course. I am sorry you were not here in time to speak to your father before he died—'

'Sorry? Was he sorry he banished me, was he anxious to make amends?'

'I believe he was.'

'That's as may be, but I have not forgiven him, nor would I have, so perhaps it is as well we did not meet again.'

She decided to ignore that. 'I have ordered refreshment. While you are having that, I will have your room prepared.'

'My father's room, I hope. The master bedroom.'

'Why, no, I did not think you would want to use that until it had been refurbished. But, of course, you may have things ordered as you wish.'

'I wish to sleep in my father's bed and I wish rooms prepared for my friends and our valets who will be arriving with our luggage before the day is out.'

'Very well. If you excuse me, I will see to it. Foster will serve you while I am gone.'

'Foster, who is he?'

'The footman. He admitted you.'

'Oh, him.' His tone was disparaging. 'What happened to Jenkins?'

'He grew old and decided to retire. He lives in a cottage on the cliff top now.'

'I think I had better interview all the staff, let them know who is master. I'd be obliged if you would gather them all together in the hall in an hour.'

She inclined her head to acknowledge the instruction and left the room in as dignified a manner as she could manage, but she was seething. The new Lord Hobart was treating her like a housekeeper, not a word of condolence or sorrow at the loss of his father, not a word of gratitude for what she had done to keep the place going, not a word of reassurance that she would be given a home. And if he did offer it, she was not at all sure she would accept—she had taken an instant aversion to him. She passed Foster bearing the tea tray, followed by one of the maids with cakes and sweetmeats, and instructed them to serve the refreshments before carrying on her way up the stairs to warn Miss Quinn to keep the girls to their own suite of rooms until she said they could come down.

Then she went back downstairs to the kitchen where the servants were gossiping and speculating about the new master. She brought them to order and gave instructions for her belongings to be moved out of the bedchamber she had used on the first floor. She had chosen it when the late Lord Hobart became ill so that she would be close at hand if he needed her, but if the new Lord Hobart meant to occupy his father's room it was not appropriate nor desirable. 'I'll use the guest room on the top floor near the girls,' she told the chambermaids. 'One of his lordship's guests can have my room and prepare another along the same corridor for the other. And rooms for the valets who are on their way, I believe.'

'And his lordship?' Betsy asked, longing to make some comment about her ladyship having to give up her room for those dreadful men, but not daring to.

'The old lord's room. I'll come and help you directly. When you have done, all the servants are to assemble in the hall to meet the new master.'

'All of us?' Cook asked.

'Yes, all. Tom, go and tell the outside staff to come too. In…' she consulted the clock that stood on the mantle '…three-quarters of an hour. Leave whatever you are doing and line up in the hall.'

There were not many servants for so large a house and Cecil, pacing up and down the row, a full wine glass in his hand, was obviously surprised. 'Is this everyone?' he demanded of Charlotte.

'It is. When Lord Hobart became too ill to receive visitors, we shut up half the house and did not need a large staff.'

'I want the rooms opened up again. I mean to entertain. As for staff, we shall see how these do before deciding on others.' He waved his hand to dismiss them all. 'Go back to your work. We will dine at five.'

They scuttled off and he turned to Charlotte 'Are you sure I have seen everyone? I recollect you have two daughters…'

'They are not servants, my lord, to be paraded before you.'

'But they do live here? They are not away at school?'

'They are too young to go away. I look after them myself with the help of Miss Quinn, their governess.'

'Who pays her wages?'

'Lord Hobart did.'

'Hmm. I am not sure that I wish to continue that arrangement. After all, your offspring have no claim on the estate, have they? I would rather employ a decent butler.'

'But they are your nieces, my lord, all the kin you have now.'

'I intend to marry, then I shall have kin of my own.'

'I see.'

'I am sure you do,' he said, smiling silkily.

She did not answer. Her head was whirling with the knowledge that her brother-in-law was not going to be bountiful, that if she stayed, she would stay under sufferance and be an unpaid housekeeper, that Miss Quinn would probably be dismissed and her girls would be faced with a life very different from the one they had known. And when the horrible man married, what would happen to them then?

'Food for thought, eh?' he queried.

'It is your business,' she said. 'May I ask when you are to be married?'

He laughed. 'When I have found a suitable bride, one who will acknowledge who is master in his own house and will do as she is told.' He looked up as his two companions sauntered down the stairs from an inspection of their rooms. 'You need say nothing of this conversation to my friends,' he murmured, then, turning to them, said jovially, 'Have you been made comfortable? Is everything to your satisfaction?'

'It'll do for now,' Sir Roland said, wafting his quizzing glass around. 'But it's devilish dull here, ain't it?'

'I warned you it would be, didn't I? You can always return to the Smoke.'

'Oh, I don't think we want to do that just yet, do we, Gus?'

'No, not yet,' the other answered. 'But I think you should put on some entertainment for us. Send for some company.'

Charlotte knew by the way they spoke that Cecil did not really want them there, that they had invited themselves and there must be a reason why he had not been able to refuse. It was a reason not difficult to guess. And did they also know the contents of Lord Hobart's will? They were in for a shock if they did not.

'All in good time, gentlemen,' he said. 'Shall I show you over the house? You will find much to interest you, I am sure.' Then, to Charlotte, 'I shall expect you to dine with us. And bring your daughters.'

'My lord, they do not usually dine with company.'

'I am not company. As you so succinctly reminded me, I am their uncle and I wish to meet them.'

'Very well. I will ask Miss Quinn to bring them down when the pudding is served.'

She turned and left him, passing the two gentlemen as she made for the stairs. She was aware that they were watching her go and she held her head high, but inside her heart felt as heavy as lead. The home she had known for the last twelve years was hers no longer; she was not even welcome in it. She made her way up the second flight of stairs to the schoolroom where her daughters worked under the tutelage of Miss Quinn.

All three turned towards her as she entered. 'Mama, what has happened?' Lizzie asked. 'Who are those men?'

Charlotte looked at Miss Quinn, her eyebrow raised in a query.

'They heard the door knocker, my lady,' the governess said. 'Such a noise it made, as if someone was determined to frighten us all out of our wits. The girls ran to look over the banister and saw them admitted.'

'One of them is your Uncle Cecil,' Charlotte told them. 'The other two are his guests.'

'The new Lord Hobart?' queried Lizzie.

'Yes.'

'I knew I should not like him,' Fanny put in. 'And I do not. I wish they would all go away again.'

'I am afraid that is unlikely,' Charlotte said. 'We must get along with your uncle as best we may. You never know, he might turn out quite charming.' She did not believe what she was saying, but she must not allow her prejudices to influence them. 'He has asked that you join us for pudding this evening, so I want you on your best behaviour. And, Fanny, please, please do not let your dislike show and speak only when you are spoken to.'

'My lady,' Miss Quinn gasped, 'surely that is hardly appropriate. Those men...'

'I know, Quinny, I know, but I shall be there, and

I shall not allow the girls to stay more than a few minutes. Bring them when I send for them and stay close at hand to take them back.'

'I don't know what the world is coming to, that I don't,' Miss Quinn went on. 'I'm with Fanny, I do not like those men. Lord Hobart is bad enough, but those two fops… They fill me with dread. I saw them poking in all the rooms, laughing and commenting on everything, saying there were some mighty fine pieces. I heard the thin one say, "We've fallen on our feet here, Gus, no doubt of it." And then they both laughed. Horrible sound it was too, like hens cackling. How long are they proposing to stay?'

'I don't know,' Charlotte answered with a sigh. She was too distressed to scold the governess for speaking her mind.

'If it weren't for my darlings needing me, I'd be gone this very night—' She stopped suddenly when she realised Lizzie was looking at her in great distress and Fanny had begun to sob. 'Oh, my little loves,' she said, gathering them into her arms. 'Quinny didn't mean that. She would never leave you, never, never.'

Dinner was a nightmare. Charlotte tried to keep up a normal polite conversation, but it was impossible. Everything she said, they seemed to twist, and they asked such impertinent questions that she refused to answer, which made Cecil laugh, though his laughter was hollow. How long had the Hobarts occupied Easterley Manor, they wanted to know, and did she know the value of everything in it? And when she said she did not know and it was the province of his lordship's man of business to provide him with an inventory, they had laughed loud and long. 'I expect him tomorrow,' Cecil said. 'Then we shall see.'

Worse was to come when he insisted she send for her daughters. 'I wish to make their acquaintance,' he said. 'After all, they are part of the job lot, aren't they? Kith and kin I must include in my reckoning.'

'You are mistaken there, my lord,' she said, reluctantly nodding to Foster to fetch Miss Quinn and the girls. 'They are my responsibility.'

'But only this morning you were reminding me of my duty towards them.'

'I did not mean you should tot them up on your inventory.'

'You mean I am not to be responsible for their keep? How glad I am of that. Food, clothes, wages for that Miss… What's her name?'

'Miss Quinn.'

'Miss Quinn. From now on you pay her yourself.'

Charlotte did not protest. She would not throw herself on his mercy, though how she was going to manage she did not know. She looked up as the door opened and Miss Quinn ushered her charges into the room. They looked very fetching in white muslin dresses, with deep satin sashes and their hair brushed until it gleamed and tied back with matching ribbons. Lizzie's was blue and Fanny's pink. Quinn gave them a little poke in the back and they both executed a neat curtsy.

'Very pretty,' Augustus chortled, surveying them through his quizzing glass. 'What say you, Roly, ain't they pretty?'

'Yes, remarkably handsome. Cecil, old man, I think you should be more generous with your dead brother's children. Put them on the inventory.'

Cecil pretended to laugh. 'Come, girls, come to me and let me see you properly. Don't be afraid. No one will hurt you. I am your Uncle Cecil, home from abroad to take care of you.'

They approached the table to join their mother, reluctant to go to him. 'They are shy,' Charlotte said. 'Not used to strangers.'

'I am not a stranger!' he shouted, banging his fist on the table, making the crockery rattle. 'I am Lord of the Manor, Squire of Parson's End. Home from abroad. Home, do you hear me?'

'My lord, please do not shout. You are frightening them.'

His voice softened, but was no less menacing. 'Then remember not to behave as if I were an uninvited guest you cannot wait to get rid of. It is you who are the guests, you and your daughters, and that one…' He nodded towards Miss Quinn hovering in the doorway. To the children he said, 'Would you like to sit with us and have some apple pie?'

Both girls, too frightened to speak, shook their heads. He beckoned to Miss Quinn. 'Take them away, they are not as amusing as I thought they might be.'

Quinn disappeared with her charges and a few moments later Charlotte made her excuses and left the men to their port and cigars and went up to her room to sit in a chair by the window, gazing out with unseeing eyes. Her head was reeling. How could she endure living under the same roof as her brother-in-law, she asked herself, supposing he did not decide to throw her out? Even so soon after meeting him, she knew him to be self-serving and pitiless. And she did not like the manner of his two companions who ogled her, almost undressing her with their eyes. And the way they had looked at Lizzie and Fanny made her shudder with apprehension. She would have to watch them and, if they stayed beyond a week or two, she would have to think of moving out—not only moving out, but finding an occupation.

It was at such a time she missed not having a husband. She had loved Grenville dearly and mourned him for a long time and because she lived comfortably under his father's roof, loved and cared for, she had never given a thought to marrying again. 'I am content as I am,' she had told Quinny. But now, now where was contentment? Where was security? Where, oh, where was love? Why did she suddenly feel so bereft, so lonely and not a little frightened? That was silly, she told herself, she feared no one. But how long dare she remain under her brother-in-law's roof while she found a way of earning a living that would have to include a roof over her head, not only for herself but her children?

Something must be done and done quickly. She sat at her little escritoire and took from it a small velvet bag. It contained a few guineas—not enough to keep the four of them for more than a day or two, for she must include Miss Quinn, certainly not enough to pay coach fares and at least two nights' accommodation for them to go to her great-uncle. She could write and ask him to send the fare, but her stubborn pride would not let her do it. He might refuse to have anything to do with her and that would be too humiliating to be borne.

Besides, she had made her home here, at Parson's End. She had grown to love the area, the cliffs, and the sea in all its moods, calm as a pond one day, raging and pounding over the shore almost to the base of the cliffs the next. She loved the pine woods carpeted with needles that crunched under your feet as you walked, and she liked the people, farming people and fishing folk, hardworking, dour and courageous. And as for their children, they were what made her life worthwhile, watching them grow, being able to help them to better themselves with a little education. It was an ongoing, self-imposed task and she did not want it to end, which it surely must if she did not have the means to continue it.

She remembered the stranger on the cliff with a wry smile. He had taken her for a schoolteacher and she remembered thinking that was what it might come to. A school was the answer, one that took boarders, young ladies from wealthy homes whose parents were prepared to pay to have their daughters educated and given some polish before being brought out. If she did that, the village children could still have their school. The wealthy could subsidise the poor. But did she have the right qualifications to attract the wealthy? She would need teachers beside herself and premises and connections. She weighed the coins in her hand and laughed at her foolishness.

She went up to say goodnight to the girls and quietly told Miss Quinn to make sure their doors were locked, though the poor lady did not need to be told; she was already in fear of her life. 'Tomorrow we will make plans,' Charlotte told her before returning to her own room and making sure that that door was locked.

She could hear the three men downstairs, laughing drunkenly. They had called for wine and a new pack of cards which was evidence enough that Cecil had not changed his gambling ways. She did not sleep until long after she heard them stumbling up to bed in the early hours and the house had gone quiet.

The next morning, she and the children slipped out of the side door to go to the village. She noticed a carriage arriving at the front as she passed the corner of the house, but, guessing it was John Hardacre, the family lawyer, she decided not to stay to receive him. Foster would alert the still-slumbering Cecil that he had arrived.

They crossed the stable yard to a path that led into the kitchen garden and from there through a side gate of the estate wall on to the road into the village. The damp hedgerows dripped onto the newly thrusting primroses at their base and the burgeoning trees in the meadows on either side moved softly in the breeze and sheltered the new lambs. It should have been a joyful time, this time of new life, but for once it did not raise her spirits. She had too much on her mind.

'My lady,' the Reverend greeted her. 'I did not expect you so early, you do not usually come until after noon.'

'No, but I need to speak to you, Reverend.'

'Then come into the church, I was on my way there.'

She sent the children to the classroom and followed him into the church. 'Reverend, I hardly know how to begin,' she said, after they had genuflected to the altar and seated themselves in one of the pews. There was a chill in there that matched the chill in her heart. 'My life has taken a dramatic turn…'

'I had heard the new Lord Hobart had arrived.'

'My goodness, news travels fast. Yes, he came yesterday morning and he is not prepared to go on as his father did and that means—'

'You will no longer be able to teach, is that it? We shall all be very sorry.'

'No, Reverend, it means that I must teach. And I must be paid for doing it.'

'You know the village children cannot pay.'

'Yes, I know that. But I must find pupils that can. And premises. The village children could be included later, when everything is up and running—' She stopped, daunted by the task ahead of her.

'I see.'

She knew he did see and was glad that she did not have to explain. 'What I need to ask you is whether you know where I might find a house…?'

'For a school?'

'Yes, but also living quarters for me and my children and their governess.'

'You surely have not been asked to leave Easterley Manor?'

'No, but I do not wish to stay. Lord Hobart is a bachelor. It would not be fitting.'

'No, I see it would not. But what about the uncle you spoke of? Would he not give you a home?'

'I do not know. I have never even met him and how do I know I won't be jumping from the frying pan into the fire? Besides, I love living at Parson's End, my children were born here and they love it too. I do not want to leave the area.'

'Then, my lady, you really do have a dilemma.' He smiled suddenly and patted her hand. 'You are welcome to stay at the Rectory until you have found somewhere. I am sure Mrs Fuller will raise no objections. But as for premises, we will have to put our thinking caps on because I do not want to lose you from the district and I am sure I am not alone in that sentiment.'

'Thank you,' she said quietly.

He rose and she knelt for his blessing. As they left the church she could hear the children arriving for their afternoon lessons. 'Will you take your class today?' he asked her.

'Yes, of course. The children expect it and I want everything as normal as possible for Lizzie and Fanny.'

'Then while you are with your pupils, I shall go up to the hall and pay my respects to his lordship.'

Charlotte managed a smile as she passed him to go into the schoolroom, wondering, as she did so, what kind of reception he would get.

The children were noisily chasing each other round the room, but quietened when they saw her. 'Back to your seats, children,' she said. 'And out with your slates. Lizzie, you can help Josh with his sums and Fanny can amuse the little ones. I will hear your reading one by one.'

The quiet industry of the classroom soothed her a little, but the worry at the back of her mind would not go away. She could not take advantage of the Rector's generosity; it would not be fair to him and his elderly wife. And though she had no qualms about being able to run a school, the problem was financing it and finding pupils. She would have to try and borrow the money against future income. If Mr Hardacre was still at the hall when she returned, she would try to see him privately and broach the matter with him. Not for the first time she wondered how he was faring with Lord Hobart.

'Miss.' She felt someone tug at her skirts and looked down to see Danny White looking up at her, anxiety writ large on his face. 'Meg wants to go home. She's got the bellyache.'

She looked at the lad's tiny sister, only a toddler, certainly not old enough for school, but if she had not been allowed to come neither would Danny and he was a bright child and deserved whatever education she could give him. Soon he would be able to join the select few who took more advanced lessons from the Rector himself. Meg was holding her stomach and crying. Charlotte scooped her up in her arms to comfort her. Her forehead was hot and she was obviously in some pain. What should she do? She could not let the child go home alone, not even if she sent Danny with her, and she was reluctant to leave her class when the Reverend was absent.

There was nothing for it but to take them all. 'Enough of lessons,' she said, suddenly making up her mind. 'We'll all take Meg home, shall we?'

The idea was greeted with enthusiasm and, having left a message with the Reverend Fuller's wife, they set off, headed by Charlotte carrying Meg, Danny beside her and Lizzie and Fanny following with the others in a double file.

The strange crocodile was greeted by smiles from the village women they met, all of whom knew the good work Charlotte did, not only for the children, but the old and infirm. She brought food and clothes, but, more than that, she brought hope. 'Mornin', me lady,' they called. Charlotte returned their greeting and went on her way, with the children singing 'One man went to mow' behind her.

The children waited outside while she took Meg into Dr Cartwright's to ask him to check on her, fully accepting that the account for his services would be remitted to her, for the poor child's parents could not pay. He felt all over her stomach. 'What have you been eating?' he asked her.

'Nuffin'.'

'Yes, you have. You've been stuffing yourself with something bad, haven't you?'

'It were beans,' Danny put in. Charlotte had not realised he had followed them in. 'I told her she shouldn't have.'

'Beans, what beans?'

'In the bag in Farmer Brown's barn.'

'Seeds,' the doctor said. 'Not meant to be eaten. They are for setting in the ground. You're old enough to know that, Danny, aren't you?'

'Course I am. Weren't my fault. She'd downed a handful afore I saw what her were adoin'.'

'I thought you were supposed to be looking out for her?' the doctor demanded waspishly.

Danny looked as though he were about to burst into tears.

'Don't blame him, Doctor,' Charlotte said. 'You can't watch children every minute of the day and he's only a babe himself. Tell me, how serious is it?'

'Not serious. I'll give her a dose to help it on its way. She'll be as right as rain tomorrow.'

Relieved, Charlotte watched while he held the child's nose and forced a spoonful of foul-tasting medicine down her throat, then they rejoined the other children and were soon at the door of the cottage where Danny and Meg lived. It was no more than a hovel; the pigs up at the hall lived in better conditions, and they even smelled sweeter, but Charlotte pretended not to notice as she explained to Mrs White why she had brought her children home.

'I'm sorry you've been troubled,' the woman said, taking the child from Charlotte's arms. Then, to Danny, 'See what you've done, you great lump. That's what all that book learnin' does for ye, makes ye forget what ye're supposed to be adoin'. Yar pa will dust yar breeks when he come home.'

Charlotte was forced to be mediator; she didn't want Danny forbidden to come to lessons again. Having soothed ruffled feelings, she returned to the remainder of her flock. It was then she saw the stranger again, standing outside the smithy, watching her with the same look of amusement that had so disconcerted her two days before.

# Chapter Three

Stacey wandered over to where she stood and swept off his hat. 'We meet again, ma'am.'

When the blacksmith had taken longer to see to his horse than expected, he had not minded, had even welcomed another night in the village, wondering if he might meet the schoolmistress again. Whiling away the time, he had found Easterley Manor, but had not ventured up the drive. His walk had taken him round the surrounding wall, and along the path to the cliff where he had seen her the day before, but the beach had been deserted except for a couple of men walking along the water's edge. They were not fishermen, being wrapped in cloaks against the wind, but then he had forgotten them to return to the village to see if his horse was ready. And here she was, followed by her little urchins, chanting a song. He was reminded of a German fairy story about a piper who lured children from their parents because they reneged on the payment they promised him for ridding their town of its rats. It made him smile.

Charlotte, who had no idea why he was smiling, felt herself blush from the roots of her rich brown hair right down to her neck, aware of the children giggling behind her. 'Good afternoon, sir,' she said, drawing her cloak more closely about her, a defensive gesture that added to his amusement. 'I am surprised to find you still in the neighbourhood. Parson's End has little to offer visitors.'

'On the contrary, I am finding my stay vastly rewarding.' His eyes twinkled again as he took in the rosy flush and the smoky blue-green eyes. She was not a seventeen-year-old débutante, but a woman of mature years with a couple of daughters, but she seemed discomforted. 'You are still giving outdoor lessons, I see.'

'I had to bring one of the children home, she was not well, and I could not leave the others.' She gave him a smile, just to prove she was in control of the situation. 'They would have caused mayhem left to themselves.'

'Ah, so they do find mischief. And here was I thinking you had them so well under control they would not dare misbehave whether you were present or not.'

'Sir, you are bamming me. Again. And we have not been introduced.'

'Oh, I see you did not mean it when you denigrated the manners of polite society. Introductions are important to you. You must not speak to a man to whom you have not been introduced. But if we had been made known to each other by a third party, then one presumes it would be acceptable to tease?'

'Your own good manners should tell you the answer to that one.'

'So I am to be given a lesson in manners, am I?'

'If you think you need one.' She was heartily sick of self-opinionated men who thought they could treat her with disdain. Cecil Hobart and his cronies had begun it, and now this man, this very superior man whose name she did not know, was doing the same. Perhaps he was one of them, perhaps that was why he was in the village, a forerunner of the congenial company that Mr Augustus Spike had asked Cecil to send for. 'Now, if you will stand aside and let me pass, I will be on my way.'

'Back to your school?'

'Is that any of your business?' She swept past him, ushering the children before her.

He stood a moment watching them, and then

strode after them. 'I am curious about it,' he said, falling into step beside her. 'At this moment there is nothing that interests me more than education.'

'Then, Mr Whoever you are, I suggest you consult others better able to enlighten you.'

'But I want you to.'

'Just leave me alone,' she hissed under her breath. The children were drinking in every word and none more so than Lizzie and Fanny. 'I have nothing to say to you, or others like you. Good day, to you, sir. I suggest you leave Parson's End and find your amusement in town, where there are those who might enjoy playing your game, for I do not.'

The strength and vituperation of her words took him by surprise and he stopped in the middle of the road and let her go. What, in heaven's name, had she taken him for? A rake? Oh, he realised he had not been particularly courteous, had teased and refused to give his name, but he had meant no harm. He really was interested in education and, though he knew her school would not be suitable for Julia, he had thought of asking her opinion on the education of young ladies and whether she knew of a good school, one that taught good manners and correct demeanour along with its lessons, one that had her sympathetic attitude to its pupils. He had gone about it in quite the wrong way.

Why had he not presented himself properly? She did not seem the kind of woman to be overawed by his rank and title. Whatever her situation was now, she had been raised a gentlewoman, if not a lady, otherwise she would not have been so top-lofty or put so much store on an introduction. Was it too late to retrieve the situation? And why did he want to? He could ask others his questions, as she had suggested; she had already given him an idea of what questions to ask. So why did he feel as if he could not let her go?

He watched the crocodile out of sight, but instead of going back to the blacksmith's, he followed, keeping far enough back not to be seen, laughing at himself for his folly while he did it.

They stopped at several of the cottages and he was obliged to conceal himself behind trees while she saw her pupils safely indoors, one by one, until there was only her own two daughters with her. Then she walked more briskly until she turned into the gates of Easterley Manor. He did not venture there, but stood thoughtfully tapping his boot with the riding crop he had been carrying when he spoke to her, then turned on his heel and went back to the village.

As she turned the bend in the drive, Charlotte saw Mr Hardacre's carriage coming towards her on its way out. She had missed him and it was all the fault of that supercilious stranger for delaying her. She stood to one side as it went to pass her, lifting her hand towards the occupant. He was looking grim and for a moment she did not think he would even acknowledge her. The interview with his client had evidently not gone well. She went to move on, when she realised the carriage was drawing to a stop. Turning, she retraced her steps as his head poked out of the door. He had removed his hat, revealing a shock of white hair. 'Lady Hobart, good day to you. Miss Elizabeth, Miss Frances, how you do grow!'

They each gave a little curtsy and stood waiting while their mother went to speak to him.

'Mr Hardacre, I am glad you stopped. I would be glad of your advice.'

'Anything I can do for you, I will, my lady. Do you wish me to return to the house?'

She smiled, realising he was reluctant to do so. 'No, there is no need for his lordship to know I have consulted you.'

'Oh.' He paused. 'But you know Lord Hobart is my client, I can do nothing against his interests.'

'I am aware of that. It is not about Lord Hobart. At least, only in as much as his arrival has presented me with a problem.' She spoke warily, wondering how much he knew or could guess. 'But I am afraid I cannot come to London to consult you.'

'I see. Then I shall put up at the Dog and Fox for the night and return tomorrow.'

'I would rather you did not come back here. Could we meet in the church? It is a public place, but quiet in the middle of the week.'

'Very well. At ten o'clock, if that is convenient.'

It was like a secret assignation and they both smiled at the idea. He was elderly and had served the Hobart family for several decades and his father before him; she was a relatively young widow and still very handsome. 'Ten o'clock will suit me very well.' She stood back as he rapped on the roof to tell his driver to proceed, and the coach rolled away.

She took the girls back to the house, entering by the side door. She had no wish to draw attention to her return by using the front entrance. But her precaution was in vain—Cecil saw her coming along one of the back corridors to the stairs. It was three o'clock in the afternoon and he was still dressed in a stained dressing gown.

'What have you been up to, my lady?' he enquired. 'Creeping about like a thief in the night.'

'I am not creeping about and it is not night,' she retorted, thrusting her chin upwards. 'It is the middle of the afternoon and I am returning from my duties in the village and going up to my room.' She gave the girls a little push. 'Upstairs with you. Go and find Miss Quinn.'

He watched them go and then turned back to her, leering at her so that the scar on his cheek deepened. She wondered idly how he had come by it. 'Duties in the village,' he queried. 'What might they be?'

'I teach a few of the village children at the Rectory. And I visit the sick and take them a little sustenance.'

'From my larder?'

'Why, yes, but only what would have been thrown away. It is no more than your own mother did in her lifetime.'

'Yes, she was a good woman, but I am sure she did not teach peasants.'

'Perhaps not, but education is something I feel strongly about. One should help those less fortunate.'

'Oh, so you do consider yourself fortunate. That is good. One should always be grateful for charity.'

Knowing he was trying to goad her into an inconsiderate reply, she did not answer. She would have passed him to continue on her way, but the passage was a narrow one and to do so meant pushing past him, too close for comfort.

'Nothing to say?' he asked.

'What do you wish me to say?'

'That you agree, that you know you are here because I, in my charitableness, have allowed you to stay and you are suitably grateful.'

'I am suitably grateful,' she said, aware of the ambiguity in the statement, though whether he realised it she did not know. He was not the most intelligent of men. How could the late Lord Hobart have sired two such different men as Grenville and this man? The one was honourable and considerate, the other the exact opposite.

'But my generosity comes at a price,' he said.

'I thought it might.'

'Until I marry, you will continue to act as my housekeeper and keep those servants in line. I never saw such a shabby collection in my life. And who told them it was permissible to answer back, to voice opinions of their own? I have a mind to dispense with the lot of them, except that I am expecting guests and there is no time to hire others.'

'Guests?'

'Yes, a real house party. So, please prepare for them. Open up the house, get in some decent food and restock the wine cellar.'

Her mind flew to the stranger in the village, but quickly returned to what he had asked. 'Very well, but I shall need money.'

'Money?' He started back in pretence of shock.

'You speak of money? Don't you know such a thing is never mentioned in polite company?'

She forbore to point out that he was hardly an example of polite company. 'Nevertheless, we have to pay for food and wine, not to mention coals, oil and candles, and laundry women. Guests make a great deal of washing.'

'Was my father's credit not good?'

'I am sure it would have been, but he made it a point of honour not to ask for it, but to pay his bills promptly.'

'He, my dear sister-in-law, had the blunt to do so. Until I have overturned that preposterous will, I have not, so until that happy day you will obtain credit. If my father was as scrupulous as you say, you should have no trouble.'

'Surely Mr Hardacre—'

'Ah, I forgot, you are privy to that ridiculous legacy.'

'I do not know anything about that, my lord,' she said quickly 'But I cannot believe Lord Hobart left you without any means at all.'

'I am supposed to have made a profit from my time in India.'

'And did you not?'

'It must be self-evident that I did not, certainly not enough to sustain the life of a gentleman.'

'I see. Then should you not postpone your house

party until you have improved the estate and made it pay again? I am afraid that when Lord Hobart became ill, it was let run down. But it will reward a little attention.'

'Do you presume to tell me what to do? No wonder the servants question their orders, when they have the example of the mistress of the house to teach them. But you are the mistress no longer.' He stopped suddenly and laughed. It was an ugly sound. 'Unless you would like to take up the role?' He put out a hand to touch her cheek and she jerked her head away.

'No, I would not,' she said and, taking a deep breath, pushed past him and went to the kitchen to see about carrying out his orders. The servants were working, but gone was the cheerful willingness that had been there when the late Lord Hobart was alive and Charlotte had the running of the house. There were frowns and mutterings and she felt they might have been disagreeing among themselves. Such an attitude would not get the work done and she tried to sound cheerful and efficient as she gave them their new orders.

'How can we do all that?' Betsy demanded. She was middle-aged, plump and red-haired. She was also the most outspoken; Charlotte guessed it was Betsy who had angered Cecil. 'Are we to have more staff?'

'I will ask his lordship,' she said.

'He's bad enough, but those other two... Ugh!' Cook said, banging the dough on the table and sinking her fist into it. This batch of bread would be well kneaded. 'They send down here, demanding food in the middle of the night, and expect it to appear like magic. Had to get out of my warm bed, I did. And I was hardly asleep again when Betsy came and woke me to be getting breakfast ready.'

'I am sorry for that, Mrs Evans, I'll ask the gentlemen to be a little more considerate. Perhaps you could leave something cold on a tray when you go to bed and their own servants can fetch it for them.' She paused, looking round at them all, some seeming unhappy, some mutinous, the younger ones sniffing tearfully. 'I know it is difficult getting used to a new master, but we must do our best to keep everything running smoothly.'

'Oh, we i'n't blamin' you, m'lady,' Betsy put in. 'We know it's as hard for you as 'tis for us.'

Charlotte smiled; perhaps she had allowed them too much freedom to speak their minds, but it was gratifying to know she had their support. If she left, what would happen to them? Could they find other positions if they decided to leave? Would Cecil pay their back wages if they did? She felt responsible for them. She sighed. Perhaps her plans should also include those servants who wanted to come with her, even if it did increase her problems. Oh, if only Cecil would decide he did not like the country after all and leave. But she suspected the death of his father had been fortuitous for him. There were probably others like Sir Roland and Mr Spike who might descend upon him at any time, dunning for debts to be paid. Perhaps one of them had already arrived. But why had he not come straight up to the house? Why skulk in the village? She gave up trying to work it out and went up to the schoolroom.

Lizzie and Fanny were at their lessons but, like the servants, they were unsettled and unable to concentrate. Miss Quinn was nearly as bad; she kept glancing towards the door, as if she expected trouble to walk through it. Charlotte smiled reassuringly. 'I shall be in my room, if you want me,' she said. 'I'll come and see you again before I go down to dinner.'

'We won't have to come down again, will we?' Lizzie asked.

'No, now your uncle has met you, I think he is satisfied you are being well cared for.'

She was becoming a liar in her efforts to keep everyone happy. Did that mean she was weak? She went back to her room and sat at her desk where she spent the time before dinner drawing up lists. And then she endured that meal in the company of men who would never have been entertained by the late Lord Hobart and afterwards left them to their drinking and retired to her own room. It was not as comfortable nor as well appointed as the one she was used to, but at least it was away from the guest rooms and near her children. She felt as if she had been relegated to the status of a servant and fervently prayed Mr Hardacre would help her to do something about it.

He was talking to the Reverend Fuller when she arrived in the church the following morning, but as soon she appeared, the Reverend bade her good morning and left them.

'I am sorry to keep you in Parson's End longer than you intended,' she told the lawyer. She was dressed in her usual mourning silk, over which she had put her black wool cloak; even though it was late March, the days were still not warm enough to dispense with it and, here in this quiet village, fashion seemed not to matter; other things were more important. 'But I am in something of a quandary.'

'I think I understand.'

'You do?' She sat in one of the pews and motioned him to sit too.

'I cannot imagine that you want to stay at Easterley

Manor. It was once such a happy home when Lady Hobart was alive and the boys were young…'

'It was still so until quite recently,' she said. 'My father-in-law's passing changed everything. I do not think I shall be able to deal comfortably with the new Lord Hobart. We do not view things in quite the same way. And I understand he is planning to marry.' She was trying to put it diplomatically. Lord Hobart was his client; it would not help to complain of his behaviour. 'I must make other arrangements.'

'What had you in mind?'

'A school. If I had a house large enough to turn into a small school, where I could take fee-paying young ladies—'

'But, my dear Lady Hobart, how can you contemplate such a thing? Your husband was a baronet in his own right and you come from a noble family— such a thing is hardly fitting.'

'I enjoy teaching.'

'I am sure you do and the Reverend has been telling me all about your work among the children, but teaching them as an act of charity is not the same as asking to be paid for it.'

She gave a strangled laugh. 'You sound like Cecil, as if the very mention of the word money is a profanity. Unfortunately it is a necessary evil, especially when you do not have any.'

'Surely it is not as bad as that? Is there no one?'

'No one,' she said firmly, dismissing the idea of applying to Lord Falconer as impractical. 'When Sir Grenville died, I was bereft and leaned very heavily on Lord Hobart. He was a kind man, he knew I had to do things my way, and so he allowed me all the freedom I wanted. It was as if Grenville had already become master of Easterley Manor and I, as his widow, was carrying on. Lord Hobart kept in the background, happy to have his grandchildren about him. I and my children have lost all that.' She blinked rapidly, trying to prevent the tears falling.

'I see,' he said, though she was not at all sure that he did.

'Then are you able to help me?'

'To find you a school?'

'More than that. To lend me the money to set it up.'

'Oh.' He looked startled. 'You meant it when you said you had no money?'

'I have three guineas and some smaller change. And some of that must go to pay the doctor for the treatment he gave one of my little pupils yesterday.'

He was shocked. 'My lady, I had no idea. How can that be? You had the portion Sir Grenville settled on you when you married. I know it was not much, but he never expected to die so young and, in any case, he knew his father would look after you.'

'I had no idea I ought to save it, Mr Hardacre. I spent it on things for the village school: slates, chalk, books, and clothes and medicines for any who needed them. They have so little and since the war their plight has become worse and worse. I often think it would do those who make the laws in this country a great deal of good to have to live among its people. They might learn the meaning of true poverty.' She paused and drew a deep breath before going on. 'That's as may be. What I had has gone.'

'I am appalled. Your daughters…'

'They want for nothing at the moment, but they are not happy at the Manor now and I must find a way to provide for them.'

'But you would need collateral if I am to approach a bank on your behalf.'

'I have none.' She paused. 'I have a little jewellery: the pearls my father gave me on my come-out, an emerald necklace that was a present from my husband to mark our betrothal and the two little brooches, one of amethysts, the other of garnets, that he gave me on the birth of our daughters. I have no idea of their worth; I never thought of them as assets, but as keepsakes.'

'My dear Lady Hobart, surely it has not come to such a pass?'

'I am sorry, I have embarrassed you, but, believe

me, it is no greater than the embarrassment I feel being obliged to ask.'

'Do not think of it.' He looked thoughtful for a moment. She must certainly be helped to leave Easterley Manor and whether she went ahead with her school idea or not, she needed money. Cecil Hobart would never provide her with any. 'As you know, Lord Hobart left money in trust for your daughters,' he said slowly. 'It was intended to be for their come-out and dowries and any expenditure the trustees felt necessary for their well-being. I think such an occasion has arisen. I will put it to them and let you know what they say. How much do you think you will need?'

'It depends how much I have to pay to rent a house, and how long before fee-paying pupils arrive, but I have worked out some rough figures.' She took two folded sheets of paper from her reticule and handed them to him. 'Do you think the trustees will agree?'

'When I put the position to them, I think they will. The welfare of your daughters must come before all other considerations and their welfare is not best served living at Easterley Manor.' It was as near as he was going to go to admitting he knew what Cecil was like. 'Can you sit tight for a week or two until you hear from me?'

'Yes. I am not a child, Mr Hardacre, I can stand

up for myself, and there are plenty of good, kind people up at the house to keep an eye on the girls, though I rarely let them out of my sight.' She paused. 'May I begin looking for a house?'

'Yes, I see no reason why you should not. But you will not be able to sign a lease or anything like that, not until I have obtained the consent of the trustees.'

'I understand.'

He rose. 'If you walk back to the Dog and Fox with me, I will advance you a few guineas. I carry very little with me because of the fear of highwaymen, but I have a little in a strong box stowed under the seat of my coach. I have to pay my reckoning at the inn and for horses and meals on my return journey to London, which is a prodigious amount, but you are welcome to what I do not need.'

'Thank you. I will repay you as soon as I can.'

He reached across and patted the back of her hand, which had been anxiously twisting the cord of her reticule. 'I know you will. I wish all my clients were as particular.' He smiled suddenly. 'But as I usually hold the purse strings and can expedite or delay at my pleasure, the situation usually resolves itself.'

'Is Lord Hobart going to have his father's will overturned, Mr Hardacre?' she asked suddenly. 'He said he would.'

'He would like to try, but I pointed out to him that,

apart from the estate, there was not a great deal of unentailed money for him to draw on and, if he took that course, the only people to gain would be the lawyers. I think he saw my point.'

'So he must marry money and have children.' Cecil's children, being the old man's grandchildren, would share the legacy of her daughters.

'I believe that is his intention. He spoke about you. He asked me if it was lawful to marry a half-brother's widow.'

'I cannot believe he was in earnest. But even if he were, I would not marry that man at any price.'

Feeling much more cheerful, she rose and they walked side by side out of the church and down the village street to the inn. They passed the smithy on the way and she noticed the stranger's beautiful white horse was no longer there. Did that mean he had taken her advice and left Parson's End? She wished she could get rid of those two toad-eaters still at the Manor as easily.

She was on her way home, with five guineas tucked safely into her reticule, when she was obliged to jump back into the hedge as two carriages came rattling along the narrow lane without a care for others on the road. Each had its full complement of passengers. She had no doubt that the first of Cecil's guests had arrived. By the time she arrived at the front door of the house, they were disgorging themselves and their luggage, shaking Cecil by the hand and being greeted by Sir Roland and Mr Spike like old friends.

She wished she could have nothing to do with them, but boycotting them was not a good idea, she decided. Until she heard from Mr Hardacre, she and her children, not to mention the servants, were at the mercy of her brother-in-law and it behoved her to try and keep the peace. But she would be very wary, polite but aloof, and if they thought she was top-lofty, what did it matter?

There were, she discovered, when she made her way into the hall, several ladies among the men; all were overdressed, all noisy. They had servants with them, and coachmen who needed accommodation. Charlotte instructed Foster to tell them where to go and concentrated on the guests.

'My sister-in-law,' Cecil said, waving his hand vaguely in her direction. 'She is housekeeping for me, so anything you need, ask her.'

'Ladies. Gentlemen.' Not by the flicker of an eyelid did she betray her consternation. 'If you will allow me a moment to take off my cloak and bonnet, I will show you to your rooms.' She divested herself of her outer garments and handed them with her reticule to Miss Quinn who hovered in the background. She went to lead the way when another guest strolled from the drawing room to join them. He stopped before her, smiling. 'Cecil,' he drawled. 'Introduce me to the lady.'

The plain clothes of the day before had gone. Now he was dressed in the height of elegance. His shirt collar had extravagant points, his starched cravat was intricately tied, his coat of blue superfine fitted his broad shoulders as if he had been poured into it and his pantaloons, tucked into shining Hessians, emphasised well-muscled legs.

'Lady Hobart,' Cecil said. 'Allow me to present Viscount Stacey Darton.'

Stacey took her hand and bowed over it. 'Lady Hobart, your servant.' He brought the hand to his lips and as his head came up, murmured. 'Is that polite enough for you, my lady?'

'My lord.' She managed to bend her knee and incline her head slightly without falling over, but the sight of him, so different from the man she had met in the village, was doing strange things to her limbs. She was shaking like an aspen, which was a ridiculous state of affairs, she chided herself. She had already half-guessed he was one of Cecil's cronies and should not have been surprised to see him. Only she had so hoped she was wrong, that he was a true gentleman. It was strangely disappointing.

'The company begins to improve,' Sir Roland said, laughing. 'A Viscount, no less. Cecil, you are a dark horse. Why did you not say his lordship was to grace us with his presence?'

'I thought it might be a pleasant surprise,' Cecil said, smirking. He went on to name his friends to Stacey, but Charlotte was not listening; she did not think it was necessary to know the names of these people. The less she saw of them the better.

'Have you brought a partner, my lord?' Augustus wanted to know.

'No, I am alone, sir. I find females distracting when there is serious play to be had.'

'But a pleasant distraction, eh, Cousin Stacey?' Cecil said and dug him in the ribs, evincing a quickly stifled recoil of distaste from Stacey.

The women laughed and one sidled up to him and smiled. She was on the plump side and her bosom was straining at the low neckline of her dress. Her hair was arranged in a complicated coiffure topped with feathers dyed blue and pink. She wore a glittering necklace and rings on almost every finger. 'I shall take pleasure in distracting you, my lord. But not until after the game.'

He laughed and pinched her cheek. 'No doubt you will. Lady Grey, is it not?'

'Oh, do not be so formal, my lord. My name is Adelia. I give you permission to use it.'

He bowed slightly. 'Adelia, I shall remember that.'

It was all too much for Charlotte; she felt sickened and curiously let down, as if she had expected better of the Viscount. He had been a much nicer person as a simple horseman, even if he did tease. 'Ladies. Gentlemen,' she said loudly, to be heard above the chatter and banter that was filling the hall. 'If you follow me I will conduct you to your apartments. Later there will be a light repast in the dining room to refresh you after your journey. We usually dine at five.'

'Five!' one of the men said. He was dressed in a ridiculous coat with a velvet collar that stood up around his ears, a yellow-and-brown striped waist-coat and a spotted cravat. 'Great God! I'm hardly out of bed by then. It ain't civilised.'

'Shut up, Reggie,' one of the women told him. Her thin dress, with its low scooped neckline and puffed sleeves, was almost transparent. 'It will give us a longer evening, more time to relieve our host of his blunt.'

So they had come to gamble. Charlotte was hardly surprised, but she wondered what the outcome might be if Cecil lost heavily. She strode between them purposefully and led the way upstairs, flinging open doors on the first-floor landing and telling them she hoped they would be comfortable.

Lord Darton was the last to be accommodated. He paused on the threshold of the room whose door she held open for him. She did not speak. 'Now that we have been formally introduced, you can have nothing against speaking to me, can you?' he asked, breaking the silence. The teasing light in his eyes was still there, but now she interpreted it differently. Now she saw it as lascivious, like the gleam of speculation in the eyes of Sir Roland Bentwater and Mr Augustus Spike, but infinitely more dangerous because she was repulsed by them, but not by this man. Viscount Darton was undeniably attractive and if she let down her guard, she might find herself liking him, responding to his teasing. And that would never do.

'I am your hostess, my lord, and not so impolite as to ignore you.'

'Ah, yes. It is an odd world, is it not, that brings a host of strangers together in one place to get along as best they may?'

Was there more to that simple comment than the words themselves suggested? Was he suggesting they might not all get along? Did he have any idea of her predicament? 'If you say so, my lord.'

'Oh, I do. It must be fate.'

'Oh, I think it more likely that Lord Hobart issued an invitation you could not resist,' she said lightly.

'There is that,' he agreed. 'But when I set out, I had no idea you would be here.'

'My lord, Easterley Manor has been my home for the last twelve years, why would I not be here? Now, please excuse me, I have much to do.'

She turned and left him, walking sedately along the corridor to go back downstairs to help in the kitchen. The servants were hard-pressed and, in their haste, falling over each other and causing mayhem. She stopped to help them, taking the platters of food into the dining room herself, where some of the guests were already assembled. Cecil was there, strutting like a peacock, full of bonhomie, pressing food and wine on to them. Not that they needed pressing; they were eager and greedy. She put down the dishes and went over to her brother-in-law.

'My lord,' she murmured. 'I must speak to you. In the library where we may be private.'

'Certainly, my dear, let us be private.' He grinned round at the company as he excused himself, then led the way from the room, along the hall and into the library. She followed him in, but did not close the door. Being shut in a room with him was something for which she had no relish.

'Well, what is it?' he asked, leaning back against the desk, a desk cluttered with papers. She supposed they had been left by Mr Hardacre, but, judging by the way they were scattered about, the contents had not pleased her brother-in-law.

'My lord, how long will your guests be staying?'

'Anxious to be rid of them, are you?'

'They are a drain on your resources and the servants cannot manage without more help.'

'Then you help them.'

'I am doing so, but I cannot be everywhere at once.'

'Now, do you know, I thought that you could.' It was said with a sneer. 'Here, there and everywhere, that is my dear sister-in-law, one minute in the house, overseeing the servants, making a fuss over her precious daughters, the next jaunting about the village, trying to teach the children of peasants to think themselves better than their masters. And cavorting on the beach with them.' He grinned at her shocked expression. 'Oh, do not imagine your antics go unnoticed. Now, I suggest you forget all about the village and concentrate on this house and making its idle servants earn their keep.'

The only person who could have told him about seeing her on the beach was Viscount Darton and she resented it. What reason could he have for doing that, except to discomfort her? 'We need at least two more kitchen maids and two chambermaids, and an extra woman in the laundry room,' she said, determined not to be side-tracked.

'Hire them, then, but don't come to me for their wages. Now, I must rejoin my guests or they will think that you and I are disporting ourselves and neglecting them.' And with that he left her.

She was about to follow him when she heard him cry out jovially. 'Why, cousin Stacey, found your way, have you? Come into the dining room and have some refreshments. Then I will tell you of the entertainment I am planning for this evening.' Standing in the doorway, she saw them go off down the hall arm in arm. Once they were out of sight, she went up to her room, grabbed her cloak and went back to the pandemonium of the kitchen.

'My lady, have you seen what he has ordered for dinner?' Cook demanded, waving a sheet of paper. 'It can't be done. I've only one pair of hands. And though Betsy is a good girl, she i'n't blessed with any more neither.'

'I'm going to the village to see if I can hire some help,' Charlotte said, swinging her cloak round her shoulders.

'Thank the good Lord,' Cook said. 'The sooner the better.'

Charlotte left the house by the kitchen door and

made her way on to the lane into the village. There were men and women there who would be glad of employment, but she could not ask them to work for nothing. Oh, they might come eagerly enough, but when they discovered the kind of people they were serving and learned that the new Lord Hobart was not as scrupulous about debts as his late father, they would think she had deceived them. They trusted her and she did not mean to betray that trust. The new servants must be paid and the ones already there too, even if it took every penny she had.

She went to the homes of those whose menfolk were out of work and, though it was not the kind of work they were used to, she offered two of them work as footmen to fetch and carry for the guests, and at two other homes she found women to come and work in the kitchens. They were not trained housemaids, but Cecil could not expect experienced servants at such short notice. She would promote Betsy to chambermaid; she was big and strong and not likely to attract the men as a young maid might and she would look after the other maids.

By the time she returned, there was barely time to see Lizzie and Fanny and instruct Quinny to keep them to their own quarters before the dinner gong sounded. She changed quickly and went down to join the guests as they trooped from the drawing room into the dining room.

'There you are, Charlotte,' Cecil said. 'Where have you been?'

'Hiring more help for the house,' she said.

'Good,' Sir Roland put in. 'I had to send twice for hot water. It nearly made me late for dinner.'

'And I asked for a bottle of cognac and was offered sherry wine,' another said. 'Don't your servants know the difference, Hobart?'

'My apologies, gentlemen,' Cecil said, as he led the way into the dining room. 'It will not happen again.'

'And my maid could not get my gown pressed,' Lady Grey put in. 'I have been obliged to wear it all crumpled from being packed.'

'You would never know it, my lady,' Stacey said. 'It looks charming, as you are yourself.'

'Why, you old flatterer,' she said, laughing and digging him in the ribs with her fan. 'For that, you may escort me into dinner.'

He gallantly offered her his arm, but he was aware of Lady Hobart, standing close by, ready to follow the last of the guests. He had been hanging back in order to escort her himself, but unless he wanted to alienate Adelia Grey and, more importantly, his host, he could do nothing but comply.

Lady Hobart appeared perfectly calm, though he

could tell by her pallor, and the way her whole body seemed tense, that she was far from easy with the situation. Poor thing! Staying in the village as he had, he had soon confirmed that she was indeed the sister-in-law he had heard Cecil speak of, heard her praised for her goodness, her generosity to those less fortunate, her commitment to educating the children, who all loved her. She was, according to the villagers, a paragon of virtue.

She had intrigued him from the start and he had found himself wondering about her, but, remembering Julia and his errand on her behalf, was prepared to leave. He had been in the inn's parlour, eating a meal before continuing his ride, when John Hardacre came in and ordered a meal and a room for the night. Stacey knew him well; he had been legal adviser to the family for years.

Finishing his business with the innkeeper, the lawyer had turned towards Stacey. 'Viscount Darton! I never thought to see you in such an out-of-the-way place.'

'I was on my way to Ipswich and was forced to stop when my horse threw a shoe.' He laughed. 'The pace of life is wondrous slow in this part of the country. It has taken more than a day to fashion four shoes, though to be honest I don't suppose they see a horse like mine very often.

And I was in no great haste. What reason have you for being here?'

'Lord Hobart lives close by. He is my client. I had business with him.'

'Oh, yes, I had heard he was back from India to take over the estate. But did he not offer you accommodation?'

John smiled. 'The business was not of long duration. I had no need to stay.'

'But I heard you order a room.'

'Yes. I also have business with Lady Hobart.'

A waiter brought food and Stacey, his curiosity aroused, nodded towards the chair opposite him. 'Please join me, I would be glad of company.'

'Thank you.' He lowered himself into the chair and watched as the waiter put out the food. Neither spoke until he had gone.

'Lady Hobart,' Stacey began, apparently casually. 'I have been hearing about her, and nothing but good. Tell me, is she as virtuous as they say?'

'She is a true lady, and I fear for her up at that house. I should not say this, but I do not think Cecil Hobart will treat her kindly. And there are a couple of loose fish up there I would not trust an inch.'

'Ah, Sir Roland Bentwater and Mr Augustus Spike.'

'You know them?' the lawyer asked in surprise.

'Hobart made us known to each other in the coach

when we travelled out of London. Can't say I liked the fellows.'

'You were right. I would say they were toad-eaters, but if they are, they will find little to pick at up there.' He gave a short laugh. 'I should not be telling you this, but you I have known you since you were a young shaver and I know I can trust you.'

'Indeed you can.' He had listened in astonishment as Hardacre recounted the terms of the late Lord Hobart's will. 'You mean he has inherited the estate, but no blunt?' he asked.

'No, but when he marries and has children, he will have the managing of their legacy. He wants me to overturn it, but it will take many months, and so he is looking for a compliant wife.'

'Not Lady Hobart?' he asked, appalled.

John gave a wry smile. 'No, I doubt she would be compliant enough, but she is dependent on him. There are two children, little girls. 'Tis a pity one was not a boy, there would never have been all this trouble. He would have been the heir…'

It was then Stacey had decided to accept Cecil's invitation and see for himself what was going on. Julia was happy and well cared for at Malcomby Hall and a few days' delay would make no difference. He was glad he had come, for no sooner had he presented himself, than other guests began to arrive, guests whose behaviour appalled him. He found himself feeling very sorry for Lady Hobart and meant to see she came to no harm, but to do that, he must go along with Cecil and pretend to be in accord with the rest of the company. He could not tell Lady Hobart that, she might inadvertently give him away, and at the moment she was looking daggers at him. He smiled at her over his shoulder as he led Lady Grey into the dining room, but that only made her thrust her chin even higher into the air and turn away from him.

'Come on, Stacey, why are you dawdling?' Cecil called to him. 'There will be time for dalliance later.'

He sighed and followed the company into the dining room.

## Chapter Four

Charlotte wished with all her heart that Cecil's uncouth guests would leave. For all their extravagant dress and superior airs, they were no more than riffraff. Even Lady Grey, if she really was a lady, was loudmouthed and frequently foxed. The only one who even made a pretence at gentlemanly behaviour was Viscount Darton, though even he sometimes indulged in Cecil's favourite pastime of baiting her.

'Come, Lady Hobart,' he said, one evening at dinner. 'Can you not find a smile for your guests?' And he gave her a wink that brought the colour flooding to her face and made the rest of the company laugh, particularly Mr Spike, who brayed like a donkey.

'You are Lord Hobart's guests,' she said, tight-lipped. 'Not mine.'

'You would not give us house room, is that what you are saying?'

'I—' She stopped. 'It is not my house.'

'No, it is not,' Cecil concurred. 'You, too, are a guest. It behoves you to behave like one.'

'Drink too much, gamble and abuse the servants, you mean,' she said with a snap. 'I am sorry if I do not conform, but I have been brought up differently. And I thought you had. Your father—'

'Ah, my father,' Cecil said. 'I begin to wonder just what my revered father meant to you. You seem to have been able to wind him round your thumb. If you wish to remain my guest, I suggest you resist the urge to bring his name into every conversation.'

She was about to make a sharp retort when she saw Stacey out of the corner of her eye slowly shaking his head, his eyes warning her to still her tongue. Although he had pretended to drink deeply, she noticed he had taken less than the others and was perfectly sober. Far from reassuring her, it put her more on her guard. What was his game? 'Yes, by all means let us refrain from speaking of the late Lord Hobart,' she said, standing up. 'Gentlemen, I will leave you to your port wine and cigars.'

She left the room, but the ladies did not follow her to the withdrawing room as they would have done in polite society, but stayed to continue drinking with the men. Later, after the table had been cleared, they would call for more wine, spread another cloth and fetch out the playing cards. It had happened every evening of the two weeks they had been at Easterley Manor.

In that two weeks, life at the Manor had become almost unbearable. Although the arrival of the extra servants had eased the situation a little, Charlotte was still expected to oversee them, to make sure the guests' many and frequent demands were met, that meals appeared on time and to inspect the guests' rooms to see that the cleaning and laundry had been properly done. That last was the most tiresome of all. The house party gambled and drank until the early hours of the morning and were still abed at the time most chambermaids would be busy making their beds and tidying their rooms. And woe betide any young girl who entered an occupied room. Even Betsy had come shrieking from Sir Roland's bed-chamber at eleven in the morning, cap all awry and face scarlet.

Charlotte had been so busy she hardly had time for her daughters, let alone the freedom to go to the village to take her classes and visit the old and sick. They would think she had deserted them. Nor had she heard from Mr Hardacre and that was worrying her. Did it mean he could not persuade his fellow trustees to release some of the girls' money to her? Were her plans all to come to naught?

She was alone in the drawing room, sitting beside a small table on which stood all the paraphernalia for making tea, the little stove and kettle, the teapot, cups and saucers, when Stacey sauntered into the room and moved over to the hearth, where a low fire burned, and stood with his back to it, looking down at her. She became disconcertingly aware of his masculinity and her breathing quickened. He was very tall and muscular, his complexion was bronzed, with fine lines about his dark eyes. His mouth was firm, his nose straight and his chin was thrust forward almost belligerently. For all that, he appeared slightly ill at ease, as if he wanted to say something, but was not sure whether to do so or not.

'Are you tired of the company in there, my lord?' she asked, inclining her head towards the dining room where a loud gust of laughter penetrated the walls. 'Would you like some tea?'

'Tea?' he asked absently, his mind on how self-possessed she seemed, but did that hide a vulnerability? After all, with few exceptions, ladies were dependent on their male relatives who could make their lives as pleasant or unpleasant as they wished. They could not handle their own money, even if they had any. He found it difficult to believe the late Lord Hobart had left her entirely at the mercy of his rakeshame of a son. Would she leave if she could? Or did she not mind what Cecil did so long as she had a home? It was an imposing and comfortable house if you did not mind its isolation. She was looking up at him, her face a picture of puzzlement and he realised he had not answered her question. 'Yes, please, my lady, that would most acceptable.' He threw up the tails of his coat and sat on the sofa opposite her, tucking his long legs under him.

She poured the tea and handed the cup to him with hands that were not quite steady. 'Are the others going to join us?' she asked.

'I doubt it. They are enjoying themselves too much where they are.'

'Why did you leave them?'

'I volunteered to fetch more wine. According to Cecil, your new footman does not know a good Bordeaux from rough mead.'

She smiled. 'I don't suppose he does, he's a farm labourer—when he's in work, that is. It's been so wet of late, the land is unworkable, and he was stood off.'

'Ah, his need for employment were more important than the needs of Lord Hobart and his guests, is that it?'

'I cannot be expected to find trained servants in a

small place like Parson's End, my lord, especially at a moment's notice,' she said sharply. 'My brother-in-law's friends must be satisfied.'

'I doubt anything will satisfy them.'

'And you, my lord, have you come to find fault? After all, you are one of them.'

He opened his mouth to deny it, but changed his mind. It was too soon to tell her the truth, that he was there because of what John Hardacre had told him, that he had at first been curious, which had turned to a surge of compassion when he arrived and had seen what was happening to her, and now wanted to protect her. She would laugh in his face if she knew. He wondered at it himself. 'No,' he said slowly. 'I do not wish to find fault. I appreciate your difficulties.'

'Oh, I do not think you do,' she said. 'Or you would not have told my brother-in-law about seeing me and the children playing on the beach. You may have thought it a fine joke, but he used it to taunt me.'

'I did nothing of the sort,' he said sharply. 'If Lord Hobart knew of it, it was not I who told him. There are others in the house, you know, and he could have seen you for himself.'

She realised he was right and her sense of fairness demanded an apology. 'I am sorry, my lord. I should not have jumped to conclusions.'

'No, things are not always what they seem, are they? I concluded you were a schoolteacher and I was wrong about that.'

'Not entirely, my lord. I do teach at the school in the village. It is something I like to do.' She stood up. 'If you come with me, I will find more wine for you, and, rest assured, I do know Bordeaux from mead.'

He put down his cup and followed her from the room, down the hall beside the main staircase, along a narrow corridor that led to the kitchens, pantries, dairy, laundry room and cellar. She stopped to light a candle standing on a small table and, opening a door, carried it down the cellar steps, sure-footed from years of practice. She knew every inch and cranny of the old house and could find her way about easily, even in the dark. At the bottom of the steps, she lit a lantern from the flame of the candle and handed it to him. 'Come, let us see what there is.'

He watched her precede him, tall, elegant, self-assured. She had a good figure, he noted, and the candle held before her added a soft glow to her hair, making a halo of it. He did not know how old she was, guessing she must be about thirty, but she was far from matronly. Without the unrelieved black she wore, she could easily be taken for a much younger woman. She stopped suddenly and he almost collided with her. He put out a hand to steady her and found himself touching the bare flesh of her arm. It was soft and warm. He felt her flinch and knew she had suddenly realised how dangerous it could be down here, alone with a man, a man she did not trust.

He took a step backwards, though the temptation was great to move forward and enfold her in his arms, to soothe her with soft words, to caress her. Even try the taste of her lips. He pulled himself up sharply—whatever had put that idea into his head? She was not a lightskirt, not like Lady Grey, who would undoubtedly allow him into her bed if he were to suggest it, but a gentlewoman. He guessed she was probably the daughter of a man of business, or a sea captain, genteel but undistinguished, which was why she saw no harm in teaching poor children. No doubt she had been elevated by her marriage to a baronet.

She pretended not to notice his touch, though it had sent shivers down the back of her spine, but pointed to rows of shelves where bottles of wine were stored. 'There is hardly any left. Last week that rack was full. I wonder you can play cards at all with the amount of wine and brandy you put away.'

'Me?'

'You and the others. I do not think there is much to choose between you.'

He did not like being lumped with Cecil's cronies,

but, as he had done nothing to make her think any differently of him, he let it go. 'One becomes used to it,' he said. 'Especially abroad in the army when it is often unsafe to drink the local water.'

'You were in the army?' She picked up two bottles and handed them to him.

'For many years I was a professional soldier.'

'I am surprised. Are you not the Earl of Malcomby's heir?'

'Yes, but my father was a soldier too. It was how he earned his earldom. I simply followed in his footsteps.'

'But you are not serving now?'

'No. There comes a time when it is necessary to stop and turn one's thoughts to duties at home.'

'Your wife?'

'I have no wife. She died many years ago.'

'I am sorry.' She paused before mounting the steps to the ground floor. 'Is Cecil really your cousin?'

'He is the son of my father's cousin, so the relationship is removed.' He gave a low chuckle. 'He seems to think it is important.'

'He thinks you are well up in the stirrups and has every intention of relieving you of some of your wealth.'

He laughed. 'He may try.'

'You do not think he will succeed?'

'I know he will not. He is a very poor player.'

'And the others?'

'They are a different matter. I fancy they have Cecil in so deep he does not know which way to turn and he is afraid.' He paused, then added softly. 'Men in that situation can be dangerous, my lady. I beg you to take care.'

She turned sharply to see his face, wondering why he should take the trouble to warn her. Not that she needed it; she knew very well the precarious situation she was in. But she had no choice. Until she heard from Mr Hardacre and could find a new home, she was stuck. For her children's sake she had to endure it. She could not tell him that and so she did not answer. At the top of the narrow stairs he turned to help her negotiate the last step just as Cecil hurried along the corridor towards them.

'Stacey, it is taking you a devilish long time to find a couple of bottles of wine. What have you been doing?' He stopped suddenly and laughed. 'Oh, I see. Dallying with my sister-in-law, are you? There's a time and place for that sort of thing, don't you know? And it is not now. We are waiting to begin.'

Instead of releasing Charlotte, Stacey, put his arms about her and drew her close. 'Trust you to come along and spoil things, Cousin,' he said jovially.

'You'll get nowhere with her,' Cecil said, relieving Stacey of the wine. 'Cold and stiff as a corpse, that one.'

'Oh, I don't know. She was thawing very nicely before you came and spoiled it.' He felt Charlotte squirm, trying to pull herself away, but he held her closer and before she could protest, had put one forefinger under her chin and tipped her face up to his, so that he could kiss her.

She started to struggle and then the sensations that coursed through her, sensations she had not felt for over eight years, overcame her resistance and she leaned into him so that their bodies touched and seemed to fuse. She did not seem able to pull herself away, though her head was telling her she was being foolish in the extreme. His lips were caressing hers, making little currents of warmth journey up and down her limbs, until they ended in one great whirlpool of desire. Her legs felt weak and she would have crumpled in a heap if he had not been holding her.

He lifted his head at last, but only to whisper in her ear, 'Do not act the outraged innocent, my lady. Remember what I said and take care.' And with that he kissed her soundly on the cheek and let her go. 'Come on, Cousin, back to the gaming table.'

Before she could find her voice, Stacey had taken Cecil's arm and propelled him along the corridor, leaving her breathless and shaking. And mortified that she had allowed herself to succumb. Now he would think he could take whatever liberties he liked. What was his game? Why did he stay? Surely not so that he could indulge in kissing her? She had no doubt he could make free with any of the other ladies if he so chose and they would not demur, they would encourage him openly.

Did he imagine there was money to be made from gambling with her brother-in-law? How disappointed he would be when he discovered Cecil had nothing. But that did not explain why he had come to the drawing room to talk to her, nor why he had pretended to be flirting with her. That was the outside of enough! She leaned against the door jamb for support, touching her cheek where he had kissed her. It felt hot. She should have slapped his face, given him a set-down; instead, she had meekly stood and allowed it. He must think her very weak, frightened of him perhaps. But whatever she felt for him, it was not fear, not in the way she feared Cecil and the others.

Slowly she made her way back to the front of the house and rang for a maid to clear away the tea things. No one else would come for it now. Then she went slowly up the stairs to her room, passing the dining room on her way. The laughter had stopped and the serious business of the card table had begun.

\* \* \*

She was in the dining room the following morning, throwing open the windows to let fresh air into the stuffy, smelly room when Cecil came in. He was dressed in a quilted burgundy dressing gown and a white night-cap. He wore slippers with curled toes, but no hose. 'Ah, Charlotte, up betimes, I see,' he said, with a pretence at joviality.

'It is half past ten, my lord.'

'Is it, by gad? Still, never mind. Need to speak to you.'

'Oh?' She waited.

'Yes. Thing is, I'm a little pinched in the pocket. Had a bad run last night, couldn't shake it off. Need to pay some of it off. Matter of honour, don't you know.'

'And?' She knew what was coming, but she wanted to hear him ask.

'And I need a bit of ready blunt, just a little to satisfy them. You can help me, can't you?'

'With money?'

'Yes, just a few guineas, to show good faith.'

'And where do you suppose I can find a few guineas, my lord? Does it grow on trees? Or perhaps in the ground along with the turnips?'

'It is not a matter for jest.'

'Indeed it is not. But you are out of luck, Cecil. I have none. Do you think I should still be here if I had?'

'I don't believe you. My father was devoted to you, so I am told. He must have left you something. Why else was there so little in the pot? You sucked it from him.'

'I most certainly did not!' She was angry now. 'Lord Hobart was never so wealthy that the allowance he sent to you was not a drain on his resources, especially in his latter years when he could not manage the estate. You may recall I told you so and that you needed to bring the land back into good heart.'

'You dare to lecture me?' He stepped towards her, so close she could smell his tainted breath and see the anger in his eyes, anger mixed with fear. Viscount Darton had been right: a frightened man was a dangerous one. But she would not retreat before him. 'You are a lying vixen,' he said, his face muscles working, making the scar stand out, a long pink weal. 'You have salted it away and I will have it.'

'I cannot give you what I do not have. You know the terms of your father's will. Everything but the house and estate in trust for the grandchildren. I have nothing.'

'Your girls are his grandchildren.'

'Yes, but I cannot touch what is theirs—' She stopped, wondering how true that was. If she could not make use of it, even for her daughters' sake, then she was truly in a coil. On the other hand, she certainly did not want to put the idea in his head that her daughters' inheritance could be realised.

'Hmm.' He seemed to consider this and then smiled. 'No doubt my father gave you presents before he stuck his spoon in the wall. Jewellery, if not cash…'

She was about to deny it—what little jewellery she owned had not been given to her by the late Lord Hobart—but stopped when she heard the door open and the Viscount strolled into the room. Unlike his host, he was properly dressed in coffee-coloured pantaloons and a brown stuff coat. His cravat was neatly but not extravagantly tied, his short hair was carefully brushed. 'Morning, Hobart,' he said nonchalantly.

Charlotte was never so glad to see him and hear his voice. Realising she had been holding her breath, she let it out in a long sigh. She stepped away from Cecil and went to the sideboard to check the contents of the breakfast dishes.

'Oh, it's you, Darton,' Cecil said, annoyed by the interruption. 'Up devilish early, ain't you?'

'If I am, Cousin, then so are you. You are here before me.' Stacey surveyed the other's garb. 'Could you not sleep?'

'I slept well enough.'

'Good. A man should never lose good sleep over his losses. There is always the morrow to recoup.

But do you not think it a little impolite to appear before a lady in a state of undress?'

'None of your business.'

'Indeed it is, if the lady in question is one in whom I have a particular interest.'

Cecil laughed. 'Particular interest, eh? You'll get nowhere with her, Darton. She has nothing, so she tells me, though I ain't sure I believe her.'

'You had better believe her,' Stacey said, moving swiftly forward and grabbing him by the front of his dressing gown, almost lifting him off the floor. 'It is not the act of a gentleman to doubt the word of a lady.' He set him down and dusted his hands together. 'I suggest you go and dress.'

Cecil pulled the gown out of Stacey's way and left the room. Stacey smiled. The fellow owed him a great deal of money and while he did and thought he could recoup, he would not turn him from the house. Besides, Sir Roland and Augustus Spike also owed him money, not quite so much, but they would not want him to leave until they had found a way of retrieving it, legally or illegally.

'So you have a particular interest, have you, my lord?' Charlotte's voice brought him back from his reverie.

'Words,' he said. 'Simply a form of words that had the desired effect. He has gone.'

'But you are still here.'

'And at your service, my lady.' He swept her a flourishing bow.

'I need nothing from you.' His intervention had been fortuitous, but that did not mean she would allow him to take liberties.

'No? Perhaps not,' he said. 'But I need my breakfast.' It was said with that half-mocking smile he had that she could never quite interpret.

'Then I suggest you help yourself.' She indicated the sideboard. 'Everything is there. I will have coffee brought to you. Unless you prefer chocolate, or tea?'

'Coffee, please, it will help to wake me up.'

'If you went to bed before cockcrow, you might find it easier to be alert during the day.'

'I could not leave the game. It would have been bad manners.' It was a statement that made her laugh aloud and he found his own mouth twitching. 'I do not want to antagonise my host, you know. It will not serve.' His voice had changed, the note of banter had gone and now he spoke quietly, as if he were in earnest, as if he were trying to tell her something. Did he mean because he wanted to continue his pursuit of her, but he wasn't exactly pursuing her, was he? He simply baited her. The others did it too; it was a kind of game to them, and he was no different, was he?

She did not understand him; he was perfectly polite one minute, downright rude the next. Sometimes solicitous, anxious for her welfare as if he knew and could sympathise with her dilemma, sometimes he was as despicable as the others, worse because they had not attempted to kiss her. She felt herself colouring at the memory. How could she have been so foolish as to allow it? Now he thought he could take liberties and she would not object. She went to push past him, but he caught her hand. 'Lady Hobart, I beg you not to reject the hand of friendship. That is all it is, you know. We all need allies at some time or other.'

She pulled herself away. 'This house is not at war, my lord. We do not have to take sides in battle.'

'Perhaps you are right, my lady.' He bowed and let her go.

He felt he was walking a tightrope. One false step and Cecil would know he was not there to play cards and flirt with the ladies. But go too far in that direction and he would make an enemy of Lady Hobart, and that was the last thing he wanted. She was either extraordinarily brave or extraordinarily foolish, but whichever it was he admired her. If they had met in a London drawing room or at a ball, they would have exchanged courtesies, danced together, and slowly, little by little, he would have learned her background, found out about her family, where she had been born, where raised, her likes and dislikes. He would have told her about Anne-Marie and Julia and about Malcomby Hall. And in the fullness of time, he might have found himself attracted enough to begin a serious courtship. None of that would happen now. They had been thrown together in circumstances far from normal and there was no going back and starting again.

What did he know of her? Only that she had been married to Sir Grenville Hobart, the elder of Lord Hobart's two sons, and that he had been killed at Corunna, leaving her with two daughters. She had made her home with her father-in-law and now he was dead she was in trouble, and though Hardacre had not acquainted him with the exact nature of the trouble, it was not difficult to guess. As for her likes and dislikes—he knew she liked order and courtesy and felt strongly about education and she loved her daughters, but that was about all. How could he be in love with her, knowing so little? But he was.

She drove all his previous convictions about women and their frivolity from his head. She made him forget he had promised himself not to marry again, that he did not like children, especially girl children. Was he a fool to let compassion for her plight cloud his judgement? He could turn his back on her, leave Parson's End and continue his journey, just as if Ivor had not thrown a shoe; he could find a school for Julia, take her to it and return home, comfortable in the knowledge that he had done his duty by her. But he could not, could he? Charlotte Hobart had changed him, made him more aware of the needs and feelings of others, made him feel guilty about Julia. But had she weakened him? He, who always liked to believe himself in control, felt it slipping from his grasp.

Sunday was the only time Charlotte was free of the obnoxious guests for an hour or two. On Sundays, she and Miss Quinn took the girls to church, and as Cecil and his friends were not churchgoers, they were able to breathe freely, enjoy the air, the service and the company of the other parishioners who gathered afterwards to pass the time of day and gossip.

It was soon apparent that the wild parties and the heavy gambling up at the Manor had become food for gossip. The new servants had not been able to resist passing on what they had seen and heard and much of it was undoubtedly exaggerated. She could tell by the way people were looking sideways at her and the way they whispered among themselves that she was the object of conjecture. Did she condone what was happening? they asked each other. She was mistress of the Manor, surely she could have refused to have those horrible people in the house if she did not like them? And why did she no longer teach the children or visit the sick? They could not believe a person they had always looked up to could change so much.

She could, of course, refute the gossip, tell them the truth, but that would mean admitting to her own helplessness and she could not bring herself to do it. She had always been the one to give succour and comfort and she could not bear the idea of being the object of pity, the receiver of whatever these poor people could give her. It would not help in any case. She needed more than they could give, she needed her daughters' inheritance, or at least part of it. These simple people would not understand that just because she lived in a big house and had enough food to eat did not mean she was not poor.

Holding her back straight and her chin high, she pretended not to notice the whispers and greeted her fellow worshippers just as she always had, with a smile and a cheery word, an enquiry here and there as to whether a child who had been ill was better, or whether an old lady was managing on her own. They did not cut her, but their answers were guarded.

'I feel like a stranger in their midst,' she told the

Reverend Fuller. 'And a not very welcome one at that. Perhaps I was wrong to want to stay in the neighbourhood, perhaps I should have taken my girls and gone to my great-uncle after all.'

'They do not understand, my lady. They cannot conceive that you, who have always looked after them, should not be able to continue as before. They know nothing of wealth and the rules of inheritance. As far as they are concerned, you are no less rich than you were before his lordship died.'

'I know.' She gave a huge sigh, then, catching sight of Stacey emerging from the dim interior of the church, bade the parson a hasty farewell and set off down the lane, followed by Miss Quinn and the girls.

'Mama, do we have to go straight back?' Fanny asked. 'It is so nice to be out. I don't like the house any more.'

'Nor do I,' Lizzie said. 'When Grandpa was alive we could go anywhere, play hide and seek in the rooms, watch the maids at work or go to the kitchen for sweetmeats. Now we may not go anywhere but our own rooms. Cook is bad-tempered and even Betsy chased me up the corridor the other day. She said I'd no call to be in that part of the house. I was only curious about the lady, the one with the black wig and the patch on her cheek. She reminded me of pictures of the Queen. I saw Uncle Cecil go into her room and he was in his nightshirt…'

'Lizzie, you know I forbade you to go downstairs without me,' Miss Quinn said, looking fearfully at Charlotte. 'It was very naughty of you.'

'I wanted to know what was going on. It's something very havey-cavey, I am sure.'

'Nothing is going on,' Charlotte said, trying not to show the unease she was feeling. Her children, her beloved daughters, were in danger of being corrupted by her brother-in-law's friends, and she must get them away. She had spent her own money paying the extra servants, which was the only way she could get them to come, and all she had left was the five guineas Mr Hardacre had given her. How far would that take them all? Would it take them as far as Hertfordshire where Lord Falconer lived? And what would she find at the end of the journey, a welcome or a refusal? It was years since she had travelled on a public coach and her children never had. How much were fares nowadays, how much did it cost to stay overnight at an inn? She would have to go to London and take a stage from there. It would take at least three days. What other costs were involved? Above all, was it safe? Perhaps it would be better to wait a little longer to hear from Mr Hardacre. 'We'll go and have a walk on the beach, shall we?'

She set off determinedly, turning off the road and down the path through the pine woods to the cliff. The day was warmer than of late, for spring had burst out in all its glory. The sky was the colour of hazy blue smoke, the sea, darker, greener, was calm and only a faint ripple at the water's edge told of a tide that could, in times of storm, be deadly. Flotsam and jetsam was often washed ashore and the villagers would salvage whatever was useful. A year or two before a body had been brought in on the tide, probably a poor sailor who had fallen overboard, for no one had ever identified him. But today the sand was clean and as golden as the sun that shone above it.

The children ran on ahead, sitting down to peel off their shoes and stockings, before dashing on to the beach and making for the pebbly water's edge. Charlotte and Miss Quinn followed more slowly.

'Poor mites,' Joan said. 'They have been cooped up like wild birds this last two weeks…'

'I know, Quinny, but what would you have me do? I dare not let them run about the house.'

'I know. How long do you think those dreadful creatures will stay?'

'I do not know.'

'Do you think when they go, life will be the same as it was?'

'I don't know that either, Quinny. I do not think

so.' They had reached the water's edge and began walking along where the tide had gone out, their conversation accompanied by the gentle whoosh and rattle as the tide came over the pebbles. 'But I have been making plans, whether they come to fruition depends on many things, but I think it would be wise to leave Easterley Manor.'

'Leave, my lady? But where will you go?'

'I do not know yet, but I beg you to say nothing of it to anyone. Until I am sure of my ground, no one must know.'

'You may trust me, my lady, but if you leave what will become of everyone, the servants and me?'

'While the girls are young, I shall need you, Quinny, though whether I will be able to pay you as well as the late Lord Hobart did…'

'That's not important, my lady, what is important is that I do not have to part from my angels.'

'Angels!' Charlotte laughed. 'Just look at them. They are like wild things, shrieking and splashing each other. Their skirts are soaked and their hair ribbons untied. Anything less like angels I cannot imagine.'

'Oh, my lady, I was so distracted by what you were saying. I'll go and—'

'No, Quinny, do not scold them. It is good to see them happy.'

Joan hurried off to remonstrate gently with the girls and Charlotte continued her walk, deep in thought. It was all very well to talk of plans, but how could she bring them to fruition? She would have to write to Mr Hardacre, find out what was happening; the uncertainty was playing the devil with her nerves. She nearly jumped out of her skin when a shadow fell across her and a voice said, 'Good morning, my lady.'

Her fist went to her heart and even through her clothes she could feel its erratic beat. 'Lord Darton.'

'I am sorry if I startled you. Did you not see me coming?'

'No. I was thinking.'

'Thinking, eh? Now what would a lovely woman be thinking about on a beautiful day like this? It is a beautiful day, is it not?'

'Indeed, yes.' Her heart was still thumping and she could hardly find the breath to speak.

'Makes you feel glad to be alive.'

'Yes.'

'You do not sound very convinced of it. Is life treating you so ill that you cannot smile?'

'It is not life that treats me ill,' she retorted. 'It is people…'

'Of whom I am one.'

She lowered her head without speaking; it was as good as an affirmation. He fell into step beside her without waiting for an invitation to do so. She walked on, gazing out to sea so that she did not have to look at him. He was so self-assured, so impertinent, as if he expected her to fall into his arms simply because he smiled at her. Well, she would not give him the satisfaction. And it was the second time too; he had done so the other evening at dinner. He had done it to goad her, and then later in the wine cellar, he had been… How had he been? Kind or insolent? Insolent, she decided, putting his arm about her in that proprietorial way and kissing her, as if she belonged to him. She belonged to no one. Why, then, was she so dependent? Whom could she trust?

'You are still in a brown study,' he said. 'What is it that fills your mind so completely, you can shut yourself off from everything around you?'

'My thoughts are my own.'

'Share them with me.'

'You would not find them interesting.'

'How can I tell if you keep them to yourself?' He paused, then, smiling, went on. 'But let me guess. You are asking yourself how long you can put up with your brother-in-law's guests. You are wondering if Lord Hobart will play so deep he will lose the roof over your head. You are wondering what will become of you. And you are debating how far you can trust me.'

'If that be so, then perhaps you, in your wisdom, can also tell me the answers.'

He sighed. 'I would that I knew. I fancy Sir Roland and Mr Spike will stay until Lord Hobart pays what he owes.'

'And if he cannot pay?'

'They will take whatever they can lay their hands on: pictures, ornaments…'

'Not the house?'

'They might try, but they are not the only ones in the game, you know.'

'I do know. What I do not know is how deep in it you are.'

'Deep enough to foil them, I hope.' He paused. 'My lady, can you not leave? I know it has been your home and you must be fond of it, but surely you are not happy with the situation.'

'You must know I am not. What I cannot understand is why you stay. You are not like the others. I do not believe you are as addicted to drink and gambling as they are. Nor that you are so pinched in the pocket that you must deprive my brother-in-law of everything he possesses.'

'Men who play as badly as he does deserve to lose.'

'You do not have to encourage him.'

'He needs no encouragement, believe me. My concern is for you.'

She looked up at him startled by his words. 'Why?'

'Because I think fate has dealt you an unkind hand.'

She laughed suddenly at the gambling connotation. 'I am not a gambler…'

'No? I think we all gamble at some time in our lives. Oh, it might not be with cards or wagers, but sometimes the decisions we make are gambles in themselves. You are gambling that the house party breaks up with no harm done and Cecil turns into an honourable man and—'

'Lord Darton, that is wishing for the moon, not gambling.'

'Then what are you going to do?' he asked seriously.

She stopped and turned towards him, looking into his face for the first time. Either he was a very good actor or what she saw in his brown eyes was a genuine concern. Did he care? Suddenly it was important that he should. She wanted him on her side, she wanted him to understand. She wanted to feel able to lean on him for support as she had once leaned on Grenville. Her husband. Not since his death had she looked at any man with longing, not until now. Surely to God she had not fallen in love again? No, she told herself, it was simply that she felt lonely and isolated and needed a shoulder to cry on. But she must not cry, she must not.

He lifted a finger and gently wiped her cheek with the back of it and she knew she had failed; the tears were gathering in her eyes and one had slipped down her face. 'My lady, I hate to see you distressed.'

'How can that be true?' she asked, suddenly asserting herself. 'When you yourself have added to it.'

'It is not my wish to do so, but I must play my part.'

'Why?'

'Now, do you know, I have no idea. Perhaps because I was bored and I enjoy a game of cards as well as the next man. Perhaps because I have taken a dislike to Cecil Hobart and his associates. I do not like a man who lays claim to kinship simply to fleece me. Or it may be that you and I never did have that conversation about education.'

'Education?'

'Had you forgot? You were expounding your views on teaching. Unusual they were too. Children should learn to be happy, you said, that life is not all work…'

She smiled at the memory. How affronted she had been at his daring to speak to her without an introduction. That seemed such a little thing compared to what had happened since. 'So I did. But you did not agree.'

'I neither agreed nor disagreed, but I was interested.'

'Why?'

'I have a daughter, Lady Hobart, a daughter who needs teaching.'

'Oh, I did not realise that, but surely she has a governess and music teachers and dancing masters, things that my poor village children do not have.'

'Is that why you stay? Because of them.'

'Partly. My wish is to open a school.'

'I thought you already had one.'

'I mean a proper school, one with paying pupils. If Lord Hobart had not come back from India, I might have asked his permission to convert part of the Manor, I could have sent him a little rent from the income.' She sighed. 'But it was not to be and now I must find other premises.'

'The village children would never pay enough to cover the overheads,' he pointed out. 'Unless you were not telling the truth when you told his lordship you had no money and you mean to subsidise it from your own purse.'

'By paying pupils I meant the children of parents like yourself who can afford the fees.'

'Are you qualified to teach them?'

'I can teach the younger ones. I would employ someone for the more advanced pupils.'

'I see. And would the children of the idle rich also be taught that life is not all hard labour? They have no conception of that, you know. Their whole lives are a round of indolence and enjoyment. The schoolroom is the only place where they are expected to do any work and, if they do not see the need for it, they rebel.' He laughed suddenly. It was a merry sound and for a little while she forgot their animosity and relaxed a little. 'That I do know.'

'Then one must persuade them of the advantages. One must make learning enjoyable.'

'Your present pupils seem to have learned that lesson already.'

'They are keen to learn.' She paused a moment, then added, 'I collect you did not find school enjoyable.'

'No, it was a harsh regime, though it did me no harm, but not what I had in mind for Julia.'

'Your daughter?'

'Yes. She is thirteen years old, thoroughly spoiled and a hoyden to boot. I hoped school might tame her.'

'A daughter is not a wild animal, my lord.'

'This one is.'

'How can you say that? She is your flesh and blood. You made her what she is.'

'I have seen little of her. She grew up with my father and mother while I was with my regiment. If there be any fault, it is theirs.'

'Perhaps, Lord Darton, you expect too much of her and of them.'

'How so?'

'You are a stranger to her and yet, I surmise, you lay down the law, demand to be obeyed, not as a father who loves her, but as if she were one of your troopers who could be flogged into submission.'

'You go too far, my lady. You have no grounds for criticising me when you do not know the whole. My patience is exhausted.'

'And you think sending her away to school is the answer?'

'Yes, but it must be the right school, that is why I was on the road, in search of one.'

'At Parson's End?' The tone of her voice told him that she did not believe that. 'Where there just happened to be a gambling den and you like nothing so much as chancing your arm at the gaming table. Your daughter, deprived of your company for most of her life, can go without it a little longer while you indulge your weakness. I misjudged you, my lord, I thought you possessed a grain or two of tender feelings, but I was wrong.'

He was furious. Not since he was in leading strings had anyone spoken so bluntly to him. At school he had been the leader of whatever pranks were played and later, in the army, no soldier would have dared to criticise him in that fashion. He felt as if she had dealt him a blow to the body and winded him. He had never had to defend his actions and he would not do so now. He stopped, turned to her and bowed. 'I see no advantage in pursuing this conversation, my lady,' he said. 'I bid you good day.'

She watched him stride away, kicking at the sand as he went, swinging his cane as if he were wielding a broadsword. She had gone too far and now she had lost the only ally she might have had. Why, if she had played her cards right, she might have found her first pupil. She laughed aloud at yet another allusion to gambling, but it was a rough, tearful sound.

'Mama, tell us the joke,' Lizzie called. The girls were coming towards her along the water's edge, with Miss Quinn in their wake. 'Did Viscount Darton say something funny?'

She gathered the girls to her and smiled. 'No, I was thinking what a beautiful day it is. It makes me feel so much more cheerful after all the rain we have had. But now we must go back.'

Back to that den of iniquity. She led them towards the path. Where would it all end?

## Chapter Five

Her room was a shambles. While she had been out, someone had made a thorough search of it. Her clothes had been thrown out of the drawers and chests and were strewn over the floor; the covers had been pulled off the bed and the mattress removed. Her small jewel box had been broken open and everything taken; necklaces, brooches, even her betrothal ring, all gone. Even the few guineas tucked away in a small bag had been taken, leaving her truly penniless.

With no word from Mr Hardacre and matters going from bad to worse, she had been coming slowly to the conclusion that she must give up all idea of a school and use whatever assets she had to get herself and her children to her great-uncle and risk his displeasure. Now she could not even do that. But who had taken them? She trusted the servants; in any case, a thieving servant would not have made this mess—he or she would have taken what they wanted stealthily and covered their tracks. Whoever had done this did not care who knew it. Cecil was desperate for money. She turned on her heel and went downstairs to seek him out, anger driving away all caution.

It was Sunday afternoon, a time for worship and contemplation in most households, but at Easterley Manor the men and women were already at the gaming table. She had not ventured in the room where they were playing before, and they all looked up in surprise as the door was flung open and she rushed in, her skirts swishing about her, betraying her agitation. The table was laid with a green cloth; there were scattered cards and piles of money, some of it at the players' elbows, some in the middle of the table, some of it holding down scribbled vouchers. But what caught her eye was not the money, but her pearls. She darted forward and grabbed them. 'These are mine! Stolen from my room.'

Cecil grabbed them back. 'Stolen from my father, you mean,' he said, sneering at her. 'Taken from my inheritance. I simply retrieved what was mine.' He lifted them out of her reach as she went to grab them again. 'Oh, no, my dear, I am afraid you must forfeit them.'

'My father gave me those pearls long before I ever came to this house.'

'Why should I believe that? I know for a fact my mother had some exactly like these; indeed, I think these are the very ones. What did you do for my father to persuade him to give them to you?'

She heard one of the women giggle. Enraged, she turned to look at them all. There was not a single friendly face among them. Even Viscount Darton, who had professed to be concerned for her, was looking bored, as if her domestic squabbles had nothing to do with him.

'I take what is mine,' Cecil went on. 'You should not have hidden them from me when I have been so good as to give you and your bratlings a home. Now go away, you are interrupting our game.'

She was not done yet. 'And the money? I had five guineas…'

'Five, was it? And you said you had nothing. I knew you were lying.'

'It was all I had.'

'Extracted from my father as he lay dying, no doubt.'

She was so appalled that she could not speak. She stared at him, clasping her hands into fists.

'I gave her the money,' Stacey deliberately drawled, controlling his anger with a huge effort.

'Good God, man, what for?' Augustus Spike wanted to know. 'Do not tell me you managed to melt the ice.'

'Is it not customary to reward the servants of one's host?' he queried mildly, though it was taking all his will to stop himself laying a facer on the man. He dare not look at Lady Hobart, though he could easily imagine the venom in her eyes. Oh, how she must hate him! But it was better to call her a servant than allow these lascivious men to call her something worse.

'Certainly, if they serve you well,' Augustus Spike said with a grin that made his meaning very clear.

'Do you expect me to believe that?' Cecil demanded of Stacey, ignoring Augustus.

Stacey shrugged. 'It matters not one jot what you believe. But I think you should give the lady back her money.'

'You know damn well, I do not have it. It went on that last hand. And if we do not proceed with the game, I never will win it back. Now, do you think we can get on with it? Your deal, Reggie, I believe.'

Charlotte, knowing she was getting nowhere and unwilling to lay herself open to any more accusations and embarrassing innuendo, turned and fled from the room.

Stacey counted out five guineas from the pile at his elbow and got up to follow her. 'I will add this to the amount you owe me, Hobart,' he said, as he went.

\* \* \*

He caught up with her on the second landing. She was in such a hurry that the only way he could stop her was to grab her arm and make her turn to face him. He lifted her hand and put the coins into it. 'Yours, I believe,' he said.

Oh, how she longed to throw them in his face, to call him every sort of name she could think of; he was no better than the rest. He had called her a servant, had implied… Oh, it was too mortifying. Did he really think of her in those terms? Not a real lady, but a servant who had married a title. She could point his error out to him, tell him she was a Falconer and watch his reaction, but why should she? She had never traded on that and would not do so now. What was worse was that she could not even give herself the satisfaction of refusing to take the money because she needed it. She clenched her fingers over it and gave way to the temptation to vent her anger and frustration on him. She hit him on the jaw, hard enough to rock his head back.

He quickly regained his balance. 'Is that your usual way of showing gratitude?' he demanded. 'For your sake I have probably made an enemy of Cecil Hobart, if not the whole company…'

'I did not ask you to do it.' She was sorry she had hit him. The edge of one of the coins must have caught his cheek; there was a red mark where she had struck him. Never before had she lost her temper so completely and lashed out at anyone. She should not have done it, especially when he, for all his faults, had tried to help her. But she could not bring herself to apologise.

He smiled ruefully, rubbing his jaw. 'You certainly pack a punch, my lady. Be thankful that I am gentleman enough not to retaliate.'

'Oh, go away,' she said. 'Go back to your playmates. Leave me alone.' But she was weeping; the tears were running down her face, salty, unstoppable. She had never felt so miserable, so alone. She was destitute and she was bandying words with this man as if it were his fault. She turned away, but not before he saw her distress. His heart, already as good as lost, went out to her. He knew that, however often they might quarrel, whatever she had been in the past—whether it was a lady's maid, which would account for her gentility, the daughter of a mushroom who had spent new money having her educated, or a governess—he loved her and would go on loving her to his dying day. Anne-Marie, for all her high and mighty manners, had not had half the character of the woman who turned from him now so that he might not see her tears.

He reached out and took her by the shoulders,

turning her back towards him. The fight had gone out of her; she did not resist. 'Oh, my dear, please do not cry. I would not for the world have made you cry.'

His soft words were her undoing. She leaned into him and he enfolded her in his arms without speaking. Now was not the time for words. She was soaking the front of his waistcoat, but he did not care. There was no longer any doubt in his mind that he loved her. He loved her for her spirit, her compassion for others less fortunate, for her consideration, her independence and her fortitude. He loved her for her beauty and her soft, pliant body, clinging to him now, needing comfort. What comfort could he give? He took a handkerchief from his pocket and dabbed at her cheeks, carefully wiping away the tears.

'Thank you.' Her words were whispered. 'I'm sorry I hit you.'

'And I am sorry to have added to your distress. I did not mean to, believe me. I would rather help you.'

She smiled shakily. 'You have. You recovered my money.'

'Five guineas will not take you very far. Is that truly all you have?'

'Yes, and my jewels. They are mine, you know, presents from my father and my husband. Cecil has no claim on them.'

'I am sure he has not, but he is desperate.' He

paused to lift her chin with his finger so that he could look into her eyes, still bright with tears. 'Do you feel better now? I must go back to the game. It is the only way…' He released her and stood back, reluctant to leave her, wanting to go on holding her, but knowing, if he did not return to the game, any gains he had made would be lost.

'What do you mean, the only way?' she demanded, but he had gone, striding down the corridor towards the stairs.

She turned and went into her room, her figure drooping with fatigue, a fatigue brought on by worry and sleeplessness. She put the money in the pocket of her skirt, the only place where it was safe, and began slowly, mechanically, to tidy up the mess. Her mind was numb. She could see no way out of her predicament.

The game continued all day and well into the night. The players stopped only to call for food and more wine, but they did not leave the table except to relieve themselves. The more Cecil lost, the more he drank; the more he drank, the more fuddled his brain became and the more he lost. Stacey remained sober, concentrating as never before on the cards, watching everyone else, memorising where the cards were. He was doing it for Charlotte Hobart, the woman he loved as he had loved no other and, if luck should favour him, then he would hand everything he had won to her. She should have her school and Julia would come to it and in the fullness of time, when his daughter was happy and settled, he would court Charlotte Hobart properly. Her didn't care about her antecedents; it was the woman he loved, not her family and whether they were high or low. The prospect brought a tiny smile to his lips. But if he lost? He did not want to contemplate that and so he concentrated harder than ever.

At midnight, Cecil threw down his cards. 'Gentlemen, you have run me aground.' Money and jewels had gone and he reached for a pencil and a slip of paper to write out yet another voucher.

'No more vouchers,' Sir Roland said.

'I have nothing else.'

'What about the inheritance?' Reginald Comins asked him. 'You said as soon as the lawyers had finished sorting it out, you would be a rich man.'

Stacey laughed. 'It is evident you do not know the terms of the late Lord Hobart's will, Mr Comins.'

'Keep your tongue between your teeth, Darton,' Cecil growled.

'Oh, let us hear the terms of this will on which we have all put so much trust,' one of the women put in.

'Hobart has inherited Easterley Manor and

whatever he can make the estate earn,' he said. 'But no ready money. That is all in trust for the children.'

'Whose children?'

'Your host's and Lady Hobart's.'

'Cecil has no children,' Adelia said. 'You haven't, have you, Cecil? I assume they must be legitimate.'

'I plan to marry very soon.'

'Then let us felicitate you. Who is the lucky lady? And when will the nuptials take place?'

'Soon.'

'And another year before we hear of an issue,' Henry Corton put in. He had made his money in the slave trade and was extraordinarily fat; his coat with its silver buttons strained across his corseted stomach. He was ahead, not by much, but enough to make him wary. 'Do you expect us to wait that long to be paid? Supposing the lady is barren?'

'You know, my friends, I think we have been bubbled,' Reginald Comins added. 'And I, for one, intend to cut my losses and withdraw.'

One by one, others picked up their winnings or signed vouchers, mostly in favour of Sir Roland or Stacey, and then left the room. Only Stacey, Sir Roland, Augustus and Lady Grey remained.

'You'll marry our friend here, won't you, Adelia?' Sir Roland asked her. 'Give him an heir…'

'Now why should I do that?'

'Because if the Viscount is correct, it is the only way to that inheritance.' He grinned. 'It would be your child's birthright. I am sure you could find ways of laying your hands on it.'

'So's I could pass it on to you. What is there for me in that? No, you find another cat's paw. I'm off with the others.' She picked up the ten guineas she had won and flounced from the room, leaving Cecil facing his two chief tormentors and Stacey Darton, who still smiled, still chinked the coins he had won.

'Then there is nothing for it but you will have to marry the ice maiden,' Augustus told Cecil with a leer. 'At least we know she ain't barren.'

'I cannot marry my dead brother's wife, it ain't allowed.'

'Then I will,' Sir Roland said. 'Might enjoy warming her up a bit.'

'You need the lady's consent for that,' Stacey said laconically, trying desperately not to let his fury show.

'Oh, I think she can be persuaded, if it means saving her precious house and her daughters. Pretty little things they are.'

Spike gave a cracked laugh. 'Can't see you as a family man, Roly, my friend, not even for a fortune.'

'There is no fortune,' Stacey said quietly. He had himself firmly under control, but it would take very little to goad him into lashing out at all three. It would, he knew, be a foolish thing to do. The three together could easily overcome him and what help would he be to Charlotte and her little girls then?

'How do you know that?' Both men rounded on him.

'Lord Hobart's attorney is also my attorney and he told me. It is no more than pin money. Cecil ruined his father years ago.'

They turned on Cecil, making him cringe. 'Is this true?'

'No, it is not,' he said. 'He's lying. There's a fortune. I'm only waiting for that damned lawyer to get on with overturning the will. He said it would be easy and not take long.'

They looked from him to Stacey, wondering whom to believe. 'I'll buy Hobart's vouchers off you,' he put in while they hesitated. 'At half their face value.'

Augustus Spike laughed. 'Why should we do that when we have the chance to be paid in full?'

'You think you will be paid in full?' Stacey queried. 'Are you prepared to gamble on that?' He let the coins trickle through his fingers on to the table. 'These and more for your vouchers. A bird in the hand, you know.'

'No,' Augustus said. 'The game continues. He still has a house.'

'I can't stake that.' Cecil said, aghast. His face was grey, his eyes wild; he was a man in a panic, a dangerous man, but the fever was still bright in him. The conviction that he could win everything back had not left him.

Stacey watched them, assessing their mood, knowing if the game went on, then he, too, must go on. He could not leave with the others, knowing he was leaving Charlotte Hobart to her fate. Would she come away with him? He doubted it. In her eyes he was little better than his companions. The fact that she had allowed him to kiss her, had cried in his arms, meant nothing except that she had no one else and he happened to be there. If he had read her character correctly, she was already regretting her weakness.

'My lady, my lady, they have called for their carriages.' The curtains were swished back and the room filled with sunlight. Charlotte blinked and sat up. Her eyes felt puffy and her head felt like wool; she had certainly not taken in what Miss Quinn had said.

'What time is it, Quinny?'

'Ten o'clock, my lady. And those dreadful people are going. I heard one of them call for the carriages.'

Ten! She remembered being wide awake when the clock struck two, and again at three. She must have cried herself to sleep after that. She threw back the bedcovers and got up. 'Help me dress. I must see this for myself.'

Half an hour later, washed and dressed in her usual black silk, her hair tucked up under a black lace cap, she walked sedately down the main staircase. The front door was open and servants were loading piles of bags and boxes into two carriages. Their owners were milling about, picking up gloves, adjusting bonnets and hats.

Lady Grey, seeing her, came forward. 'Ah, Lady Hobart, you have come to see us off. I am leaving with Mr and Mrs Comins. There's nothing worth having here, after all.'

'Then I wish you a pleasant journey.'

'And good riddance, eh?' The woman laughed. And when Charlotte did not answer, added, 'Oh, I do not blame you. Nor do I envy you. Cecil Hobart is about the worst rakeshame I ever met and I've met a few, I can tell you. You are welcome to him.' She turned as her maid approached. 'Is everything in? Then let us be off.'

Charlotte watched them depart, but realised almost immediately that Viscount Darton was not among them, nor Sir Roland Bentwater and Mr Spike. She turned to Foster, who had been overseeing the stowing of the baggage. 'Have the others also left?'

'No, my lady, they are still abed. The game did not break up until dawn.'

So they had not all gone. No doubt those that remained would continue gambling until Cecil had nothing left, not even the Manor. What then? She hardly dare think of the house in the hands of Sir Roland or Mr Spike, nor, come to that, Viscount Darton, though of the three, he was the most likely to give her time to make other arrangements.

Almost dragging her feet, she went along the hall to the small parlour near the kitchen, which, in times gone by, had been the housekeeper's and more recently the room where she instructed Mrs Evans about the meals for the day and gave orders to the servants. It was small and cosy and Cecil never ventured there. She needed to think.

She was standing at the window, looking with unseeing eyes as the pot boy crossed the yard with a bucket of scraps for the chickens, deep in contemplation, not of the scene but of her predicament, when she heard a light tap of the door. Thinking it was Mrs Evans, she turned and called, 'Come in.'

It was not the cook, but Stacey Darton. He was dressed for riding and her heart gave a sudden leap of alarm. Was he leaving like the others after all?

Having bled Cecil dry, was he abandoning her to her fate? Had he come to say goodbye? 'Lord Darton.' She could not keep the tremor from her voice. She had not realised until now, when it seemed she was losing him, how much she had been depending on him to curb the excesses of her brother-in-law and his cronies, and if he left she would be more at their mercy than ever. Or was there more to it than that? Did she want him to stay because of something else, something deep inside her she refused to recognise, but which insisted on pushing its way to the surface of her mind? She pulled herself together, stiffened her spine and looked him directly in the eye. 'What can I do for you, my lord?'

He bowed. She looked exhausted, which was hardly to be wondered at. 'Good morning, my lady. Forgive me for intruding, but I have something of yours to return to you.' He held up a small velvet bag; because she did not put out her hand to take it, he stepped forward and tipped its contents on to the cloth covered table. There lay her necklaces and brooches and betrothal ring.

She was so taken aback she could only gasp. She longed to pick them up, but something held her back, a sense of fairness or it might have been pride. 'But, my lord, you must have won them in play. That means they are yours.'

'And I choose to give them to you. I would not have you believe I could steal from a woman or condone it in others.'

'I did not think it,' she murmured. 'Was that what you meant when you said it was the only way?'

'Yes.'

'Is Cecil quite ruined?'

'I believe so.'

'In debt to you?'

'Not by much, I took the jewels as my share. His main liabilities are still with Sir Roland and Mr Spike.'

'Then I must press forward with my own plans.' She picked up her jewellery and put it back in the bag. 'I do not know how to thank you for these. They will enable me to pay an advance on the rent of a house.'

'You cannot mean to sell them? Surely they are of great sentimental value?'

'I cannot afford sentiment, my lord. I must go to Ipswich and get what I can for them and then I must look for a home for me, my daughters and whichever of the servants want to come with me. And I must earn a living. A school is the only way.'

He looked closely at her. She was nearly at breaking point, her lovely eyes clouded with worry, her posture drooping. Dare he tell her what was in his heart? Dare he say, 'I love you and I want to take care of you, so that you need never worry about a thing again? I want you to be my wife.' Would she be convinced? And there was still the problem of Julia, the problem that had made him set off from home over two weeks before, a problem that had been pushed to the back of his mind, but which insisted on coming to the fore. Could he, instead of finding a school for his daughter, confront her with a new wife? However sympathetic Charlotte was, Julia would hate her. Unless they could be brought together in a different way.

'My lady,' He enclosed both her hands in his. The gesture was so natural she did not pull away. 'Let me do it for you.'

'Do what?'

'Take your jewels and exchange them for hard cash. I know a man. He would give you a fair deal, a better one than you might obtain by going alone.'

He was right. She knew no one and would be prey to any scoundrel who tried to pull the wool over her eyes, but even so she hesitated. 'I don't know what to say, my lord.'

'Do you trust me?'

She looked into his brown eyes gazing into hers and knew she did. Knew she loved him. Knew if she allowed him to do this for her, he would not be lost to her because he would have to come back when his errand had been accomplished. 'Yes, my lord, I do, but it is a great deal to ask. You must be anxious to go about your own business. Your daughter will be wondering what has become of you. I cannot think why you have stayed so long.'

'Can't you?' he asked softly.

'Gambling,' she said. 'You said you enjoyed it as well as the next man.'

Her answer made him realise he had not entirely won her over and it was too soon to say what was in his heart. 'So I did, but that does not mean I cannot help a lady in distress.' He paused. 'Let me do this for you. A lady travelling alone, carrying valuables, would be a target for every ruffian in the county and I can see to my business at the same time.'

'Then I thank you from the bottom of my heart.' The velvet bag was transferred from her hands to his.

While their hands were still touching, he bent forward and kissed her forehead. 'I will be there and back in no time, my dear, but take care, won't you? Keep out of the way of those mountebanks. If you have to get out in a hurry, go to the parsonage until I get back.'

He had called her his dear, had kissed her again, oh, so lightly on the forehead. There had been nothing objectionable about it, nothing lustful, but she did not dare hope that it meant any more than a compassionate concern for the predicament she was in. 'Thank you,' she whispered.

And then he was gone. She turned and gazed out of the window again, and a few moments later saw him cross the yard to the stables where one of the grooms brought out his big white stallion, saddled and ready to go. She watched him leap easily on to its back and clatter out of the yard to disappear round the side of the house. How long would he be gone? Oh, she hoped he would be quick, because now she was more than ever at the mercy of Cecil's cronies. Had they won the house from him? Were they about to turn him out and her along with him? She did not care what happened to Cecil, but she did care what happened to her daughters and the rest of the household. What price jewels compared to that?

She hurried up to the schoolroom, where Joan Quinn was endeavouring to teach her pupils. They knew there was something afoot; they had heard the first of the guests leave and could not concentrate on their lessons for trying to decide whether that meant they were all going and life could go back to being what it had been before, or that others might come in their place. Charlotte was unable to enlighten them. 'Never mind them,' she said, making up her mind that there was no time to be lost.

'Come, put on your coats and bonnets, we are going to the village. It is time we went back to school.'

They obeyed with delight and all three were soon making their way along the lane to the village. The Reverend was taking her class and looked up with a delighted smile when she entered. 'Why, Lady Hobart, how good it is to see you. Children, greet her ladyship properly.'

The children stood and chanted, 'Good morning, my lady.'

She smiled as she answered. It had been hard to get them to be natural with her. At first they had been overawed that she was a lady and she had not wanted them to address her as 'my lady', but the Rector insisted they must use the proper form of address and she could not think what else they should call her. Most of them had become used to it, but some of them forgot now and again and called her miss or missus. They did not hold grudges and were pleased to see her. Of course, it might be because she was not as strict as the Reverend Fuller and her lessons more fun.

'Are you come to take your class?' the Rector asked her.

'If it is agreeable to you.'

'Of course it is. Afterwards, I should like to speak to you. I have some news you might find interesting concerning the request you made of me two weeks ago.'

The only request she had made that she could remember was about finding a house to use for a school. Did that mean he knew of somewhere? She could hardly wait to find out, but forced herself to concentrate on hearing the children read and gently correcting their mistakes.

As soon as the children were freed to go home, she stepped over to the Rectory. The parson greeted her with a warm smile and, while his wife took Lizzie and Fanny with her to the kitchen to see some new kittens, he conducted her to the drawing room and asked her to sit. It was a large comfortable room, but a little shabby. The Reverend was not a worldly man and much of his stipend went on charitable work. 'Did the lessons go well?' he asked, seating himself opposite her.

'Yes. It was good to be back with the children.'

'Does that mean Lord Hobart's guests have left?'

'All but two, but the problem remains. I must move.'

'You have not changed your mind, then?'

'No, I am more determined than ever.'

'Do you know Captain Alexander MacArthur, my lady?'

'Captain MacArthur who lives in the house on the

cliff near the lighthouse? The Crow's Nest, isn't that its name?'

'Yes. His wife died last year. Her funeral service was held here at this church.'

'Yes, I remember, but he is at sea so often, I can hardly say I know him.'

'For all his blustery ways, a Christian gentleman.' He paused as his wife came in carrying a tea tray, which she set down on the table in the window.

'The little girls are amusing themselves with the kittens,' she said, pouring tea for her visitor and offering her a piece of cake. 'Good as gold, they are.'

'Thank you,' Charlotte said, knowing that Lizzie and Fanny had had the stuffing knocked out of them in the last three weeks, just as she had. She would rather have them noisy and mischievous than so subdued they were afraid to open their mouths. 'I do not want to trouble them with thoughts of more upheaval until I have everything settled.'

'Very wise,' the Reverend said. 'But perhaps it might not be too long if what I suggest is agreeable to you.'

'You were speaking of Captain MacArthur,' she said.

'Yes. He is off back to sea, being sent to the Indian Ocean, he told me, and he has decided to let his house. I told him about your plans and he expressed an interest.' He paused to let his words sink in, then added, 'It might only be for a year, but it would give you time to find something more permanent.'

'He knows what I intend to do? That it will be used for a school?'

'Yes, I told him. He was a little reluctant at first, but I explained there would only be a handful of young lady pupils from the very best backgrounds and you would make only minimal alterations to accommodate them, and so he agreed.'

'You did not tell him I want to include the village children?'

'No.' He smiled suddenly, his grey eyes lighting with mischief, making him seem years younger. 'What the eye does not see the heart cannot grieve over. In any case, there is an extensive stable block which will make a fine classroom for the village children. They need not mix.'

That was not Charlotte's idea at all, but she decided not to tell him so. She must do nothing to jeopardise her plans now there seemed a chance they might be brought to fruition. 'Did he mention the rent?'

'No, that is up to you to negotiate. He is a generous man and, as I said, a true Christian and I do not think money is his first consideration. I will be disappointed in him if it is.'

'Then I must see him at the first opportunity.'

'He is in London at the moment. He told me he had

to go to the Admiralty for his orders, and then see to the outfitting of his new ship, but he intends to come back before he sails. You will be able to see him then.'

Her heart sank; as soon as he had told her the news she wanted to rush off and make all the arrangements—now she must wait again. She rose to go. 'Thank you very much, Reverend. I shall wait patiently to hear from you that Captain MacArthur is back and will see me.'

He rose too and conducted her to the kitchen where Mrs Fuller was busy making bread, a great deal more than could possibly be needed for two people, Charlotte noted, guessing that the extra was destined for the poor. It reminded her that it was over two weeks since she had taken a basket of food to the village. She would have to sneak some out from under Cecil's nose. She smiled wryly to herself. Did the larder and its contents still belong to Cecil? It was a measure of her returning confidence that she could smile at all.

The girls were reluctant to be dragged from the kittens, but came away on the promise they could visit them again in a day or two. Once on the lane, heading towards the Manor, Charlotte took stock. She had to stay there a little longer, so whoever was now in charge must not be antagonised, not until she was ready. How much would the Captain want in rent? How much would Viscount Darton get for her jewellery? Who would come back first, the Viscount or the Captain? She had better write to Mr Hardacre to acquaint him with the latest developments. He would, as her man of business, have to sign the rental agreement and he might still be trying to persuade the trustees to release some of the girls' legacy. If the sale of her jewels did not realise enough, she might still need some of that. But it would be paid back with interest, on that she was determined. Lizzie and Fanny would not lose their dowries or their come-out. That was the most important thing in a young lady's life apart from her betrothal and marriage.

'Can we go for a walk on the beach?' Fanny asked. 'I don't want to go home yet.'

'Yes, why not?' she said. She did not want to go back to the Manor any sooner than she must and while she was on the cliff she would take a look at the outside of The Crow's Nest.

The house was a little way from the village on the southern side of the Hobart estate. It stood close to the edge of the cliff and she made a mental note that it would have to be fenced. With the children trailing behind her, she walked all round the property. It was a large house, with a strange turret at one end, from the top of which, on a good day, she surmised, one could see for miles out to sea; no wonder the Captain had dubbed it The Crow's Nest.

The house was nothing like as big as Easterley Manor, but, as far as she could see by peering in those windows that were not shuttered, there were several reception rooms downstairs, two of which were big enough to be used as classrooms. There was a coach house and a stable and a small garden. Its isolation was, perhaps, a drawback; there were no other buildings in sight except the lighthouse and the little cottage where the old footman, Jenkins, lived. Later, she might go and see him; she would need a man about the place and he might be glad of a few shillings to supplement the tiny pension the late Lord Hobart had arranged for him.

Having seen all she could, she gave in to the girls' entreaties to be allowed to go down the path to the beach. Walking along the sand, she was reminded of the last time she had walked there and been accosted by Viscount Darton. She had been unsure of his motives, prickly as a hedgehog, mistrustful, wary. But then he had not made it easy to trust him, had he? He was often uncivil and as much of a gambler as Cecil, the only thing that was different was that he seemed to be more successful. Had he really been thinking of her all along, wanting to act the knight in shining armour, or was that something he had dreamed up after he arrived? He could not have known anything about her before he arrived.

But he *had* given her back her jewels. And taken them away again. She had meekly allowed him to ride off with them. Supposing he didn't come back? Supposing he simply took the last, the very last, of her possessions and kept them for himself? She had only his word that he meant to sell them for her. How he would be laughing at her naïveté! The thought drained the blood from her face and made her stumble.

He wasn't like that, she scolded herself, as she regained her balance. She had looked into his eyes and seen only compassion; she had stood in his arms and he had comforted her. He had won the jewels at the gaming table and would have been entitled to keep them and had no need even to tell her of it. Instead he had brought them to her. He had asked her if she trusted him and she had said she did. She had been absolutely sure, when she spoke, that it was the truth. Why the doubts now? 'Dear God, I hope and pray I was right to trust him,' she murmured. 'Otherwise we are undone.'

She turned back to the girls, who were standing at the water's edge, gazing out over the sea at a ship riding at anchor in the bay, trying to guess whence it came. 'The *Orient*,' Lizzie said. 'It is loaded with silks and tea and spices to be sold in Ipswich.'

'No, it's a pirate ship,' Fanny said. She liked to read adventure stories in which pirates and captured princesses figured largely.

'Or smugglers,' Lizzie said. 'They are going to come into the bay when it gets dark and unload their contraband while we are asleep.'

Charlotte smiled. It was good to hear her daughters chatting happily again. Soon, God willing, the last few weeks would be nothing but a bad dream. 'Come, girls, we must go,' she said, holding out her hands to them. 'The tide is coming in and we don't want to be caught out by it.'

God willing, she repeated, as they made their way up the cliff path and back to Easterley Manor, a house, a roof over their heads, a source of sustenance, but no longer a home. God willing the nightmare would soon be over. 'Stacey Darton, if you have an ounce of compassion, come back to me,' she said to herself. 'If you cannot love me, at least have mercy on me.'

Stacey had every intention of returning, just as soon as his errand had been accomplished, and no intention whatsoever of selling Charlotte's jewellery. He had known when he suggested it that he could not bring himself to do it. Instead he had ridden to Ipswich and taken the London mail from the Great White Horse, leaving Ivor at the inn to be picked up on his return.

Luckily there were no incidents on the journey, no highwaymen, no broken wheels, no trees blown across the road and all the changes of horses and picking up of the mail went smoothly so that they arrived at the Spread Eagle in Gracechurch Street just before seven the following morning. The speed with which they had travelled precluded sleeping comfortably, but he was too fired up, his head too full of whirring thoughts to be able to do more than nod off now and again, only to be awakened at their next stop. As soon as the coach was at a standstill at its destination he was out of it and looking for a cab to take him to John Hardacre's home in Piccadilly.

'My lord,' the lawyer greeted him when he had been shown into the breakfast room where John was sitting over ham and eggs and coffee. 'I did not know you were in town.'

'A flying visit, only. I am sorry to disturb you so early.'

'Oh, you are not disturbing me. Will you join me?' He rang for a servant to lay another place. 'All is well at Malcomby Hall, I trust.'

'As far as I know. I sent them my direction in case I should be needed urgently, but I have not been home since I saw you last. I have been staying at Easterley Manor.'

'Good heavens! Why?'

'Because of what you told me of your concern for Lady Hobart. I wanted to see for myself what was going on.' He had rehearsed the answer to this question as he rode. 'Hobart is a second cousin and, though the relationship is not close, I did not like the idea of him sullying the family name, even at a distance. And a lady in distress…' He shrugged. 'I could not ignore that.'

John smiled; it was why he had told Stacey of his concern. The young man was a hard-headed soldier, not given to sentimentality, but he was also a chivalrous man who could not pass by and do nothing when he knew there might be someone needing help. He had a large measure of curiosity too. John had told him just enough to arouse it. 'What happened?'

The servant arrived with more hot dishes and a fresh pot of coffee and Stacey waited for him to go before answering. 'He had the most evil collection of house guests it has been my misfortune to meet, all there to gamble. Hobart was in deep, very deep. He is a poor player and does not have the cool demeanour needed to deceive his opponents. I could read his expressions like a book and no doubt the others, who have known him longer, could do so too. He should never have sat at a gaming table.'

'There you have it. It was why his father banished the young rakeshame and nearly ruined himself paying off his debts. So what was the outcome? I assume he lost.'

'Everything. I believe even now the winners are stripping the house of everything valuable.'

'I feared that might happen. And Lady Hobart. How is she?'

'Almost breaking under the strain. Hobart even stole her jewellery and what little money she had and gambled that away.'

'Good God! She must be got out of there at once. I will have to write to Lord Falconer.'

'Lord Falconer? You mean old Falconer of Rickmansworth?'

'Yes, Lady Hobart's great-uncle, younger brother to her maternal grandfather. He came to the title when her grandfather died without a male heir. Did you not know that?'

Stacey was taken aback. That Charlotte was a lady in the true sense of the word he had never doubted; that she came from so illustrious a family had not occurred to him. Such a one would, in his opinion, never have lowered herself to teach in school. How wrong he had been! And he had been so condescending, had taken liberties he never would have done had he known. But why had she never told him? 'No, I did not,' he said. 'I knew she was a lady, that much is easily deduced, but I had no idea she was so well connected.'

'I am surprised you never learned of it. It is hardly a secret.'

Except from me, Stacey thought, and wondered why. 'Why did she never apply to him when she found herself in straitened circumstances?'

'I believe her mother was estranged from him. He is a stickler for protocol and proud that the Falconers can trace the family back to Henry the Eighth's court and he heartily disapproved of her marrying Captain Delaney.' He smiled a little. 'Called him a no-good Irish sea captain.'

'Was he?'

'No, he was an honourable man and a baronet, went down with his ship at Trafalgar. His wife, Lady Hobart's mother, died of a fever soon afterwards and then Lady Hobart lost her husband at Corunna. You did know that?'

'Yes. Poor lady. The death of Lord Hobart must have seemed as if everyone was being taken from her. Is Lord Falconer likely to help her?'

'Might, might not. He certainly said he never wanted to see his niece again. Age may have mellowed him, but it might have made him more obdurate.'

He was tempted to rush straight off and confront Lord Falconer, make him see that it was his duty to acknowledge his great-niece, but decided that would not serve. The man would ask him what business it was of his, might not even admit him and that would be a waste of time. It would be better to stick to his original plan. 'Then we cannot wait to find out. I persuaded her to trust me, which wasn't easy since I was gambling too. I won her jewellery back for her and have told her I would sell it for her, so that she can rent a house. She means to start a school.'

'Yes, she told me of that, but I fear the pieces are not very valuable, they will only fetch a modest amount.'

'I guessed as much, but, as I do not intend to do as she asked, it does not matter.'

'What will you do, then?'

'Keep them safe for her and see that she has enough money to achieve her goal,' he said.

'That is very generous of you, my lord, but do you think you are doing her any favours encouraging her? After all, teaching is hardly an occupation for a lady, you surely must agree.'

Stacey pondered on this for less than a minute. 'No, I don't, and the lady herself evidently does not think so, or she would not have endured the insults of her brother-in-law's guests. I believe the school is something she feels very strongly about.'

'That does not make it right. It is one thing to teach as an act of charity, quite another to make a business of it.'

'I know that. It is why I am here. I will help her,

but it must appear to come from you. You are one of the executors to the late Lord Hobart's will, are you not? You could make the money over to her and pretend it came from the inheritance, something you had previously overlooked.'

'I did tell her I would approach the other trustees with a view to releasing some of her daughters' legacy…'

'And have you?'

'Unfortunately it needs the consent of all three trustees and, though I have written to them, I have not yet had a reply from Lord Swindon, who is out of the country until late in the year. My main aim was not to fund a school, but to help her to live quietly and bring up her daughters until they came of age. I cannot believe that she would consider running a school if she were not in straitened circumstances.'

'Then you cannot have seen her with the children as I have,' he said. 'She is so at ease with them, not lofty, but not indulgent either. She has them well disciplined. And they love her. She is just the sort of person I could entrust with Julia.'

John laughed suddenly. 'Oh, I see, you have a personal motive.'

Stacey smiled. If that was what the lawyer wanted to believe, so be it. But even as he had been speaking, he knew what he had been saying about

Charlotte was the truth. But if she was as dedicated as he said she was, how could he win her for himself? Did he really want to take on a dozen other children as well as Elizabeth and Frances? That was what it amounted to. How could you love the woman and not embrace her aspirations? How could you say you did not like children and let them swarm all over you? On the other hand, how could you let her struggle on alone, when she was determined to go ahead? 'While we dither, she is in danger, and so are her children. What harm can it do to let her have her way, if only to set her free from Cecil Hobart and those two rogues he has brought to Easterley Manor? If it fails, there is no harm done, we will argue with her when that happens.'

John, unable to stand out against Stacey's persuasiveness, smiled. 'Very well. If you have finished your breakfast, we can adjourn to the library and get down to business. I assume you mean to return as soon as it is concluded.'

'Yes, tonight if possible. And I pray no harm has come to her while I have been away. I made her promise to go the parson if staying at the Manor became intolerable, but the sooner I return the better.'

John concealed his smile this time; Stacey Darton had fallen in love and for that reason alone he would agree to do as he asked.

## Chapter Six

Charlotte had expected Stacey back the following evening or the very latest the day after. After all, Ipswich was only a day's ride away, but three days passed and he did not appear and she began to wonder if she had been right to trust him. How long did it take to sell a few trinkets? If Viscount Darton proved to be as big a mountebank as her brother-in-law and his two confederates, her inherent trust in the goodness of human nature was cast into doubt. She had always believed the best in everyone; had even tried to find excuses for Cecil when his father condemned him. Cecil was weak, the other two were evil, but she did not want to believe it was also true of Stacey Darton.

He had been kind to her, kissed her, called her his dear, given her back her money, told her he wanted to help her. And she had fallen in love with him, longed to feel his arms about her again, to feel safe and warm and cherished. Not since Grenville had gone off to war had she felt like that. Her father-in-law had had great affection for her, she knew that, her children loved her, the servants respected her, the parson admired her, but none of that compared with the love of a man. Until Stacey had arrived, she had not realised what was missing and now she had, she felt the emptiness all the more. She wanted him, longed for him, desired him. Surely, surely, she was not such a bad judge of character as to love a rogue? But where was he? Why had he not come back? She kept telling herself anything could have happened to detain him and she was being far too impatient.

With no help for it, she carried on with her housekeeping duties and because there were now fewer guests she was able to resume teaching in the village, which went part of the way to preventing her from brooding. And in the evening, while Cecil and the two men continued to gamble—though what Cecil was using for stakes she did not know—she sat in her room and made plans for her school, knowing they might never come to fruition, but doing it just the same. There was the house to be made ready and equipment bought, and she would need staff, not only servants but other teachers, specialists in their subjects, all of whom would expect good salaries. Was she being too ambitious? But if she could not offer everything a wealthy parent wanted for his daughter, how could she attract pupils? And what about the pupils? Where would she find those? Word of mouth would not be enough, she would have to advertise, discreetly, of course. And it all took time. And time was running out. Was it all a pipe dream? If Viscount Darton did not return, she feared it might be.

She had been sitting at her escritoire, making notes, but now she put her quill down and stared into space. What if something dreadful had happened to him? Supposing he had been waylaid and the money he was bringing to her taken from him? There were frequent reports in the newspapers of highwaymen, footpads, out-of-work soldiers, disgruntled labourers, thieves of every description attacking and even murdering wayfarers for the sake of a few coins. She would not put it past Cecil to do that if he got wind of the Viscount's errand. Had he done it already? Was that what he was gambling with? But if he had, Stacey would have come back and exacted revenge. Unless he was too injured. Or dead. She put her hand to her mouth to stifle the groan that threatened to become a full-blown wail of anguish and told herself firmly she was being fanciful.

Unable to sit still, she began pacing the room and

when that did not serve to calm her, she went downstairs. She would take the men some more wine and perhaps she might learn what Cecil was using for a stake. The other two might have relented over taking his vouchers. After going to the cellar and extracting the last two bottles of Burgundy, she made her way to the dining room, where the men had been ensconced since dinner. She stopped and hesitated outside the door, debating with herself whether it was such a good idea, after all.

'Hobart, my old friend, you are dished up.' This was Augustus Spike's voice. 'Now admit it.'

'The next hand…'

Sir Roland laughed. 'It is always the next hand with you, Cecil, is it not? There will be no next hand, not now we have this pile of brick and stone and everything in it, including the coach and horses, and the lady.'

Charlotte gasped and moved closer to the door.

'The lady?' Cecil asked. 'Roly, you surely did not mean it when you said you'd marry her?'

'Why not? You have gambled her daughters' inheritance as well as your own. How else am I to get my hands on it?'

'She won't have it.'

'Then how do you propose to settle your dues?'

'I don't know. I'll find the blunt somehow.'

'Cecil, old man, what happens if the lady were to meet with an accident, an untimely end?' Augustus asked. 'Wouldn't you be her bratlings' guardian?'

'I suppose I would, but what of it? She's young, youngish anyway, and healthy. And what would I do with a brace of infants?'

'Oh, you could be the loving uncle for a couple of years, couldn't you? Then who knows what might happen?'

Charlotte, glued to the door, stuffed her fist in her mouth to stop herself crying out. She was in terrible danger, more than she had ever imagined. The temptation was to rush in and confront them, let them know she had heard every word, but she held herself in check. If they thought she knew about it, they would not hesitate to do away with her and what would happen to her girls then?

'No.' Cecil sounded more vehement than she would have expected. 'I may be no great shakes as a gambler and not averse to a bit of humbuggery, but I draw the line at that. I don't fancy preaching at Tyburn Cross.'

'Accidents do happen.'

'I won't have anything to do with it. It's too risky.'

'And it would take too long to come to fruition.' It was Augustus, speaking quietly, as if all they had said so far had been leading up to this. 'And, if Darton was telling the truth about his lordship's finances, not worth the candle. There is another way for you to come about.'

'Go on,' Cecil urged him warily.

'We, that is, Roly and I, have an interest in a certain cargo ship. It comes and goes, you understand, and though it is fully laden, it cannot put into port.' He paused before adding, 'You do understand me, I hope?'

'Contraband.'

'Right, my friend. But things have become a little hot of late. The Coast Blockade is suddenly a mite too efficient and we cannot put in at our usual spot at Dungeness. Your little cove, being isolated as it is, will make an ideal landing place. And this house, with its deep cellars, a fine warehouse.'

'Oh, I see. It has been your purpose all along. When I told you about my inheritance, you seized your chance.'

'It could not have come at a better time, my friend, and you were so easy to gull and such a poor gamester, it was child's play. Now, we do not want to deprive you of your house, so all you have to do is to cooperate. You will do that, won't you?'

'And Lady Hobart?'

'She is safe so long as you do as you are told. If not, we shall make sure her demise is laid at your door. I am sure you understand.'

Charlotte heard the scrape of chairs and made good her escape, running up the stairs, clutching the bottles of wine. Reaching the safety of her room, she locked the door and sank on to her bed. What could she do? To whom could she turn? 'Oh, Stacey, Stacey, where are you when I need you so?' she murmured, but there was no one to hear her, no one to help her. She was on her own and she must get herself and her children away. Now. At once.

She put the bottles on the chest, pulled a portmanteau from a cupboard and began stuffing clothes into it and then she stopped. Running away was not the answer. If they saw her leaving the house with her children and a lot of baggage, they would realise she had discovered their secret and would stop her. She must be more subtle than that. She put everything back, then went to bed and spent hours and hours going over her dilemma again and again until she dropped off to sleep with nothing decided.

The morning dawned bright and clear, the sun shone and the sparrows twittered in the eaves, but Charlotte, heavy-eyed, her very soul weighed down with grief and bitterness, could hardly rouse herself. But rouse herself she must. Perhaps today Stacey would return. If he did not, then she was truly alone and must save herself and her children as best she could.

'Whatever happened to your clothes, my lady?' Betsy, who had brought her hot chocolate and pulled back the curtains, was busy looking at the gown her mistress would wear that day and was appalled by the untidy way they had been bundled back into the drawers and closet. 'Those men haven't been in here again, have they?'

So even the servants knew what had happened. It was hardly surprising. 'No, Betsy. I was looking for something. A shawl. I'm sorry I did not put things away as tidily as I should.'

''Tain't surprisin', my lady,' the maid said. 'With all you've had to endure, 'tis a wonder you manage to get up of a morning, let alone see to them men. I was never so glad to see the others go, though the two what's left are the worst of the lot.'

'Sometimes we have to make the best of things, Betsy.'

'Is it true the master has lost the house?'

'I don't know. I hope he would not allow matters to reach that pitch.'

'If it weren't for you needin' me, I'd leave, my lady, an' tha's a fact. And so would the others. We talked about it and decided we'd stay, so you need have no fear of being left without help, but if you was to decide you'd had enough, then we'd understand, but we'd go too. Beggin' your pardon for speakin' so free.'

Charlotte smiled, though behind the smile the tears lurked. Their loyalty was touching and, at a time when she was at her very lowest, it made her want to cry. 'Were you elected as spokeswoman?'

'Yes, my lady, seein's as I look after your room and can talk to you easier than the others. You never know who's listening.'

'I do not know what I am going to do, Betsy, but be sure I shall tell you as soon as I can. Now, can you find the least crumpled of my dresses? I must appear to be going about my daily tasks.'

Dressed and looking her usual cool self, even if her insides were churning, she went down to breakfast. Unusually, the men had been up some time and gone out, on foot, so Foster told her. Glad not to have to face them, she forced herself to eat a little breakfast, then went up to see the girls, who were just beginning their lessons. Satisfied that they were safe and well, she returned to her room to write to Mr Hardacre. She dare not tell him the true state of affairs, but asked him if he had been able to sort out her 'little problem'. She almost laughed at that. It was not a little problem, it was a huge dilemma. After that she wrote to her great-uncle without any hope that she would receive a reply. She should have done it long before. Why had she delayed?

Could it be because she still cherished her dream? Or had the arrival of Stacey Darton had something to do with it? Had she been hoping…?

She pulled herself up short; it was no good dwelling on what might have been. Sealing both letters, she put a short cape over her dress, set a black bonnet on her curls and set off for the village. She would give the letters to the Reverend Fuller to be forwarded with his mail. A carrier took all the village post to Ipswich every afternoon to be put on the London mail and brought back the incoming letters the following morning. It would be safer to send her post that way than trust it to the young lad at the Manor whose task it was to take the post. She had a feeling her letters might be intercepted by a curious Cecil.

The Reverend was just coming out of his gate when she arrived. 'Good morning, Lady Hobart,' he greeted her. 'I was on my way to see you. Captain MacArthur has returned. He is only here until tomorrow, so, if you still want the house, you must see him today.'

She hesitated. Could she go ahead with her plan after all? Dare she? The Captain's house would be vacant after tomorrow—would he allow her to move in before the contract for the lease had been signed? Did he even need to know she had taken possession?

After all, he would have to leave her the keys. She smiled to herself—what had Stacey said about some of the decisions we had to make being a gamble? This was most definitely a gamble, a gamble that somehow or other she could produce the money for the rent and have enough left over to keep her and her children until the school was up and running. 'Then perhaps I should go now,' she said, stuffing her letters back into her pocket.

'Would you like me to accompany you?'

'That is kind of you, but no, I can manage alone and there is my class. Can you take it today?'

Captain Alexander MacArthur was a bluff, weatherbeaten man of middle years. His hair and beard were white as snow, his hands brown and gnarled, though when he took her hand to bow over it, his grip was gentle. 'My lady, come in. Please excuse the untidiness.' He waved his hand at the piles of bags, boxes and chests that were piled up in the hall and drawing room. 'Coppins, leave that and fetch the lady some tea,' he told his manservant. Then to Charlotte, 'Let us go into the back parlour, my lady. That is less disturbed.'

He led the way and settled her into a chair, passing comments on the weather in a way that left her in no doubt he was a seaman; it was all about winds and tides and moons being in the right quarter. 'Got to catch the tide tomorrow night, so need this business cleared up today.' He paused while his servant brought in the tea and dismissed him before continuing. 'I had it in mind to employ a caretaker to look after the house, never had to do it before, of course, when Mrs MacArthur was alive, God rest her soul.'

'My condolences, Captain.'

'Thank you. As I said, I thought about a caretaker, don't do to leave a house standing empty, does it? But when I asked the Reverend if he knew someone to take on the job, he told me about you. He tells me you are Captain Delaney's daughter. A fine seaman and a good man to have at your side in a fight. Lost at Trafalgar, I collect.'

'Yes, he was.'

'And now Lord Hobart has handed in his accounts you want to leave Easterley Manor?'

'Yes. I do not choose to live with my brother-in-law.'

'Understood. You need say no more. But what about this school idea? I must know more about that.'

She explained her idea as succinctly as she could, her enthusiasm for her subject overriding her unease about being able to finance the project. Knowing her background, he would assume she was not without funds and the fact that he had mentioned her father meant he set some store by that relationship.

'And your pupils?' he asked, at the end of the recital. 'I do not want my home wrecked.'

'Of course not. They will come from the very best families. I have good connections…' she paused '…and I have my first pupil. Viscount Darton, who is distantly related to my late husband, is going to entrust me with his daughter.' She hoped Stacey would forgive her for the fib, if she ever saw him again. If… Oh, Stacey, my love, please do not desert me, not now.

He stood up. 'Then let me show you over the house. You need to be sure it will be suitable before we go any further.'

She had already made up her mind that she could not afford to reject it, but she followed him dutifully from room to room, mentally deciding which could be classrooms and which her private quarters. It was a shambling old house that had once been quite small, but which had been added to over the years to make a home for a sea captain. It was furnished with heavy, serviceable pieces in a mixture of styles and she guessed he had picked much of it up on his travels about the globe. It reminded her of her childhood home in Portsmouth, not elegant, but comfortable. She was not looking for elegance and what was there looked as though it could stand up to a knock or two by exuberant children. Anything valuable or flimsy could be stored away until the Captain returned.

From one of the upstairs room she could see the roof of Easterley Manor, from another the pine woods that protected the village and from yet another, the bay on which a few fishing boats were moored, and beyond them the distant sea. 'I can see why it is called The Crow's Nest,' she said.

'Oh, you can get a much better view from the tower. Would you like to see it?'

'Yes, please.'

The stairs were steep and winding, but she lifted her skirts clear of her ankles and climbed after him. At the top was a circular room with a large bay window in which a telescope was stationed. He put his eye to it and made one or two adjustments, then turned to her. 'Take a look, my lady.'

She put her eye to it. 'My goodness, you can see the men working on the decks of those vessels. How far away are they?'

'Four or five miles, I should say.'

She swivelled the instrument round and looked along the coast. There were three men walking along the cliff top and she had no difficulty in recognising Cecil and his two friends. They did not appear to be doing anything except talk, but every now and again one of them gestured out to sea.

From up here she had an excellent view of the bay, except she could not see the beach and cliff immediately below her on account of not being able to depress the angle of the telescope enough. 'It is amazing,' she said, deciding to say nothing of the men. 'You must know about everything that comes and goes past this little bit of coastline.'

'Yes, I do. But a word of warning. If you take this house, the tower is out of bounds. I want no one up here. That is a very sensitive instrument and very valuable.'

'Of course. I understand.'

'Then let us go downstairs again and complete our bargain.'

If she was agreeable, he was prepared to let her have the house for a year, he told her, when they were once again seated in the comfortable little parlour that she had decided would be her private sitting room. The rent would reflect the fact that he had been prepared to pay a caretaker and that salary would be deducted from what she would pay, but any alterations she made to the house to make it suitable for use as a school must be paid for by her and, at the end of the tenancy, everything restored to what it was. It was more generous than she could have hoped for and she expressed her gratitude. 'I will write to Mr Hardacre today, and he will tie up the details,' she said, trying to sound businesslike, though she was sure her mounting excitement was showing on her face. She was positively elated. Was this how a gambler felt when he thought he was on to a winning streak? If it was, she had better cool her ardour at once; she had not won yet. 'There is just one thing. When may I move in?'

He smiled, knowing, as everyone else did in the village, about the dreadful goings-on up at the Manor, and he did not blame her for wanting to leave. 'Whenever you like, my lady. I depart tomorrow and must leave the keys somewhere, so why not with you? Your caretaking duties can begin as soon as you like. As for the legalities, I do not have time to see Mr Hardacre, so a simple agreement between you and me will suffice. I have no fears about trusting you.'

'Thank you. Would you like me to come for the keys?'

'I leave at noon. But if it is more convenient for you, I can pass them to the Reverend Fuller.'

'That would be better. I take a class at the Rectory every day.'

She left, treading on air, but she had not gone above a dozen steps when she came down with a bump. She still did not have the wherewithal to pay the rent, little as it was and she was thankful that the

Captain had not asked for an advance. He trusted her, he said. But was she worthy of that trust? She had every intention of moving in, knowing she could not pay; if such action was not illegal, it was certainly dishonest. She was overwhelmed with guilt, but there was a great deal of anger too. Anger at Viscount Darton for letting her down. Where, oh, where was he?

And there was Cecil to be overcome. What would he say when she told him she was moving out? She was a hostage to his fortune though she was not supposed to know it. Would those men insist she stay at the Manor? How soon before the contraband ship arrived? Up at The Crow's Nest she was in a prime position to see it arrive and being unloaded. She knew it and so would they. On the other hand if they did not know she listened at doors and had discovered what they were scheming, she was probably safe enough. Oh, what a tightrope she was walking!

The Reverend was teaching her class when she returned, but she waited until he had dismissed the children before approaching him. 'It is all arranged,' she told him. 'The Captain will leave the keys with you for me to collect. I can move in as soon as I like.'

He smiled. 'Good. I knew he would agree. I am

glad you called, it will save me coming to the Manor. I have a letter for you. The carrier brought it half an hour ago.' He looked round the classroom to see that all was as it should be before ushering her out and locking the door behind them. 'Come over to the Rectory and I will give it to you. It was franked, so I did not have to pay for it.'

Her fortunes must have taken an upward turn at last, she decided when she took the correspondence. It was not from Stacey, as she had hoped it might be, but from Mr Hardacre. He had been looking at Sir Grenville's papers again and come across an item he had missed at the time of his death. There was money available from a fund her husband had set up many years before, when he first went soldiering, and it had been gaining interest ever since. It had nothing to do with the late Lord Hobart's will and was hers free and without encumbrance to spend as she liked. 'My lady, please accept my humble apologies for not seeing it before,' he concluded. 'If you have found a house, then let me have the details and I will do whatever is necessary to procure it for you.' By the time she finished reading it, she was in tears. She had been saved, not by Viscount Stacey Darton, but by her own husband.

'Oh, Grenville,' she murmured, remembering his crookedly indulgent smile when he wanted to please her with some small gift or an unexpected treat.

'Not bad news, I trust,' the Reverend asked, looking concerned.

'No, not bad at all. Good news. Very good. All is well. I shan't wait to make the alterations but move into The Crow's Nest the day after tomorrow. I am going to have my school, Reverend.'

He breathed a huge sigh of relief; like everyone else in the village he had been worried sick about her. But she would still need protection, people to look out for her, and he could organise that with some of the village men. He wouldn't tell her that, though, it would hurt her pride.

'I wonder if I might beg writing paper and pen and ink to reply to this letter before I go home,' she said, unwilling to let anyone at the Manor know what she was about, certainly not about her windfall. 'Then I can leave it with you for the post. It will save time.'

'Of course.' He led the way to his study, provided her with the writing materials and left her to compose her letter. When it was done, she returned to the drawing room and gave it to him. 'Thank you. Now I must go home and tell the girls.'

He offered her his escort, but she declined it, saying it was only a step and she had no qualms about walking about the village alone, which was true. It was not in the village the danger lay, but at the Manor. And that, praise be, not for much longer.

She hurried home, her mind racing with all the things she had to do. She would tell the girls and Miss Quinn first, then speak to the servants. Betsy, she felt sure, would want to come with her, but what about Mrs Evans? She could do with a good cook, not perhaps to begin with because she could cook a little herself, but later when she had pupils; prospective parents would want to know all about her domestic arrangements before entrusting her with their daughters. And that was another task; she must draft out a prospectus and an advertisement, and send for books and writing materials and beds. She must have more beds. And she would need references. Oh, there was no end to it.

And she must tell Cecil. She was not looking forward to doing that, knowing his temper, but she would stand her ground and not allow him to intimidate her. Whatever happened, she must not let slip that she knew about the free-trading. Her life might depend upon it. She wished Stacey Darton had not gone away. He had no need to sell her jewellery, after all, but it was too late to tell him so. Again she wondered where he was. But listening at doors had proved one thing; Cecil had not waylaid him or he would not have been entirely without funds and would not have been forced to agree to the smuggling scheme. So where was the Viscount? In Ipswich, perhaps, enjoying the proceeds from selling her trinkets, gambling it away, forgetting all about her.

She must not think of him, she told herself as she turned in at the gate of the Manor. She must put him from her mind, forget his gentle voice, forget the comfort of his arms, forget his kisses and his promise to come back. He was no more to be relied on than Cecil and his cronies, less so when she considered that she knew they were rogues and Stacey Darton had bamboozled her completely.

Cecil was surprisingly sanguine about her intention to move out and he did not protest about Miss Quinn leaving with her, nor Betsy with whom he had crossed swords on more than one occasion, but he refused to let Mrs Evans go. 'I can't be without a cook,' he said and promptly offered the woman the post of housekeeper-cum-cook with a higher wage, which she could not resist, though Charlotte wondered how he proposed to pay it. The cargo of contraband must be a very lucrative one, but how big a share was her brother-in-law expecting? That was why he had not tried to stop her, she decided; if she was out of the way, she would not witness what was going on.

Forgetting all about Cecil and his friends and smuggling, and trying desperately not to think of

Viscount Darton, she set about packing her clothes and personal possessions and arranging for a carter to carry them to The Crow's Nest.

The next few days were so busy settling in, she had no time to brood, would not allow herself to brood. The past—her privileged childhood, marriage and widowhood—was all behind her and she must live the life she had now and enjoy it, she and her children.

The house needed little in the way of alteration. It was largely a question of moving out and storing the Captain's furniture from the two large rooms she intended to be classrooms and installing desks and chairs and bookcases. There were several bedrooms, one of which was quite large and could be made into a dormitory when she had more pupils. It meant removing the heavy four-poster that stood there and replacing it with six small beds. Six was the number of boarders she had fixed upon; the village children would naturally live at home. Lizzie and Fanny would share one of the smaller bedchambers.

Armed with Mr Hardacre's letter to a bank in Ipswich to release funds to her and a long list of her requirements, she borrowed the parson's gig and set off, taking Lizzie and Fanny with her. They had not been out for days and deserved a treat. If the thought crossed her mind that she might see Stacey in Ipswich, she resolutely pushed it from her. It was two weeks since he had left Parson's End with her jewels and he must surely have moved on to exercise his charms elsewhere. She tried not to be bitter about it, but sometimes it was hard not to feel anger and resentment. More fool she for trusting him!

'Now, girls, we must go to the bank first,' she said brightly, after they had left the gig at the Great White Horse inn. 'And then I must find a printer and do the shopping and then we will do whatever you choose.'

'I want to see the ships,' Lizzie said. She had seen vessels from the beach, plying up and down, their sails stiff with the breeze, and she was always curious about where they had come from, where they were going and what they carried, perhaps because Charlotte had talked to her daughters about their seagoing grandfather.

'And I want to have a cordial drink and a honey cake,' Fanny added, making Charlotte smile. Fanny was always hungry.

'Then we will do both.'

The expedition was a great success, especially as there was a new ship being built in the docks and the girls had been fascinated by the builders and workmen swarming round it. All three were exhausted when they returned to the inn for the gig. A stage had just arrived and the yard was busy with passengers alighting and others taking their places, horses being changed and luggage being unloaded and loaded, making a great deal of bustle. Charlotte had not told the ostler what time she intended to be back, so the gig was not ready for her. She made her way through the throng to the stables. The parson's pony was contentedly munching hay in a stall next to a magnificent white stallion.

There was no mistaking the grey blaze on the stallion's nose and its proud head as it whinnied on seeing her, almost as if it recognised her. 'Ivor?' she queried, reaching forward to stroke his nose. 'What are you doing here?' She turned as a groom came into the yard, carrying an armful of tack. 'This is Viscount Darton's horse, isn't it?'

'Yes, ma'am.' He hung the tack on a hook beside a stable door.

'Is he staying at the inn?'

'No, ma'am, just left his horse here.'

'When? How long ago? Where did he go?' She could not keep the eagerness from her voice.

He looked sideways at her, as if wondering whether he ought to answer this barrage of questions, but she was obviously Quality with a capital letter and his lordship had not said he was incognito or that his business was secret. Still... 'What do you want to know for?' he demanded.

'I am Lady Hobart and I have been expecting him at Easterley Manor and his non-arrival worried me. Anything you can tell me will be helpful.' She opened her reticule and took out a handful of small coins to offer him.

'Well, my lady, can't say as I can tell you anything,' he said, pocketing the money. 'His lordship left the horse here about a se'ennight ago, I disremember exactly. He took the London mail, not that I can swear to that being his destination, o' course. He came back two days later, but then he was off again. Said he didn't know when he would be back, but if he needed the horse he'd send for it. We ain't seen hide nor hair of him since.'

'Was he well? Did he seem troubled or anxious, or in a hurry?'

'Oh, he were in a hurry all right, but I can't rightly say whether he were anxious.'

'Where did he go the second time?'

'Don't know, my lady, an' that's the truth, but if he don't come back after that horse soon—' He stopped when he saw the head groom come towards him. 'I must get on with my work, my lady.'

She thanked him and asked him to harness the gig; ten minutes later, having paid her dues, she and her girls were trotting out of the town in the direction of Parson's End. She was no nearer to discovering the whereabouts of Stacey Darton than she had been before; in fact, the mystery deepened. Where had he gone after leaving Ipswich? Why had he come back and then gone again? Had he been coming back to her? If that were so, why had he gone off again? He would never abandon that horse; it was a valuable beast and he prized it above everything, more than humans, she thought. So had he met with a terrible accident? But where was he going in such a hurry? Not back to her or he would have ridden the stallion.

Her new found tranquillity had been blown away on the wind and now she was as unsettled as she had been before. Her mood must have conveyed itself to the little pony, for it laid back its ears and broke into a gallop, swinging the light vehicle all over the road.

'Mama!' Lizzie cried. 'You'll have us over.'

Charlotte returned her attention to the pony and brought it under control and for the rest of the journey concentrated on driving. Nothing had changed, she told herself, as they clopped gently through the Suffolk countryside, nothing. She was just as much alone as ever. She could have left a letter at the inn to be given to Viscount Darton when he returned for his horse, but then what could she have said? She had too much pride to tell him she missed him and too much independence to demand to know what he had done with her jewels. After all, he had won them fair and square in the first place. Why, oh, why could she not banish him from her mind?

Stacey sat by his daughter's bed and watched her thrashing from side to side, trying to loosen the covers that were wrapped tightly about her. A fever of the brain, the family doctor had told him, brought about by being out all night in the damp air. It had been said in a tone of disapproval that had not been lost on Stacey. His daughter was out of control and he was to blame. Oh, he had told Charlotte he blamed his parents, but that was unfair. They were elderly and Julia was too high-spirited for them to manage. He should have done something about it when he came home at the end of the war and saw what was happening. But years away from home, dealing with men whom he could shout at and flog—not that he believed in too much of that—had taught him nothing about bringing up a motherless child. It had taken Charlotte Hobart to make him begin to see and that made him feel more out of his depth than ever.

Charlotte. How was she faring? She would have received Hardacre's letter long ago, a letter the lawyer had been loath to write. 'It makes me look incompetent,' he had said. 'What will she think about a man of business who can overlook something as important as a mystery fund?'

'We can tell her the truth later, when it doesn't matter any more,' he had answered. 'What is more important, Lady Hobart's safety or your pride?'

And so the letter had been written and Stacey had signed over twice what Charlotte had noted she needed, and set off back to Ipswich, looking forward to seeing her again, seeing the pleasure on her face when she realised she would not have to part with her jewels. He was supposed to have sold them, but he could easily say he had only pawned them and then pretend to return to Ipswich and redeem them for her. He would put them back into her hands and see her lovely eyes light up and he would suggest helping her to set up her school and then bring Julia to be her first pupil.

The mail left Gracechurch Street at half past seven in the evening, which meant he had some time to spare and he had spent it at White's, where he had a good meal and dozed off in an armchair afterwards. He had been at the Spread Eagle in good time and the journey of the night before had been made in reverse. It seemed to take much longer than it had in the other direction, although when he checked the time on their arrival at the

Great White Horse, he discovered they were only five minutes later than their scheduled time of a quarter past three.

Before he returned to Parson's End he must visit the school to which he had been heading when he first met Charlotte. He had told her he would do so and it was only common courtesy to tell them he had changed his mind about sending his daughter there. It was far too early in the morning for that and he had been dog-tired, so he had taken a room at the inn and gone to bed, asking to be roused at eight.

The servant had to shake him hard to wake him but, remembering his errand and looking forward to being back in Parson's End by nightfall, he completed his ablutions in record time and went down to the dining parlour to a welcome breakfast.

'Darton!' He had looked round to see Gerard Topham grinning up at him from a nearby table.

Stacey went over to him and shook his hand. 'What are you doing here, Gerry?'

'I told you I was going to ride along this coast, don't you remember?'

'Oh, so you did. Any luck?'

'Not so far. Join me?' He indicated the chair opposite him.

Stacey sat and beckoned the waiter, ordering coffee and bread and butter. 'No time for more,' he said.

'You look as though you've been on the march a full se'nnight,' Gerry had said.

'It feels like it.' He had explained all that had happened since they had last met and Gerard told him of his lack of progress at catching smugglers. 'They're wily as foxes,' he said. 'And half the population ready to shield them. As far as they are concerned, the free-traders are doing a good service. They don't see the other side of it, the intimidation and violence and the damage they do to the country's economy, or if they do, they are prepared to shut their eyes to it for the sake of a few bottles of brandy and a half a pound of tobacco. It's more than a few bottles of brandy and a half a pound of tobacco, it's a huge business. I know there's something in the wind, but I haven't had a whiff of it yet.'

'Perhaps you are looking in the wrong place.'

'Perhaps. There's no sign of them in the usual spots, so I'm going to ride north. Shall we travel together as far as Parson's End?'

'I'd say yes, but I have a call to make first. Maybe I'll catch you up.'

'Right. I'll be off then.' He stood up, a huge man, strong as a bear, not one Stacey would like to tangle with. 'If you should hear anything, let me know, will you? A letter sent to the Customs House here will reach me.' They had shaken hands and parted, though Stacey had expected to catch up with his friend long before he reached Parson's End.

But it was not to be; he had found his father's letter waiting for him when he arrived at the school at ten o'clock. 'Come home at once,' it said. 'Julia very ill.' Nothing more. No explanation.

He had started back to fetch Ivor, but decided riding would be too slow and instead paid the livery stable to keep him a little longer and had taken the mail to Norwich and hired a chaise from there, his head in a torment of anxiety and guilt. And his father was no help. 'What that child needs is a mother,' he had told him almost as soon as he had put a foot in the door. 'You should be doing something about that, not gallivanting about the countryside on that great horse of yours, pretending to look for schools. We sent for you over a week ago, wrote to that school you went to see in Ipswich, but, according to the man I sent, they had not even seen you. Where have you been?' It was only his worry talking, but it had annoyed Stacey when all he wanted to know was what had happened to his daughter.

'I have been looking for a school, and found one a hundred times better than that establishment in Ipswich.' He was tired and worried and snappy, torn between his duty—no, his love—for his daughter and his love and concern for Charlotte, left to the mercies of those three rogues. She should by now be in possession of funds to enable her to set about finding a house. Had she done it? Had she left the Manor? If she had, where had she gone? It would be perfectly understandable if she left no forwarding address, so how was he to find her again? And he could not go looking for her until he knew Julia was safe and well. He felt as if he were being split in two.

'What happened?' he demanded, watching a nurse bathing his daughter's brow with a cloth wrung out in water.

'She was out all night in the rain,' the Earl said.

'All night in the rain?' Stacey felt his voice rising and changed it to a fierce whisper. 'Why? Where were you? How could you let it happen?'

'My lord,' the nurse remonstrated. 'If you cannot keep your voice down, I must ask you to leave.'

'Come downstairs, we'll talk down there,' the Earl said. 'The nurse will call us if there is any change.'

Stacey had followed him down to the large airy drawing room, where his mother sat waiting for them. 'How is she?' she asked, looking up from her Berlin work.

'About the same,' her husband answered. 'We can do nothing but wait for the fever to break.'

'Sit down, Stacey,' she said, as he stood with his back to the fire. It was a big old house and a beast to keep warm so, except on very hot summer days, there was almost always fires in the rooms. 'You can do nothing fidgeting about like that.'

He flung himself down on to a chair. He was still agitated, still feeling helpless and guilty, but his temper had cooled. It was no good blaming his parents. 'Tell me what happened?' he asked wearily. 'How did Julia come to be out all night?'

'It all began over a runt of a puppy,' the Earl had explained. 'You know how soft she is about animals…'

Stacey didn't know, but he let it pass. 'Go on,' he said, quietly.

'I told her it would never be any good, that it ought to be put down. After all, if it was allowed to grow, it could weaken the strain.'

'You mean it was one of a litter of hunting hounds?'

'Yes, of course it was. What other dogs would I be breeding? Anyway, she took a fancy to it and when Bolton went to deal with it, she grabbed it up and ran off with it. He chased after her, but he's full of the rheumatics and she easily outran him. We thought she would come home when she was hungry, that's usually what she does, but she didn't. I sent every able man off the estate out looking for her and went myself, but we couldn't find her in the grounds, nor the village and we started to search the heath, but when it got too dark to see, I had to call off the search until the morning. If you had been here, you might have carried on all night, but you weren't, and she might have been anywhere. I hoped and prayed she would seek shelter and come home as soon as it was light…'

'So where was she?'

'Out on the heath almost as far as the marshes, further away than we expected. She is as stubborn as a mule and had decided she was not coming home until we had forgotten all about doing away with the puppy. There was a heavy mist when we set out next morning and we could hardly see a hand before us, but we kept calling and calling. It was the dog told us where she was. We heard it barking. She had sheltered under the lee of a rock, but it was not enough to keep the damp off her and she had not taken a coat. The dog was in her arms and must have afforded a little warmth. She was only half-conscious. She's been like it ever since.'

'Where were you?' his mother asked. 'It is not like you to be neglectful of your duty.'

He smiled wryly, thinking of the answer Charlotte might have given to that question. His duty and his love should go hand in hand, so why had they not? Did he think bringing up daughters was not a task for a man? Did he resent the fact that his wife had died giving birth to her and he had wanted a son? If that were true, it was despicable of him and he must do his best to make amends. *If* he was given a second chance. His daughter was flickering between life and death and only now did he realise how much she meant to him. 'I'll explain later,' he said and left the room to return to Julia's bedside.

He was still there twenty-four hours later when she opened her eyes. Not that he saw them open; he was slumbering uncomfortably in the chair he had drawn close to the bed, too exhausted to stay awake. His hair was tousled and he had a three-day stubble on his chin.

'Papa.' The soft voice woke him at once. 'Is that you?'

He stirred and stretched his cramped limbs and leaned forward to take her hand. 'Yes, Julia, sweetheart.' Her eyes were bright, but the fever had gone and only a soft blush stained her cheeks. 'How do you feel?'

'Strange. I'm thirsty.'

He helped her to drink from the cup the nurse had left by the bed and gently laid her back again.

'What are you doing here?' she asked, as if it was the last place she expected him to be. The question screwed his insides up in painful guilt.

'Watching over you. You gave us all a fright, you

know.' He was about to ask her why she had been so foolish as to run off like that and frighten her poor grandparents to death, when he heard Charlotte's voice, as clearly as if she had been in the room with them. 'The poor child does not need a scolding. She was cold and frightened, but she stuck to her guns. It was very brave of her. You should reassure her, not ring a peal over her.' He smiled. 'But you are safe and that is all that matters.'

'The puppy. They took him from me.'

'You were ill and had to be put to bed, but do not worry, he is safe and being looked after.' He stood up, patted her hand and left the room. Five minutes later he returned with the puppy in his arms.

The nurse had come in while he was away and, seeing the puppy, drew herself up to her haughtiest. 'My lord, you cannot bring an animal into the sick room.'

'Oh, yes, I can. My daughter nearly died trying to save it and it repaid her by saving her life. It will aid her recovery to have it by her.' And, ignoring the nurse's protests, he dropped the puppy on to the bed beside Julia. She hugged it to her. 'Oh, Papa, thank you.'

It was the first time he could remember her smiling at him in any sort of friendship and he felt a glow of sheer happiness spreading through him.

'You were a brave girl, sweetheart, and now you must get better. Later we will talk. But now I must wash and shave and change into some clean clothes. I feel like a tramp.'

She giggled suddenly. 'You look like one too.' Then, still tired and drowsy, she murmured, 'But I think I like you when you are not so stern and correct.'

'Oh, Charlotte,' he murmured as he went to his own room. 'You were right and I cannot wait to tell you so. But I must be patient. You, of all people, will understand that.'

# Chapter Seven

The carriage came to a halt at the door of The Crow's Nest and Stacey jumped down without waiting for Jem to climb from the driving seat and to let down the step. 'Wait there,' he said to Julia and strode up to the front door and knocked.

He had written to Charlotte at Easterley Manor as soon as he knew Julia was on the mend, but had received no reply. It left him wondering if she had moved without leaving a forwarding direction, or if she was still there, still unable to leave. Supposing those men had intercepted her mail and, knowing she was now in funds, had found a way of depriving her of them? The uncertainty had driven him nearly insane.

He had longed to set off to find out for himself, but he had made a vow not to go away and leave his daughter again. It was a promise he meant to keep and so he had watched over her day by day, sat at her bedside, brought her little treats, until she grew strong enough to be dressed and come downstairs. He was still awkward with her, didn't know what to talk to her about, had started to tell her things and then suddenly realised they were not stories for young girls.

What on earth did you talk about to girls? Her lessons? They bored her. Fashions and society? She declared she had no interest in them. Animals? That was better. His father had been right and he had been wrong, she did have a feminine streak—she was soft-hearted when it came to birds and animals. Susan Handy had told him she had once risked being torn to pieces by the hounds in order to rescue a young fox they had chased into a corner. And she loved to ride. That was something they had in common and, as soon as she was well enough, they had taken long rides together, galloping across the open countryside that surrounded the Hall. There were several riding horses in the Malcomby stables, but he missed Ivor and meant to fetch him as soon as he could and find a way to restore Lady Hobart's jewels to her, but in the meantime he must concentrate on Julia.

Little by little she had thawed, and he found her to be a delightful and intelligent companion who knew more about nature and the countryside than he did and very little literature and mathematics, geography or history. She had no interest in female pursuits like needlework and, when forced to do it, the result was a mess of lumpy, misplaced stitches, though she could draw well. He had seen sketches of rabbits and stoats that were admirably executed.

She still did not like being curbed and hated discipline of any kind. It was going to be a long road, this getting to know his daughter, and, although he had found a love for her he had not realised he had, he ached for Charlotte. It did not help to tell himself that she was strong and if she could manage a dozen children she could surely manage three ill-mannered men, and that her brother-in-law, for all his faults, would not allow the other two to lay hands on her.

It was not only that he was concerned for her welfare, it was his own feeling of having let something good slip through his fingers, something he had been looking for all his life, that he found so unbearable. He wanted to be with her, protecting her, arguing with her, holding her and oh, yes, kissing those red lips and exploring every inch of her. And it was not raw desire, though that figured hugely, but a real, enduring love of her as a person, the woman she was. And he cared not one jot what her rank was; that she was well-born enough to be approved by his parents was simply a bonus.

But if he went back, would she be there? Would she give up her grand plans to be his wife? Would she jump at the chance to escape the life she was leading to become a viscountess? And there was Julia to consider. Her opposition could make his wife's life very uncomfortable indeed. It was all conjecture, of course. He had no idea what Charlotte herself thought of him. He had let her down and, although he had written to explain, it was evidently not enough to appease her or she would have written saying she understood and forgave him.

It all came to a head one day in late April when he saw an advertisement in a London newspaper, which his father had sent down to Malcomby every day. 'The Sir Grenville Hobart School for young ladies has limited vacancies for the daughters of gentlemen,' it said. 'The school is ideally situated in its own grounds and has excellent facilities for the proper education of young ladies.' He smiled at the use of the word proper. He would take a wager Charlotte's idea of proper was very different from her pupils' mothers. The announcement went on to list the curriculum and invited interested parents to send for a prospectus. The address given was John Hardacre's. So Charlotte had her school after all. He had written at once to Hardacre, asking for her whereabouts.

'Would you like to come on a trip with me?' he asked Julia the day he had John's reply. She had fully recovered, but as he had decided he could not leave her again, she would have to come with him. Knowing she was capable of dressing herself, they had left Miss Handy at home.

Now he stood on the step of The Crow's Nest, unsure of his reception and as nervous as a schoolboy on his first day at school. Had she received his letter and decided to ignore it? Had she given him up as not worthy of a second thought? Did she hate him for breaking his word to her? Did she think he was a thief? He fingered the small bag of jewels he had in his pocket—would they convince her he was not?

The door opened and he found himself facing one of the servants he had seen at Easterley Manor; Betsy, he thought her name was, and she did not look at all welcoming, no doubt associating him with Lord Hobart and his guests. He gave her a reassuring smile and touched his hat. 'Is Lady Hobart at home?'

'No, my lord.' It was said firmly.

'When will she be home? I have come a long way and I have my daughter with me.' He nodded towards the carriage where Julia sat with her head out, bonnet askew, looking about her. 'Do you think we might come in and wait?'

'I can't let you in when her ladyship a'n't here,' the woman said, almost filling the doorway with her bulk. 'It's more'n I dare do. Come back later.'

'This is a school, how can there be no one here?' He was becoming impatient with her, though he realised that was unjust. Betsy was only protecting her mistress and had probably been given instructions not to admit anyone, especially anyone from the Manor.

'They are all down on the beach.'

'Oh, I see. Thank you.' He turned away and went back to the carriage he had bought expressly for the journey, a light chaise drawn by two horses and requiring only Jem, his personal servant, to drive it. 'Come, Julia,' he said, opening the door. 'We are going for a walk.'

Charlotte had, as yet, no fee-paying pupils, but she told herself she must not expect too much too soon and as her teaching methods were a little eccentric, she must prove they worked. Mr Hardacre had promised to put in a word for her with a couple he knew who might send their daughter, but as yet she had heard nothing.

The village children came every day to take their lessons with Lizzie and Fanny, trudging up from the village at nine in the morning and returning at two in the afternoon. The arrangement seemed to be working well and she was kept busy, preparing lessons and teaching, because so far she had not engaged more staff, relying, as before, on the help of the Reverend for those lessons she did not feel qualified to take. She was reluctant to spend more than was necessary of the funds Mr Hardacre had put at her disposal because she did not know how long they would last. Without an income from paying pupils, perhaps not very long.

On a practical level her life was on an even keel, but on an emotional level, it was as topsy-turvy as ever. Her disappointment in Stacey Darton was profound and, though she told herself it was simply because of his duplicity and the way he had tricked her out of her jewellery, she could not banish him from her thoughts. He invaded her sleep and her awakening, invaded the school room and the kitchen where Betsy worked as her only household servant, invaded the children's bedroom when she went to see that they had settled down for the night, even thrust himself into her prayers. Especially he was in her prayers.

He had been the one bright light in the gloom of her time at the Manor since the arrival of Cecil and his cronies and she could not believe that he was as black and malicious as they were. Time and again she remembered his kind words of warning, the way he deflected the other men's offensive attention from her, the way he had returned the five guineas Cecil had stolen from her and won her jewels. She could feel again the pressure of his lips on hers and heard again in her head his murmured endearment when he said he would come back. But he hadn't, had he? How he must be laughing at her! But why had he left that valuable horse at the inn? Was the animal still there or had he fetched it? Where had he gone? Had something dreadful happened to prevent him returning? She did not want to think of him being hurt, but was that preferable to thinking he had tricked her?

She told herself over and over again to stop torturing herself with questions like that and for a large part of most days she succeeded. But today, for some reason she could not fathom, she could not think of anything else. She found it so difficult to concentrate, she decided to take the children onto the beach for some exercise. But it was worse there, for that was where she had first met him, had first been the object of the scrutiny of his humour-filled brown eyes. He seemed to be everywhere, in the wind blowing off the sea, in the waves that crashed on to the shore, in the air she breathed, walking towards her along the strand. A figment of her imagination, she told herself sternly.

But the image refused to dissolve into nothingness as figments had a habit of doing; this one was very substantial. He came slowly towards her, so slowly she was able to take in every detail of his dress and manner. He wore a dark green coat with a high collar, light brown pantaloons and highly polished Hessians. He was carrying his hat to save it being carried from his head in the wind, which ruffled his dark hair. He was here! He had come back!

Her emotions went into a spin and she could not move. The incoming tide was lapping around her feet and the children had stopped their excited chatter to stare at the elegant newcomer, but she could not stir. Love and anger did battle in her head and heart. She did not know what to do. She wanted to run into his arms and cry with joy, at the same time to beat her fists against his chest and call him a thief, a deceiver, a mountebank. But her voice had gone; nothing came out but a croak.

He stopped three feet from her, scanning her face. 'Lady Hobart. How do you do?' It was said quietly, almost tentatively, except that he was too sure of himself to be nervous. It annoyed her. Did he expect her to welcome him with open arms?

'My lord.' She came to her senses enough to acknowledge him. 'I did not expect to see you again.' She surprised herself with how calm she sounded.

'I said I would return.' He looked about him for signs of the kind of pupils she hoped to have, but all he saw were her two daughters and the village children. Did that mean her school was not yet up and running?

'So you did, but there is a mile of difference between saying and doing. Six weeks' difference.'

'I am sorry for that.' He turned from her and, for the first time, she realised he was not alone. There was a girl behind him, dressed in a pale pink muslin dress and silk cape. Her hair, beneath the straw bonnet she wore, was as dark as Stacey's and her eyes were the same golden brown, but without the humour of Stacey's. In fact, she was looking decidedly mulish. He took her hand and drew her forward. 'May I present my daughter, Julia, my lady? Julia, this is Lady Hobart.'

Charlotte smiled at the child. 'Julia, how do you do? I have heard so much about you, it is good to meet you at last.'

Stacey gave the girl a nudge and she gave a reluctant bob before murmuring, 'My lady.'

'Come and say hallo to the others,' Charlotte said, taking her hand and drawing her towards the children. 'This is Elizabeth and this is Frances. This scamp is Danny and the little one is his sister, Meg.' She went on to name them all, then added, 'We were gathering shells to see how many different ones there are and later we are going to look them up in some books. Would you like to join in?'

The village children simply stared at her, but it was Lizzie, who was nearest to her in age, who took her hand and began to show her their finds so far. Charlotte, who had decided to be cool and dignified, turned back to Stacey. 'Well, my lord, what brings you back to Parson's End?'

'I have unfinished business in the neighbourhood.' Why, in heaven's name, was he being belligerent when all he longed to do was take her in his arms? He could not do that in front of the children, but he could have made himself more pleasant. 'You may recall I told you I was searching for a school for my daughter.'

'Yes, but we agreed you were unlikely to find it in Parson's End.'

'I do not remember agreeing that. On the contrary, I recall being interested in your ideas. I assume you have a school, since you have adver-tised its existence—'

'It exists.' She was sharp and snappy and didn't seem able to help it, but then it was he who was in the wrong and she had no intention of humiliating herself by letting him see how hurt she was. 'It was fortunate that I did not, after all, need the money from those jewels. For all you knew or cared, I could have still been at the Manor, still being insulted by those horrible men, could even have come to harm at their hands.'

'God forbid.'

'It was as well He did, for it was no good relying on you, was it? What I cannot understand is why, since you absconded with my jewellery, you bothered to come back at all?'

'Is that what you thought, that I had made off with your jewels?'

'What else was I to think?'

'You could have trusted me.'

'I did and have ever since been wondering why I did. It was fortunate that Mr Hardacre discovered that my own dear Grenville had provided for me after all.'

He almost winced when she spoke of her husband in such glowing terms. Now was most decidedly not the time to tell her whom she really had to thank for the change in her fortune. 'So you decided to use it to go ahead with your school?'

'Yes, of course. Why would I not?'

'If your husband left you well provided for, there was surely no need—'

'No need at all,' she said waspishly. 'But it was

something I have wanted to do for a long time. I thought you understood that, but there, I do not think I can be a very good judge of what men think. They appear to say one thing and mean another...'

She was looking at him, studying his face, wishing desperately that they could begin this conversation again, that he would explain, show a little humility, convince her she had been wrong to doubt him, but he said nothing, simply met her gaze and made her feel weak. She did not realise that the tide was coming in and that the wind was whipping up the waves. He was facing the sea and saw a breaker that was about to engulf them and suddenly scooped her up in his arms and carried her to safety.

Without putting her down, he turned to see that the children were safe. Squealing with a mixture of delight and fear, they raced ahead of the breaker, until they were out of its reach. They turned open-mouthed, to see Charlotte in the arms of the man who was showing no sign of setting her back on her feet.

'Put me down at once, sir,' Charlotte hissed in an undertone.

'If I must.' It was said with a sigh and a mischievous smile.

'Of course you must. We are not alone. The children...'

The children, yes, he could not forget their

presence; it was why he had not been able to speak openly to her about his feelings. And she had been so unwelcoming, so ready to castigate him, he suddenly realised those feelings were not reciprocated. He set her down, but kept her hand in his as another breaker, bigger than the first, surged towards the land. 'Run, children, run,' he called and, scooping little Meg up with his free arm, herded them all to the safety of the foot of the cliffs, where he reluctantly released Charlotte's hand and set Meg on her feet. It was while the children were putting on their shoes that he realised that Julia was standing a little to one side, glaring at him. His actions had obviously upset her and the last thing he wanted was for her and Charlotte to be at odds with one another. He went and put his arm about her shoulders and they climbed the cliff back to The Crow's Nest together.

His conversation with Charlotte had been abruptly halted and nothing had been explained or clarified. And the jewellery still nestled in his pocket. Impatient as he was, he would have to wait for a more propitious moment. 'Lady Hobart has a school,' he explained to his daughter as they walked, a little ahead of the others. 'But it is a very unusual school.'

'Indeed it is,' she said. 'A school for vagabonds and peasants…'

'And young ladies. Elizabeth and Frances are young ladies. Did you not find them pleasant companions?'

'Pleasant enough considering how common they are. And the other children are so dirty and ragged…'

'They cannot help being poor, Julia. You are fortunate that you will never know poverty, but that does not mean you cannot show compassion towards those who do not have your advantages.'

'Papa, you are surely not intending to put me to school here?'

'Do you not think you should like it?'

'It will be like all the others. You will hand me over like a worn-out portmanteau and leave me. And then everyone will be horrid and expect me to sit still and learn stuffy lessons and I shall be forced to run away.'

'I think that would be a very foolish thing to do.' He paused. Julia had been so much more amenable lately he had thought, had hoped, she would raise no objections, especially when she discovered how easygoing Charlotte was.

'I do not see why I have to go to school at all. I can learn all I need to know at home.'

'You know why,' he said and could not keep his irritation from his voice. He had made such plans, had so many dreams, had hoped, oh, how he had hoped, that his daughter would learn to love

Charlotte as he did. What would he do if they could not deal well together? More to the point, what would Charlotte do? She would refuse him, of that he was certain. Her own children had to be considered too. Oh, why was love so complicated? There had been nothing complicated about his marriage to Anne-Marie, but then that had not been based on love. 'You do not behave properly when you are at home. It is not only literature and mathematics you need to study, but how to conduct yourself as a young lady—'

'By consorting with peasants. Papa, you are so inconsistent. You did not like me associating with that village boy at Malcomby, but those—' she tossed her head backwards at the children toiling up the path behind them '—are no different. Except, of course, for the lady, though I must be very ill informed, for I did not think it was quite the thing for ladies to allow themselves to be picked up and carried by gentlemen—'

'That is enough, Julia,' he snapped. 'You have far too much to say for yourself.'

'Miss Darton.' Charlotte had come up behind them without either of them realising she was there. He wondered how much she had heard. 'It is not as a schoolgirl that I would like you to stay, but as a pupil teacher for the little ones. I really need some help.'

Julia turned to look at her in surprise. 'Why me? I am ignorant. Papa is always telling me so. And are you not afraid I should lead them astray? I am also very wicked, you know.' She spoke almost as if she were boasting.

'Wicked?' Charlotte queried, pretending to take her seriously. 'Who says you are wicked?'

'Everyone. Grandmother and Miss Handy and Papa.'

Charlotte gave Stacey a withering look that stopped him from speaking, just as he opened his mouth. 'But what do you think? Do you think you are wicked?'

Julia sighed. 'I must be or I should not be at such odds with everyone.'

'I am sure you are nothing of the kind,' Charlotte said. 'But perhaps you would do better if you could get away from all these people who are for ever finding fault. I really do need some help with the little ones, you know.'

'You mean it?'

'Oh, yes. You help me and I will help you to overcome this shocking reputation you have.' It was said with a genuine smile and Charlotte was rewarded with a little giggle. 'Shall we make a bargain?'

'What bargain?'

'A month's trial and if you do not like it, then I shall ask your papa to take you home and you may find somewhere more to your liking.' She stopped. 'But you have not seen the school yet, have you? My goodness, I would not expect you to make such an important decision without first inspecting the premises. Come, we are nearly there.' Putting the onus of making a decision on Julia herself had a wondrous effect on the child. She was actually smiling as they reached the top of the cliff and Charlotte led the way back to the school, ignoring Stacey who followed in pensive silence.

The tour of the school was undertaken after Charlotte had sent the village children home and Stacey's horse and carriage had been taken to the stable where Jenkins, who had been pleased to come and work for a few hours each day, showed Jem where everything was and afterwards conducted him to the kitchen where Betsy provided him with a meal. Then Stacey and Charlotte left Julia to talk to Lizzie and Fanny in the schoolroom and adjourned to her sitting room, where Betsy brought in the tea tray. They had said very little since coming into the house; there was a constraint between them that made every thought, every opening gambit too full of pitfalls to utter. She busied herself making the tea to cover their awkwardness.

'The establishment is satisfactory?' she enquired

at last, raising her head to meet his gaze and wishing that she had not. He was studying her intently, his brown eyes watchful as if he wanted to catch her out, to discover what was in her mind. If only he knew! She squirmed inwardly. Oh, why did he have to come back and upset her hard-won equilibrium all over again? Why could he not have stayed away and left her in peace? But only half an hour before she had been longing for his return, praying for it. Did she know what she wanted?

'You mean for Julia?'

'Of course I mean for Julia. We are not talking about anyone else, are we?'

'No, no one else,' he said. 'And the school will do very well, but why did you tell her you needed help? How can she be a teacher? She is—'

'The daughter of a viscount and granddaughter of an earl,' Charlotte finished for him. 'And therefore above such a lowly occupation.'

He decided not to tell her he knew of her own aristocratic connections. She had never mentioned it and would want to know how he knew and he could not tell her of his visit to Hardacre. Besides, he did not want her to think he was influenced by such things. 'I was not going to say that at all, my lady. I was thinking of what she might teach your pupils. She may lead them astray, as she said she might.'

'She said nothing of the sort. She asked me did I think she would, which is a very different thing. And she will not be left unsupervised, you may be sure.' She handed him a cup of tea, sitting in its deep saucer. 'Julia needs to feel valued, my lord, and by asking for her help, I am trying to show that she is.'

He smiled suddenly. 'Here endeth the second lesson.'

'I am sorry, my lord, I did not mean to preach at you, but why the second—has there been a first?' She handed him a plate and offered the cakes.

'Indeed there has,' he said, taking one, though he did not begin eating it. 'That is why I have been so long away. Lesson one was that I should spend more time with my daughter.'

'Oh.' She felt deflated and then suddenly stiffened her spine. 'That does not explain why you did not come back to Parson's End before you went home.'

'No, but I wrote to you at Easterley Manor, which was the only direction I had. I explained that I had received an urgent summons to go home because Julia was gravely ill. I am afraid I abandoned my errand of selling your jewels in my haste to go to her. I thought I would sell them in Norwich instead and send the money to you, but she was so ill, I did not leave her bedside for two weeks and then I felt I ought to wait until she was strong enough to travel.'

Charlotte was stricken with guilt and forgot her animosity. 'Oh, my lord, I am so sorry. Please forgive me…'

'I assume you did not receive my letter?'

'No. Oh, dear, and did you enclose the money? If you did, then I am afraid—'

'No, I would not be so foolish as to do that, knowing how matters stood at Easterly Manor. In any case, by the time I was able to leave Julia for a few hours, I had seen your advertisement and concluded you had found funds elsewhere and decided you might not wish to sell your valuables after all and so I have brought them back to you.' He reached in the pocket of his coat and drew out the velvet bag that contained them. 'Of course, if you still wish—'

'Oh, my lord!' She took the bag he offered and tipped the contents into her palm, her eyes alight with joy. 'Oh, I am so very glad you did not. Thank you. Thank you. I am sorry I ever doubted you.'

He sipped his tea and watched her lovingly fingering the jewellery, precious not in monetary terms, but because they reminded her of her husband whom she had loved. It gave him a stab of pain, not only because she was not yet ready to look favourably on him, but because he had not enjoyed a similar experience in his own marriage.

'I collect you said your late husband had provided

for you,' he said, when she returned them to the bag. He must evince some curiosity or she might wonder why he had not asked. 'How did that come about?'

'Oh, it was Mr Hardacre who discovered it when he was going through Grenville's papers. My husband made some investments just before he went to Spain, which were left to me. I cannot conceive how he over-looked them before, but it was fortuitous, for I could not have stayed another night at the Manor.'

'Are those men still there?'

'Cecil and Sir Roland and Mr Spike are and like to be for some time, I think. I heard them plotting more mischief.'

'I've a mind to visit them.'

'Why?'

'I told you, unfinished business.'

'Then I am very disappointed in you, my lord.' She rang a little hand bell on the tea tray. 'I would have thought you had learned your lesson.'

He burst into laughter. 'Lesson number three. Do not gamble. But my dear Lady Hobart, surely it is permissible if one is winning.'

'You cannot always be winning.'

'No,' he said suddenly serious. 'One cannot always win, cannot always achieve one's heart's desire.' He stopped speaking as Betsy came into the room in answer to the summons.

'We have finished with the tea things,' Charlotte told her and they silently watched as she gathered the cups and saucers and plates and piled them on the tray before carrying it from the room.

'Will you take Julia, my lady?' he asked after a long silence when they were both busy thinking about his last remark. He knew what he meant, but did she?

'If she is willing.'

'I am reluctant to leave her.' He saw her little smile and laughed. 'Oh, I know what you are thinking, that I had no compunction about leaving her before, but it is different now. In the last few weeks, while she has been so ill, I have come to understand her a little better.'

'But there is still a long way to go.'

'That is exactly what I was about to say. We are in accord, my lady.' He smiled a little wryly.

'But you cannot stay here with her, my lord. It would be most…'

'Improper?'

She laughed. 'Yes, it would raise a few eyebrows and I cannot afford that. I am already considered a little out of the ordinary and I must find fee-paying pupils; the funds I have must be husbanded carefully until I am making a profit. And if you were here, it would disrupt the whole routine of the school when it is important for everyone, Julia included, to be settled.'

'I know that. It is why I said I would go to the Manor. If I am there, I will not be in your way and I can still see Julia occasionally.'

'Oh, I see,' she said, disappointed that he had not said he wanted to see her. Something had changed since he had left Easterley Manor and she supposed it was that he had decided his daughter was more important than making love to an eccentric school-mistress. And he was right, wasn't he? She endeavoured not to let her misery show. She stood up shakily. 'I will go and find Julia.'

He rose too and stood by the hearth, his hand on the mantelshelf, wondering how they were to go on from there. Seeing her again had only confirmed his love for her, his need to have her in his life, but she had shut him out, talking about the school and Julia and her damned husband, almost as if she were trying to stop him saying what he wanted to say.

He went to the window and looked out towards the sea. It was very rough out there, the waves were crashing against the shore, he could hear them as they came on and drew back and came on again, a timeless rhythm. She was like that, he decided angrily, battering him, making him believe he might hope, then flinging him from her when his usefulness was done, when she had her jewels back in her possession and her school was up and running. What would she say if he told her that it was he and not Sir Grenville who had funded it? It might give him a certain satisfaction to see the shock on her face, but it would be the end of any hope of winning her.

He turned as the door opened and Charlotte and Julia came into the room. 'Well?' he said, addressing his daughter. 'Will you stay?'

'Do I have a choice?'

He heaved a sigh. 'Yes, you have a choice.'

She laughed suddenly. 'That is all I wanted to hear.' Then, seeing the angry cloud gathering in his eyes, added, 'Yes, I will stay. Lady Hobart has convinced me that she needs me and you know there is nothing like being needed.'

'Lesson number four,' he murmured, but no one heard him.

Leaving the carriage in the coach house at The Crow's Nest and Jem racking up with Jenkins, he set off to walk to the Manor alone.

'Well, well, if it isn't Cousin Darton,' Cecil said when Foster conducted Stacey to a back parlour, where the three men sat about a table. Curiously they were not playing cards, though there was a glass of cognac at each elbow. There were papers on the table that Sir Roland hastily swept to one side as he entered. 'To what do we owe the honour of this visit?'

'Unfinished business,' Stacey replied. 'I have a pile of vouchers—'

'Too late.' Augustus laughed. 'There's nothing left.'

'You should not have continued to play, knowing the vouchers I hold have first claim.' It was said quietly, but there was venom in his voice.

'You left.'

'I had other business to see to.'

'Ah, yes, my lady's jewels. I'll wager they did not fetch as much as you thought they would and that's why you are back. We had the last laugh, after all.'

Stacey pretended to smile in agreement. 'But I still have some of Lord Hobart's vouchers and I will be paid for those, one way or another.' Before he left Charlotte, she had warned him about the smuggling. It was a worrying development, not only because he had brought Julia into the middle of it, but because Charlotte might be in danger from them. Gerard had warned him how vicious the so-called free-traders could be. He intended to find out what he could and then send for him. In the meantime, he would make Hobart squirm.

'You can't squeeze blood from a stone, Viscount,' Sir Roland said. 'Cecil has nothing.'

'Oh, but I have,' Cecil said, proving what they already knew—that for him gambling was a disease and he would never be cured of it. 'I'll play you for those vouchers. I win, you tear them up.'

'And if I win?'

'I'll pay for the vouchers and half as much again.'

'What are you proposing to use for a stake?' Stacey asked. 'The house?'

'Don't be a fool, Hobart,' Spike broke in. 'We need the house.'

'Oh?' Stacey queried, showing mild interest. 'What is so special about it? It is old and draughty and miles from any society worthy of the name.'

Cecil suddenly laughed. 'That is its chief attraction, Cousin.'

'Shut up, Hobart!' Augustus growled.

'Well, my lord?' Cecil addressed Stacey.

'I will play, but only for cash, your blunt against the vouchers, at their face value, not the amount I paid for them.' He was well aware as he spoke that it would double his losses if he lost, but it was a risk he was prepared to take. He wanted to see where and how the man would procure the money. 'But tell me, if you are dished up, where are you going to find enough cash to cover the vouchers?'

'I shall have it.' Cecil tapped his nose in reply. 'But it needs arranging. Shall we say three days from now? We will sit down to play after nuncheon on Sunday. Shall it be hazard or piquet?'

'Piquet,' Stacey said promptly. Hazard was a game of pure chance and he wanted the game to have an element of skill. 'I assume I may reside here in the meantime?'

'Yes, but my lady ain't here to act the hostess, if you were thinking of continuing your dalliance with her.'

'Pity,' he said laconically. 'Where did she go?'

'Oh, not far,' Cecil said. 'Just to a house on the cliffs. Seems she prefers the company of children to grown men with more to offer. Will you call on her?'

'I might,' he said laconically. 'I've nothing to do until we begin our game. That is, if you have no other entertainment planned.'

Cecil giggled and Augustus silenced him with a look. 'Nothing,' he said. 'Go and visit the widow, keep her occupied.'

Mrs Evans arrived at that point to say dinner was ready and should she lay another cover for Lord Darton.

'Yes,' Cecil told her. 'And have someone make up a bed for him too.'

The cook had too much pride in her skill to provide poor food for all she loathed her employer, and they dined well on roast beef followed by an almond tart. Afterwards they played whist for cob nuts from the dish on the side table. Stacey gave them the satisfaction of losing all his very quickly and then got up, yawned, and said he was tired after his journey and meant to retire.

He left them arguing about who had started with the most nuts and whether large ones counted for more than small ones, and made his way to his room. But he did not undress, and, after a few minutes, crept down again to listen outside the door. The panelling was thick and he could make out nothing more than an odd word or two. 'Moon and tide' figured more than once and he heard 'tub carriers' mentioned, which indicated a large cargo needing men to carry it inland from the spot where it was landed to its hiding place. He guessed they would recruit helpers from the village who would be prepared to take the risk. It left him with a dilemma. If he alerted Gerard Topham and his Coast Blockade, they would arrest everyone in the vicinity, not just the ring leaders and did he want that to happen? He returned to his room and went to bed to mull it over.

Next morning after a good breakfast, he strolled over to The Crow's Nest with no sense of urgency or haste, to be told by Betsy that her ladyship was taking a lesson and she would not thank her for interrupting it.

'I have no wish to interrupt,' he said, removing

his hat. 'I will sit on this chair until she comes out.' And before she could protest, he lowered his tall frame into a small chair outside the room where she was teaching.

'As you wish,' she said, huffily. 'I don't know what the world's coming to, that I don't, when a *gentleman* don't know when he's not wanted.' And she marched away towards the kitchen and the meat pie she was making for everyone's dinner.

Stacey could hear the murmur of Charlotte's voice and the piping voices of the children as they answered her questions. It was evidently a geography lesson, for he heard her speaking about the early discoverers of America and how the country had once belonged to Britain but had fought for its independence, and about the goods that were imported and exported. He could not resist the temptation to put his eye to the keyhole.

She was facing the door, dressed in her usual mourning attire. It was so plain it emphasised her curves, the trim waist, the full bosom, the shapely hips. He allowed himself to imagine her in a fashionable gown—deep cerise, he thought, or perhaps blue, the blue of a spring sky, or lemon. Yes, lemon, trimmed with the palest green and cream. The severe hairstyle she wore as a schoolmistress became, in his mind's eye, a soft Grecian style, and the black lace cap a tiny bonnet, one of those that sat well back on her head and revealed her shapely brows, lovely eyes and long neck.

'Can anyone tell me how long it takes to sail from America to Ipswich?' she asked, using her finger to trace the route across the Atlantic on a globe on the table beside her.

'Why, missus, it would depend on the wind and the tide, wouldn't it?' Danny White piped up.

'Indeed it would,' she said, ignoring the way he had addressed her. 'But if both were favourable?'

'Eight weeks, my lady,' said another, though Stacey could not see him, could not see Julia either. 'That's what my pa says anyhow and he oughta know seein's he be a seaman.'

He saw Charlotte smile at the boy and it was as if the sun had come out after rain. If only she would smile at him like that! But she reserved it for her pupils; when she was with him, she was nearly always angry, or fighting back tears.

He heard someone coming and reluctantly took his eye from the keyhole and sat up straight, smoothing the pile of his hat to give his hands something to do. A maid passed him with a pile of bed linen and climbed the stairs. Behind him the schoolroom door opened and the children tumbled out, to be followed by Charlotte and

Julia, so deep in conversation they did not see him.

'Perhaps we will be able to go out later,' Charlotte was saying. 'After the other children have gone home, and you shall tell me all about yourself.'

'I thought Papa had told you everything.'

'No, indeed not. And I want to hear it from you.' She laughed lightly. 'Papas do not know everything, you know. They are men, and often they do not understand what we ladies think and feel inside ourselves—' She stopped abruptly when she saw Stacey rising from the chair to greet her. Her face was suffused with bright pink colour. 'My lord. I did not know you were here.'

'Evidently not,' he said, pretending severity. 'Or you would not be teaching my daughter to be unfilial.'

'Not at all, my lord. It was merely woman-to-woman talk.' Julia was giggling, but Charlotte's pretty blush had suddenly become a flag of anger.

'Oh, Papa, what are you doing here? Have you come to check on me already?'

'No, merely keeping my promise not to abandon you.'

'We are about to have dinner,' Charlotte said. 'I know half past one is nearer the hour for nuncheon than dinner, but I like to give the village children a good meal before sending them home and that is why we have it so early. Will you join us?'

'You mean you sit down and eat with them?' he asked in astonishment.

'Yes. It is part of their education to learn table manners. It is not enough to tell them what is right and wrong, one must set an example. It is a philosophy I apply to most things. I included it in the prospectus, which I assume you have studied.'

'I agree our daughters might benefit from such teaching, but surely it is not for peasants.'

'They might not always be peasants. The more intelligent among them might aspire to higher things.'

Julia was laughing and he turned to her in exasperation. 'And what do you find so amusing, madam?'

'You sitting down to table with children. Why, until we set out on this journey and we stopped at that inn for refreshment, I had never had a meal with you at all. I was never allowed into the dining room, was I?'

'It is not the custom for children—'

'If you do not wish to share the children's meal, my lord,' Charlotte put in quickly, before father and daughter could begin an altercation that would undoubtedly result in Julia being punished, 'perhaps you could return after the little ones have gone home. The Reverend is coming later to give a Latin lesson to the older ones and I shall be free to talk to you. That is, if the object of your visit was to speak to me.'

'Yes, I must.' He smiled suddenly, deciding he might as well humour her, if only to restore himself to favour. 'I shall be delighted to join you for dinner.'

She turned from him and ushered the children into pairs, then turned back to him, smiling. 'Shall we lead the way, my lord?'

They trooped into the dining room and it was all he could do not to laugh at the exaggerated politeness of the boys as they held the chairs for the girls to be seated before taking their own places. Charlotte helped herself from the dishes Betsy offered her and, once everyone had been served, picked up her knife and fork. The children watched her and copied her, though some who were not used to so much food gobbled it up quickly, afraid it might be snatched from them. Charlotte did not admonish them. 'They will slow down when they realise there will be more tomorrow and the day after that,' she whispered to Stacey who was seated on her right and who had been gazing at the children in a kind of numbed incredulity that he was there at all. They were evidently overawed by this big, handsome man with his fine clothes and smooth white hands, for they dare not open their mouths.

'Do you not think you could make a little polite conversation to put them at their ease?' Charlotte suggested when the silence became prolonged.

'Good heavens, what about?' he asked.

'The weather—some of their fathers are seafaring men and the weather is always of some concern, as it is to the farmers. Or you could tell them about your life in the army, though no gruesome details, please.' She smiled at him and spoke aloud. 'My lord, I believe you have travelled on the Continent, is it so very different from England?'

To please her, he tried, but he was thankful when the meal ended and the village children were sent off home, leaving Julia, Lizzie and Fanny to return to the classroom to work on the Latin exercises set by the Reverend Fuller. At last he was alone with Charlotte.

## Chapter Eight

Having exhausted his supply of small talk at the table, he was left with nothing to say except what was in his heart, but she had given him no encouragement. She treated him politely, as she would treat the father of one of her pupils, and he knew he had a long way to go before she was ready to hear an offer from him. Rank, breeding and wealth, all the things his parents set so much store by, meant nothing at all to her; she had not thought fit to tell him her own antecedents, as if it did not matter. Did it matter? Had it ever? 'Shall we go for a walk along the cliffs?' he asked her. 'We may be private there.'

Her heart jumped before settling again to its usual beat. Wanting to be private did not mean what she wanted it to mean. He had never given any indication he loved her; she was not such a green girl as to imagine an endearment and a kiss meant anything to a man like Viscount Darton, who would not stoop to marry someone as lowly as a schoolteacher. If he could not accept her as the person she was, then she was better off without him. She must, she really must, convince herself of that or she would be lost. But she would go, hear what he had to say. 'Very well. I will fetch my bonnet and cloak. The wind is still quite keen.'

He waited in the hall while she ran lightly upstairs. Five minutes later she returned ready to go out and they set off along the cliff-top path in silence. It was an uncomfortable silence, but neither knew how to break it. He glanced at her when he thought her attention was elsewhere and noticed she looked weary, but that was hardly to be wondered at considering all the worry she had had, and not until today had he realised how tiring it was to look after a dozen young children; the short time he had spent with them had exhausted him. He would rather drill a regiment or charge the enemy.

She turned and saw him studying her and hastily turned away again. 'Did you go to the Manor?' she asked him, looking straight ahead.

'Yes.'

'And was his lordship surprised to see you? Did he make you welcome?'

'I believe he was surprised, but as to a welcome,

I cannot be sure, but he invited me to stay. After all, I hold a few of his vouchers and he is anxious to win them back.'

'I cannot understand what makes a man continue gambling even after everything is lost.'

'I believe it is a compulsion, a feeling that one more card, one hand, one throw of the dice will set all to rights. When it does not, he must risk more in the hope his luck will change, and, on the rare occasions when it does, instead of stopping, the true gambler risks it all again.'

'Is that how you feel about it?'

'No, I have no need to make money in that fashion and I have never chanced more than I am prepared to lose.' Was he gambling now? Was he gambling his happiness and peace of mind on being able to bring her round?

'I collect you said we all gamble one way or another when we make a decision. I am afraid I did that when I agreed to take on The Crow's Nest, even before I learned of my husband's legacy. It gave me sleepless nights, I can tell you. I was never so relieved and grateful when I found I could afford it. I certainly would never dream of doing anything so rash again.'

He smiled, wondering again what she would say if she knew where that legacy had really come from. 'That proves you are not a true gambler, my lady.'

'I have always thought Cecil was simply weak and easily led and without the other two we might have come to some accommodation.'

'You may be right.'

They walked on companionably. 'How long do you intend to stay at the Manor?'

'I do not know. It depends…'

'On what, my lord?' The wind was whipping her cloak about her legs and a wisp of hair escaped her bonnet and blew across her face. Unconsciously she pushed it back with one gloved finger. It was such a little gesture, but it wrenched at something deep inside him and made him ache to protect her and love her so long as he had breath in his body.

'On you,' he said softly.

'Me?' she asked, so startled she stopped and turned to face him. He was smiling, his brown eyes holding hers, so that she was obliged to look away. 'Oh, I infer you mean how I perform as an instructress for your daughter.'

He had not meant that at all, but he refrained from contradicting her. 'Among other things. How does Julia?'

'I have not had her with me long enough to make a judgement,' she said carefully, resuming walking.

'But you must have formed an impression. Do not be afraid to tell me the truth. You are her teacher and mentor and I would expect nothing but honesty from you.'

'You would get nothing but honesty,' she said sharply. 'From what I have observed so far, Julia is an intelligent and vivacious young lady, but I can see that she would be headstrong if thwarted or if asked to do something she does not wish to do.'

'It did not take you very long to discover that. What has she refused to do?'

Charlotte smiled. 'Nothing very dreadful. She did not want to go to bed at the same time as Lizzie and Fanny, claiming she has always been allowed to stay up until she felt like retiring and she was old enough to know when she was tired enough to sleep.'

'That is my father's fault, I am afraid. He likes her company and he would keep her up, telling her tales of his battles. Miss Handy, her governess, is too afraid of the Earl to insist. How did you overcome the problem?'

'I told her that if she was old enough to know when she was tired, she would also know that a long journey, new and strange surroundings and meeting new people was about the most tiring thing on earth, and did she not agree.'

'And did she?'

Charlotte laughed. 'She was dead on her feet, but she flung her head in the air and said she would go to bed, but she did not expect to sleep and would read if I would allow her a light. She took Sir Walter Scott's novel *Waverley* to bed with her, but when I went to her room to say goodnight to her only five minutes later, she was fast asleep and the book not even opened.'

'And today?'

'She has performed all the tasks I set her.'

'Without complaint?'

'Why should she complain when she wants so very much to please you? She thinks that if she pleases me and I pass on a good report, you will be pleased with her and allow her to go home.'

'Did she tell you that?'

'No, of course she did not, but it is not difficult to deduce. All little girls love praise.' She paused, laughing a little. 'Even little boys. Sometimes quite big boys too. Did you not strive to please your father, so that you might bask in his praise?'

'*Touché,*' he said.

They had reached the path that led down to the beach and he stopped to look about him, wondering which path the free-traders might use—probably the one through the pine woods, he decided, that would give more cover, although it was not the most direct one to the Manor. 'Shall we venture down? There is something I want to look at.'

He took her arm to guide her down the path, ready to steady her if she should slip, and that small gesture was nearly her undoing. She had managed to keep a tight hold on her emotions until then, mainly by being professional and talking about Julia and the school, but she did not know how she would manage if he spoke to her on a more personal level. Not that he had given any indication that he meant to and paradoxically that disappointed her.

She wanted to know how he had felt about leaving her to her fate and going to his sick daughter. It wasn't that she blamed him for that, it was the only thing he could have done and as he had written to her to explain, even if she had not received the letter, she had no cause for complaint, but it would have been good to know that he had had a little qualm about it and that he had thought about her since. But all he seemed concerned with was settling his daughter into school and returning to his life of drinking and gambling.

As soon as they reached the beach, she moved away from him so that his hand dropped to his side. She felt its loss keenly, but steeled herself to continue speaking normally. 'Did you learn anything about the smuggling while you were at the Manor, my lord?'

'Very little, they were careful to say nothing in front of me, but I did overhear a little. I think the contraband will arrive in the next three days, moon, wind and tide being favourable.' He looked out over the sea. There were several ships on the horizon, their sails driving them on a brisk south-westerly. Was one of them the contraband ship? He had no way of knowing.

'What are you going to do? Have them arrested?'

'I do not know yet. There is more to consider than catching three free-traders. One of them is your brother-in-law and the scandal would reflect on everyone at the Manor, including you and your school.'

'But I have left.'

'Yes, but it could be said that The Crow's Nest is an ideal spot for a lookout and that you took it on purpose to help them.'

'No one who knows me would believe that and I am astonished that you could even think it.'

'I did not say that was what I believed, did I? Do not be so swift to take offence, my lady. I am only pointing out what the world might say. And I collect you told me Sir Roland proposed using you to make Cecil conform, though whether that weighs with him or not, I do not know.'

'I think he is a little afraid of them.'

'Yes, I believe he is, which is one of the reasons I must do nothing to put you or the children in danger.'

'Danger, surely not? Why would they want to trouble themselves with us?' She did her best to sound convincing, but was not at all sure she had succeeded.

'I sincerely hope they do not, but I beg you, please keep away from the beach and cliffs and make sure the children do not wander down there. They are desperate men.'

'What, those three?' She managed a light laugh, but a shudder passed through her. Sir Roland had not been specific, but the threat had been there. 'They are all wind and no substance.'

'It is not only those three, they are not working alone. They will have recruited others, ex-soldiers, rough men used to handling weapons and prepared to use them. They will do anything to avoid capture, including murder.'

'Murder?' She stopped and turned to him in such distress he reached for her hands and held them.

'If anyone stands in their way, I think they would. And the men from the village might be involved. It would not be difficult to persuade hungry, unemployed men to help land the goods and carry them to the Manor for a fee. And even those who are employed would jump at the chance to make more in one night than they can earn in a month. If they were all arrested, their families would suffer, the very children you teach, my lady.'

She did not draw away from him, but stood looking up into his face, trying to read his mind and failing utterly. Did he mean he would do nothing to prevent their activities, might even collude with them? That was the easy option and if it meant nothing dreadful happened to the villagers—wives did not become widows and children like Danny and Meg White, her particular favourites, were not deprived of fathers—would that not be best?

'So are you going to turn a blind eye and allow it to happen? I believe that is what many people do.'

'I don't know what I am going to do, but rest assured, I will let nothing happen to you, I promise, or to Julia, or any of the children.' They continued to walk, but now he tucked her hand beneath his elbow and held it close by his side. Clouds scudded across the horizon, threatening rain, and the wind was churning up the sea into foam-topped waves. 'Not tonight,' he murmured. 'The sea is too rough.'

'You know,' she said. 'You were right about The Crow's Nest being a good vantage point. There is a splendid view from the top of the tower and Captain MacArthur has a powerful spyglass up there. You can see miles out to sea and most of the paths on the cliffs, though not the beach immediately below the house. The Captain said the children were not to go up there, but I could. I could keep watch.'

He smiled indulgently and pressed her hand closer. 'And then what?'

'I could let you know what I have seen. I would not come to the Manor, of course, but we could arrange a signal, a light perhaps.'

'No. It might be seen by others. The smugglers would think you were betraying them to the Coast Blockade and the Coast Blockade, if they are anywhere about, would be sure to conclude you are in league with the lawbreakers. No, you must keep right out of it. I forbid you to become involved.'

'Forbid, my lord?' she said, sharply. 'How can you forbid me? I am not answerable to you.'

'Oh, yes, you are. You are—' He stopped, knowing he had made a grave mistake. How could he make her understand? How could he tear down the barrier she had built up around herself? She had changed since he had left her at Easterley Manor. Then she had been a woman with her back to the wall and he had admired her courage, fallen in love with her, kissed her and she had not objected, not vehemently, not like a woman would if she thought she had been insulted. He had imagined, hoped, that meant she welcomed his advances; she had certainly accepted his help, said she trusted him. Now she no longer needed him, she seemed to be casting him aside, deliberately keeping her distance. He had let her down, he knew, but he had apologised and she seemed to have accepted it, so why had they not been able to resume where they left off?

He became aware that she was looking at him, her head a little on one side, waiting for him to continue. 'I beg your pardon,' he said, bowing formally. 'That was presumptuous of me, but you must know that the safety and happiness of you and those about you are important to me and I would be the biggest scoundrel of them all if I let anything happen to you when I could prevent it.' Oh, how stiff he sounded!

'I see.' She thought she did. He was concerned for his reputation, for his pride, for his honour, for his daughter. 'Rest assured, my lord, I will do nothing to put Julia, my daughters or any of the other children at risk.' If he could stand on his dignity, so could she, with more justification.

They walked on, moving down to the water's edge. He looked straight ahead, his stance upright, his whole body tense; she was subdued and miserable, blinking back tears, but managing to keep her head up. They stopped when they could go no further, standing silently side by side contemplating the breakers rolling shorewards. The tension between them was almost unbearable.

'Shall we go back?' he suggested.

'I thought there was something you wanted to look at?'

'I have seen all I want to see.' His voice was clipped.

'And said all you wanted to say,' she retorted. 'I do believe you brought me down here to deliver a lecture.'

'No, but as you are not prepared to listen, I will not waste my breath.'

How did they come to this pass? he asked himself, as they turned to go back the way they had come. Nothing had gone as planned, and he had been a fool to expect her to fall into his arms, simply because he returned her jewels. Why had he bothered to come back? He could have found another school for Julia if he had tried hard enough and he could have sent a courier with the jewellery. He knew the answer to that. He could not stay away. His life was tied to hers irrevocably and, sooner or later, she must come to realise that herself.

The village children were more than a little in awe of the Honourable Julia Darton, which was her proper title, so she informed them loftily. And when her father became the Earl of Malcomby, she would be Lady Julia in her own right. Her baggage, which they had watched being unloaded from the carriage, consisted of a huge trunk that Jenkins and Betsy had hardly been able to lift, and two portmanteaux. They could not imagine anyone having so many clothes. Even Lizzie and Fanny were impressed. 'I am here to teach you,' she told them, as they crowded round her, waiting in the classroom for the next day's lessons to begin. 'You must all do as I say.'

Charlotte, approaching the room with her arms full of books, overheard this and wondered whether to make some comment or let it go. She pushed open the door and stood looking round at everyone. Julia looked smug and the others guilty as they quickly returned to their places.

'Good morning, children,' she said.

Danny sprang forward. 'Take the books, missus?'

'Missus,' said Julia scornfully, imitating his accent surprisingly accurately. 'Don't you know how to speak to a lady? You should say, "May I take the books, my lady."'

He looked perplexed, but brightened when Charlotte handed the books over to him with a smile. 'Thank you, Danny.' He had always called her missus, and she had not corrected him. But now she had a paying pupil, whose papa would not approve of such slipshod ways; it behoved her to teach them to address her, and anyone else with a title, correctly. On the other hand, Julia's smirk annoyed her.

Danny, his face flaming, set the books down on

the table at the front of the class and returned to his seat. Charlotte followed him and stood facing the class. Except for Julia and her own girls, they were ill clad and undernourished and could probably look forward to nothing more than hard work and little joy throughout their lives. The promise of being able to better themselves if they had an education had a hollow ring, but when she started out on this venture she had truly believed it. Had she been wrong to expect high and low to integrate, that one would learn from the other? The Reverend was the only one who had encouraged her; Cecil had told her she was mad when she told him what she intended to do and even Viscount Darton only humoured her because it suited his purpose to have his daughter near at hand when he wanted to gamble with her brother-in-law.

'Julia, Lizzie, Fanny,' she said. 'I believe the Reverend Fuller set you some exercises yesterday. You can do them in the dining room.'

'What, now?' Lizzie asked.

'Yes, now.'

'But you said I was to help teach the little ones,' Julia put in.

'So you shall. We will discuss what you will teach them after dinner.'

The girls left the room and Charlotte turned to the

remaining children. 'Now, do any of you know the name of the King of England?' she asked.

'George,' one of them said. 'But he's mad, my pa says so.'

'He is ill, but he is still our king. Now, how would you address him if you were to meet him?'

They laughed at such an absurd idea.

'Mr King?' suggested one.

She smiled and corrected him and from there went on to explain the different titles in order of precedence: king, duke, marquis, earl, viscount, baron and baronet, and how each should be addressed. She did it quickly, knowing it was unlikely they would remember or even needed to, and then moved on to a reading lesson. Teachers of poor children usually confined themselves to using the bible as their text in order to make good little Christians of their pupils, but in her opinion the language was difficult for the children to comprehend and therefore did not hold their attention. She picked up Sir Walter Scott's *Waverley*, an action-packed adventure that might motivate them to want to read it on their own. 'Come and stand out here, Danny,' she said, wanting to make up for the humiliation he had received. 'Let us see what you make of this.'

He did very well, slowly at first but gaining in confidence as he went on, then she asked the others to take over, one at a time, until they had all read a passage. At the end of the lesson she led them to the dining room for dinner where they were joined by the older girls.

Charlotte, sharing their meal, could not stop herself thinking of the smugglers and wondering if the children's parents were even now receiving their instructions. Would such transactions be kept from their offspring or would they make no secret of what they were doing, perhaps enlist the help of some of the older ones? How much contraband was expected? A few barrels of brandy and a box of tobacco or a whole shipload? Surely it could not be brought ashore without anyone seeing it?

'Go straight home,' she told the village children after the meal. 'Do not stop and talk to strangers.'

'Why not, missus…I mean, my lady?' Danny hurriedly corrected himself, which made the others giggle. 'They might be lost and want to know the way. We don't ever get people come here but they've lost their way. It don't lead anywhere, you see.'

'Except the sea,' put in Joseph Bowker, whose father was a seaman.

'I know,' she said, and, not wishing to alarm them, added, 'Of course you may direct someone who is lost.'

And there was no one more lost than she was, she reflected as she watched them go, some running, others dawdling, unwilling to go home to the chores that awaited them.

'I wish I had my mount here,' Julia was saying as Charlotte rejoined the girls in her small parlour where they were sitting with their sewing. Lizzie was mending stockings, Fanny was trying to embroider a cushion cover, though whether it would ever be fit to put on a cushion Charlotte doubted. Julia was nursing a piece of canvas and a pile of skeins, but her hands were idle. 'I would love to have a gallop along the beach. I think I shall ask Papa if he will send for Ebony. We could go for a ride together.'

'I collect when the Viscount was here earlier in the year, he was riding a big white stallion,' Charlotte said, wondering if he had fetched the horse from the inn at Ipswich.

'Yes, that was Ivor. He is named for the Russian Count who sold him to Papa.'

'I did not think he had him here with him now.'

'He hasn't. I do not know where the horse is. Papa left him somewhere when he came home last time. I don't know where, but he told me he was in such a hurry to come to me he decided to travel on the mail. I was very ill, you know.'

'Yes, I did know. But you are fully recovered now, I trust.'

'Oh, yes. I have never been ill before, though I was always used to go out and about in all weathers. The doctor said it was my strong constitution that pulled me through it.'

'Then I am very glad.'

'If we cannot ride, can we go for a walk?'

'No, not today. Remember we are to discuss what you are to teach the children. We must plan the lessons properly and we must not forget that you are learning too.'

'How can you teach and learn at the same time?'

'Oh, easily. I am doing it all the time.'

'You?' Julia laughed.

'All life is a learning experience,' Charlotte said. 'From birth to death we are learning, experiencing new things, new sights, new tastes, learning about people, and if we are wise we try to understand them. We are all different, but we are all human beings with our own strengths and frailties, from the highest in the land to the lowest. And we can all be hurt by someone else's cruelty.'

'Oh, I see, this is meant to be a jobation.'

'Do you think you deserve a scolding?' Charlotte asked mildly.

'No, why should I?' It was said sharply. 'If people

cannot stand being corrected—' She stopped. 'Why are you smiling?'

'Don't you know?'

'No.'

'Mama means that if the shoe fits, then you should wear it,' Lizzie said. 'You corrected Danny White and Mama is correcting you.'

Julia turned on her. 'Do you not mind that little urchin calling your mama missus?'

'Not if Mama doesn't. He was not disrespectful. But you are. You are odiously rude.'

'Lizzie!' Charlotte admonished.

'And you are a toady, a jumped-up little mush-room,' Julia shouted.

'That is enough!' Charlotte clapped her hands together.

Both girls subsided and looked down at the work in their laps. Lizzie began stitching with great fury, but Julia flung her work from her. 'I do not have to stay here to be insulted.' And with that she flounced from the room. Charlotte went after her.

She found her sitting on her bed, staring at the wall with a mutinous expression on her face. But her eyes were filled with tears and though she tried manfully to blink them back, they chased each other down her cheeks. 'Oh, Julia, do not cry.' Charlotte sat down beside her and put her arm about the girl's shoulders. 'Lizzie did not mean it.'

'I am not crying, I am not!' Her voice rose, but then, suddenly deflated, she sank back against Charlotte. 'And it isn't Lizzie…'

'Then what is it?'

'It's… Oh, I don't know. I miss Grandpa and Grandmama and Malcomby and Miss Handy, and all my animals. I want to go home. I hate being cooped indoors, but I said I would stay to please Papa, but he will not be pleased.'

'Why would he not?'

'You will tell him I have been naughty and he will beat me.'

'Beat you?' Charlotte asked, unable to believe that, however exasperated Viscount Darton might be, he would lay hands on his daughter. 'Has he ever beaten you?'

'No, but he said he would if you gave me a bad report.'

'I am sure he did not mean it.'

'Oh, he did,' the girl said with conviction.

'Then we must endeavour not to send him a bad report. Now, dry your eyes and come downstairs again. We have still to plan your lessons.'

Julia regained her usual aplomb remarkably quickly and accompanied Charlotte downstairs, where they spent some time talking about her role as a teacher's helper. It did not take Charlotte long to discover that the girl was well versed in things to do with the natural world, wild flowers, the animals of the countryside, birds and their nests, and as the village children also had a little practical knowledge she decided to put the two together and see what transpired. By teatime, Julia was showing real enthusiasm and settled down with a book on bird recognition in order to prepare for the next day's lesson. Charlotte breathed a sigh of relief and decided there was no need to tell Stacey about her behaviour towards Danny White and the subsequent contretemps with Lizzie, who had voluntarily said she was sorry and had received a grudging apology from Julia.

Next morning, with the smaller children crowding round Julia, absorbed in the bird book, and Lizzie and Fanny writing an essay on the Jacobite rebellion of 1745, and why it had failed, Charlotte felt safe leaving them in the care of Betsy, Joan Quinn and Jenkins while she went into Parson's End. She needed a few provisions and might at the same time learn if there was anything unusual happening there. Viscount Darton had told her to keep out of it, but he hadn't told her she should not venture into the village; his concern had been that they should not go on the beach. In any case, why should she do his bidding? The villagers all knew her and none would harm her.

She had not been in the village long when she became aware of an atmosphere of veiled excitement. Everyone was going about their usual business, working on the land, tending animals, or hanging out washing and sweeping the dust from their houses, but they looked more animated than usual, often stopping to look about them and Mrs White was singing as she beat her mats in the yard. Oh, they knew what was afoot, all of them. Should she say something? Should she warn them of the dire consequences of being caught with contraband goods? But they knew that already.

'My lady, good morning.' Stacey stood before her, doffing his tall hat. His dark hair curled about his ears, his dark, arched brows lifted a little at the sight of her, his dark eyes with their glinting golden lights swept over her.

She felt the colour flood her face, but managed to hold his scrutiny with her own candid, aquamarine eyes. 'Good morning, my lord.'

'Is all well at The Crow's Nest?' She was in her usual black cloak and bonnet and he wondered how long it would be before she decided to throw off her mourning. He hoped it was for her father-in-law and could soon be put off, and not her husband, who had been dead nearly eight years. A woman with her beauty and figure should not go through life swathed in black.

'Yes, my lord. I have come into the village for a few provisions.' She lifted the basket on her arm, which held a meat pie which she intended to take to an old lady who was housebound by rheumatism before filling the basket with her shopping. The village children rarely refused anything, but the older girls were more particular and Betsy always cooked more than was needed.

'Do you need to do that yourself? Surely there is someone you might send?'

'I like to do it. I like to visit the sick and do what I can to help them. The children are all occupied with their lessons and Miss Quinn and Betsy are there to watch over them.'

'Have you made your purchases?'

'Not yet, my lord. I go to the farm for fresh eggs and a plucked chicken for the children's dinner.' She indicated her direction and began to walk. He took her basket and fell into step beside her. Mrs White stopped singing to watch them go.

'The weather is calmer today,' he commented.

'Yes. Do you think it will happen tonight?' She

found herself whispering, though she did not know why, there was no one close enough to hear.

'No, I have my ear to the ground and what I hear indicates some delay. I am not quite sure what it is, perhaps a diversionary tactic to put the revenue men off the scent.'

'Are they on the scent?'

'I do not know.' He shrugged, then suddenly changed the subject. 'Would you not obtain better and cheaper produce in Ipswich?'

'Possibly, but I like to support the local people where I can and, in any case, I have no means of going there, unless I borrow the Reverend's gig and I do not like to ask for it too often. But I shall have to go soon because I need things for the school not obtainable in the village. I heard today that a Mr and Mrs Tyler are interested in sending their daughter to me.'

'I will be pleased to take you in my chaise. I have an errand there myself.'

'Oh, I did not…I was not asking…' She stopped, confused.

'I know that, but I need to go and so do you, so why not?' He paused, smiling. 'I promise not to lecture you.'

The idea was tempting, but as she looked about her and felt the tension in the air, though no one had said a word of anything afoot to her, she felt it would be wrong to leave the children without some supervision, especially if their parents were intent on helping the smugglers. She wished the whole desperate business was over and done with and they could get on with their normal lives. 'That is obliging of you, my lord, but I cannot leave the children.'

'I am sure the Reverend will be willing to take your classes for one day and his wife will look after our daughters until we return. What do you say?'

She hesitated. She really did need to go into Ipswich and the idea of being conveyed there in a comfortable chaise was enticing. 'Could we not take the girls with us? I am sure they would enjoy the outing. And Lizzie needs a new pair of shoes; she complains that the ones she has are pinching her.'

It was not what he had intended at all, but it was better than not taking her at all, and he might observe for himself how she and Julia dealt with one another. 'It will be a squeeze, the carriage is only meant for four.'

'But they are all quite small.'

'Very well. We will go tomorrow.'

'You do not think anything will happen before then?'

'No, and certainly not in daylight.'

'Then I will complete my errands and speak to the Reverend.'

She did not expect him to stay with her, but he accompanied her to old Mrs Warton's cottage and waited outside while she took the pie to her and then went with her to buy the eggs and chicken. Then he carried her basket to the Rectory, obviously determined to have his own way.

'Why, of course I will, my lady,' the Reverend Fuller said when she made her request. He had invited them into the parlour and asked his wife to provide refreshments and all four were sitting enjoying tea and cakes. 'Do you go to the May Day Ball?'

'Ball?' she queried. Balls and social events of any kind had passed her by in the last two years, since old Lord Hobart had needed her constant attention, though when Grenville was alive, they had sometimes gone to balls. It was how they had met: her father had taken her and her mother to a ball in Portsmouth given by the Admiralty. She had been so happy then. But that was in the past, a happy memory. It made her a little sad to think she might never dance again. If she had met Viscount Stacey Darton in the capital at one of society's many social occasions, how different their relationship might have been! If—

'Yes.' The parson interrupted her thoughts, which was just as well for she was off into the realms of fantasy. 'You collect, they have one every year in the Assembly Rooms.'

'Yes, I do remember, but I cannot go to a ball, Reverend. I am in mourning for one thing and, for another, we would have to stay overnight.'

He smiled at Stacey, who was sitting next to her on a sofa, balancing a cup and saucer in his big hands and saying nothing. 'They are all problems that can easily be overcome, my lady. Is that not so, my lord?'

Stacey realised with a little start of surprise that the Reverend was matchmaking and felt himself smiling. 'If Lady Hobart wishes to attend a ball in Ipswich, then I will be happy to escort her,' he said. 'As for staying overnight, I think that can be arranged, if her ladyship's maid were to come too. I am sure accommodation can be arranged in a hotel for Lady Hobart and the girls and I can stay at another establishment.'

'And I am sure the late Lord Hobart would not wish you to refuse on his account,' the Reverend added, deciding that he approved of Viscount Darton. At least he had the wisdom not to suggest staying at the same establishment as her ladyship. 'He would say, as I do, that you deserve a little respite.'

Charlotte looked from one to the other; both were smiling. 'This is a conspiracy,' she said, only half-annoyed, because she knew the old cleric meant well.

'Not at all,' he said. 'But you have been working too hard and it is time you had a little leisure. I will see to your pupils tomorrow and the day after that is Saturday and they would not be in school in any case.'

'But there will no be room in the carriage for Miss Quinn as well as the girls.'

'I can easily sit beside my driver,' Stacey said. 'How many more objections are you going to raise?'

'None. I accept your kind offer.'

It was only when the arrangements had been made and they were once again on the road and walking towards The Crow's Nest that it occurred to her that the parson knew about the smugglers and was determined, with the Viscount's connivance, to send her away from trouble. She was not at all sure she liked being manipulated in that way.

Stacey arrived after breakfast the next morning and the girls, who had been ready and waiting for at least an hour, piled into the carriage that Jem had brought to the door from the stables. Julia and Miss Quinn sat on one side and Fanny, who was the smallest, between Lizzie and Charlotte on the other. They were chattering excitedly, planning what they would buy with the coppers they had to spend. Stacey put Charlotte's small portmanteau under the driver's seat along with his own and climbed up beside Jem, who handed him the reins. He liked to drive when the opportunity offered itself and they were soon bowling along the narrow country lanes towards Ipswich.

Fortunately the weather was fine, though still a little blustery, and they made good time, arriving in the town in the early afternoon. Charlotte had been wondering what they would do if Stacey could not find suitable accommodation for them, but she need not have worried—his name and presence, with the added inducement of a handful of gold sovereigns over and above the usual tariff, procured them a suite of two bedrooms and a sitting room at the Great White Horse.

'Unless you need me, my lady, I will leave you to do your shopping while I go about my business,' Stacey said, once he had seen them safely to their rooms. 'I will call back at eight o'clock to escort you to the ball.'

'That will be convenient, my lord,' Charlotte said, matching his formality with her own.

'Ball, Mama?' Lizzie queried, as soon as he had gone. 'I did not know you were going to a ball.'

'It was the Reverend's idea,' she said, smiling to reassure her. 'He thought I had been working too hard and needed a little recreation. He asked Lord Darton if he would escort me and, being the gentleman he is, his lordship could hardly refuse. You do not mind, do you? We shall have all the afternoon and dinner together and this evening Quinny will look after you until I return.' She looked at Julia as she spoke, watching for her reaction, but her face remained impassive.

'I am hungry,' Fanny put in, unaware of any undercurrents in the conversation and accepting her mother's explanation at face value.

'Then we shall order refreshments and then go shopping and see the sights. And when the time comes, if you like, you can help me dress.' Her shopping and the girls would keep her occupied until the time came to get ready for the ball, so she would have no time to worry whether the gown she had brought with her would be suitable, about what Lord Darton would wear and how they would deal together in an atmosphere very different from the one at Parson's End.

If it were not for the presence of her daughters, she would be feeling like a seventeen-year-old, going to her first grown-up outing, which was foolish. Why should the prospect of being escorted by Viscount Stacey Darton fluster her? But it did and she knew why perfectly well.

Stacey went to the stables and was reunited with Ivor. 'He's become fat,' he told the head groom.

'Beggin' your pardon, my lord, but there've bin none to exercise 'im. The lad did try, but he's too strong for 'im. Threw 'im off, he did.

'Was the lad hurt?'

'No, my lord. Landed on a heap of straw.'

'I'll take the horse out as soon as I've enjoyed some of the inn's excellent food,' he said. 'So have him saddled and ready in an hour from now.' He strode into the inn followed by Jem and bespoke a hearty meal, after which he sent Jem to book rooms for them at the Lion and the Lamb and set off for the docks and the Custom House. He did not hurry; Ivor had become unused to exercise and he would have to get him back into peak condition gradually.

He pondered on his errand as he rode, his hands lightly on the reins. Ivor knew who was on his back and whinnied in pleasure at being out of the confining stable. If Gerard was not readily available, he was not sure whether to leave a message; the situation was a ticklish one and he did not want a clumsy force of men to rush in arresting all and sundry; ten to one the real culprits would escape, leaving the villagers to be rounded up and punished. The alternative was to say nothing and let events take their course. It meant Sir Roland and Augustus Spike might escape scot-free, but could they be apprehended the next time?

Would there be a next time? He felt sure there would be; such a neat hiding place as Easterley Manor would not be used just once and abandoned, but the risk to the villagers increased with every run and Charlotte, stuck in The Crow's Nest in the path of the run, would be in danger. If he had known about the smuggling before he came back, he never would have brought Julia with him and he would have tried to persuade Charlotte to look elsewhere for her school, but it was done now and he must do what he could to prevent anyone being hurt.

The town was not the once great seaport it had been, but it was still a busy place and there were several ships in the docks. One was a brand new vessel and he paused to speak to one of the men working on it. 'Yes, sir, a fine ship,' the man agreed. 'It's one of the largest of her class, one hundred and fifty-three feet from stem to stern, she is.' The man was evidently proud of the hand he had had in her construction. 'Are you a seagoing man, sir?'

'No, a soldier. I am looking for the Custom House, can you direct me?'

He followed the man's directions and made his way to the Custom House on the Quay and, to his immense relief, Gerard was there, conferring with a colleague. He greeted Stacey enthusiastically.

'What happened to you, old friend?' he demanded after introducing him to Lieutenant Tarrent. 'You said you would catch me up.'

'I would have done, but I was prevented.' Stacey went on to explain what had happened. 'I have just come from Parson's End,' he concluded.

'She must be prodigious beautiful to attract you back to that dead place.'

'It is not exactly dead,' he said, ignoring the jibe and then, appearing to change the subject, added, 'How goes the free-trading business?'

'It goes better than it should. The trouble is that the general populace see no harm in it and will not come forward with information and, even if they disapprove, are too afraid of being identified and punished by the rogues.' He sighed. 'But we make progress, little by little. According to a reliable informant there is even now a ship crossing from the Continent loaded to the gunnels with contraband, but we don't know where it intends to land.'

'I do,' Stacey said quietly.

'You do?' Gerard exclaimed. 'Out with it, man.'

'The situation is a little delicate.'

'It always is. Are you involved?'

'Certainly not, though I am well in with the principals. My fear is that the innocent will be taken up with the guilty and that would be a pity.'

'Do you think my men are so ill trained they cannot tell the difference?'

'They might not. Let me tell you the whole and perhaps we can devise some way of taking up the villains and leaving the misguided to return to their homes and ponder on the lucky escape they have had.'

Gerard and the lieutenant listened to what he had to say, nodded their heads now and then, and, at the end, agreement was reached about how they should proceed. It was six o'clock when Stacey left them to return to the inn to change into evening clothes. What impulse had made him pack an evening suit when he left Malcomby he had no idea, but he was very glad he had. He meant to forget all about smugglers, recalcitrant daughters and make it a night to remember.

# Chapter Nine

Long before eight o'clock, Charlotte was in a state of feverish excitement mixed with quaking trepidation. The prospect of a little self-indulgence, dressing up in something other than mourning black and dancing with a handsome man, did battle with her image of herself as a matronly widow for whom such things should be mere memories. She began to wonder if she had been wrong to agree to go to the ball at all, never mind with Viscount Stacey Darton. After all, he had not suggested it, the Reverend Fuller had and, as she had said to the girls, being a gentleman he could not refuse when perhaps he would rather not have offered his escort.

They had quarrelled only two days before and she had climbed on her high horse and berated him for forbidding her to go on to the beach, so why should he continue to bother himself with her? It was unkind and ungrateful of her to treat him as if he had been one of Cecil's cronies. But was he? Had he seized the chance to remove her and the girls from Parson's End while the contraband was run ashore? Did he intend to let it happen while he danced with her at the Assembly Rooms? Should she be grateful that he had brought her and the girls out of danger? How much did the Reverend know? The Reverend Fuller would not be the first clergyman to accept a half-anker of brandy in payment for turning a blind eye.

But even while these thoughts were buzzing round in her head, she was sitting in her chemise and under-petticoat, having her hair brushed by Miss Quinn while the girls sat on her bed, watching the preparations, almost as excited as if they were going themselves.

'Papa went to a ball almost every week when he first came home from the war,' Julia said, putting her head on one side to see Charlotte's reflection in the looking glass. 'I heard Grandpapa telling Grandmama he had agreed to look for a new wife and that Lady Hortensia Carstairs would suit him very well. She was the daughter of a Marquis and would give him an heir, which I collect is of all things desirable.'

'What happened?' Lizzie asked, putting the question Charlotte herself longed to ask. Julia's words had brought home to her that the Viscount had no male heir and that would be a prime consideration if he were ever to marry again. At nearly thirty she would not be considered a candidate, even if he had known of her connection to Lord Falconer. As it was, he imagined her to be well below him in rank and, perversely, she had decided not to disillusion him

'She came to Malcomby Hall to stay,' Julia answered. 'But I did not like her and she did not like me, so nothing came of it.'

'Why did you not like her?' Fanny asked. 'Was she ugly?'

'Oh, excessively so. And top lofty. You have no idea how top lofty. She had a very long nose and looked down it at me and said I should not be allowed to run free about the house and if she had the managing of me I would be confined to the nursery.' She laughed suddenly. 'I think it annoyed Papa to be criticised, though he did not show it. He sent me to my room and that made me angry.'

'What did you do?'

'I climbed out of the window and down the ivy and went to the coach house and threw horse muck into her carriage on the fine velvet seats.'

'Oh, you never did!' Lizzie exclaimed and the other two looked at each other, unsure whether to laugh or be shocked.

'I did. You should have heard her when her coachman told her of it, screeching like a witch she was, and packed her bags and set off home just as soon as the men had cleaned it out for her. Papa blamed one of the stable boys.'

'That was unfair of you to let a stable boy take the blame,' Lizzie said.

'Oh, I didn't. As soon as Lady Carstairs left, he came to my room to see me and I started to tell him not to blame Saul, but he said he didn't, he knew it was me. He confined me to the house for a week, though I think he was secretly glad I had got rid of her for him.'

'Julia, it is not a matter to be proud of,' Charlotte rebuked her mildly.

'Well, just so you know.'

Was there menace in the girl's voice, a warning to leave her father alone? Charlotte suddenly felt sorry for the child. She was so insecure in her father's affections, she saw everyone as a threat and behaved badly as a consequence. 'And now we know, we will find something else to discuss. What would you like for your supper?'

They all wanted something different and Miss Quinn was despatched downstairs to order it to be brought to their sitting room. While she was gone Charlotte slipped into her ball gown.

It was three years old, but it had been a favourite of hers in the days when she had gone to balls. The material of the overskirt was a pale blue-green gossamer covered with tiny embroidered flowers in silver thread; the underskirt was blue silk. The effect was one of shimmering lightness, like the waters of a lake with the moonlight shining on it. The high waist was bounded by a deep blue ribbon and the hem of the skirt was scalloped so that it showed the bottom of the underskirt. The boat-shaped neckline was rather more revealing than she remembered it, but there was a long, deep stole in the same blue-green gossamer that she could drape over her shoulders.

'Oh, Mama, you look beautiful,' Fanny said, a sentiment echoed by Lizzie, who added,

'You will have to fight off your dancing partners.'

'No, she won't, for my papa will be escorting her,' Julia said, reminding Charlotte that he would be calling for her at any moment and setting her nerves jangling again.

Miss Quinn returned and stood just inside the door, surveying Charlotte from head to foot. 'Oh, it is so good to see you out of black,' she said. 'And that gown, I remember it well. You wore it when Lord Hobart took you to London for the ball to celebrate Napoleon's first defeat. I collect thinking then how it matched your eyes.'

The jubilation had been short-lived; the defeated Emperor had staged a return and it had taken Wellington and the Battle of Waterloo to show him what a mistake that had been. She had not celebrated the second time because, by then, Lord Hobart's health was failing. Little had she suspected that his demise would change her life so radically. She looked round at the children and felt a sudden surge of love for them all and, never one to stifle her feelings, hugged them one by one, even the difficult Julia, then sat down at her dressing table and took her emerald necklace from its case and, turning to Julia, smiled. 'Would you fasten it for me, dear?'

The girl jumped up from the bed and went to obey, her expression revealing her pleasure at being chosen for the task. It was no sooner round her neck than a knock came at the outer door and they all trooped into the adjoining parlour as Miss Quinn admitted Stacey.

He stepped into the room and stood a moment, looking at Charlotte as if he had never seen her before. She was out of black and wearing something light and soft that clung to her figure and swirled about her feet. He realised, with a start, that apart from their first encounter on the beach, he had never really seen her hair; it had always been covered by a black lace cap or a bonnet and any escaping tresses had been firmly tucked away. But now he saw it in all its glory, beautifully arranged so that it coiled about her ears and was drawn up on top of her head where it was held with combs, allowing loose curls to fall about her ears and onto the nape of her neck, such heavy, shining hair and such a long, white neck. The schoolmistress had gone and in her place was the most beautiful, the most majestic woman he had ever set eyes on.

He took a step towards her and then suddenly became aware that they had an audience. Miss Quinn and the girls were all watching. He had not expected a reception committee, but it was typical of Charlotte to allow them to be present and his face twitched into a smile as he executed a flourishing leg for their benefit. 'My lady, your obedient,' he said.

She dipped a small curtsy, suddenly shy. He was in an evening coat of black superfine, a white single-breasted waistcoat and black breeches with white stockings. His neckcloth was pristine and elegantly tied, which made her wonder fleetingly if he had tied it himself or whether Jem, among his other tasks, fulfilled the role of valet. His hair, though not overlong, was carefully brushed into a style that curled about his forehead and ears. 'My lord.'

'Your carriage awaits, my lady.'

Julia giggled and that set the other two off and

then Miss Quinn's lips twitched and that made Charlotte suddenly relax. 'I am ready, my lord.' She smiled and offered him her hand, which he took and laid upon his sleeve.

'If you are good while we are gone,' he said, addressing the girls over his shoulder, 'I will take you to the harbour to see a brand new ship tomorrow.' He surprised himself with the suggestion. Viscount Stacey Darton, who had little time for children, had voluntarily promised to entertain three of them!

'Are you not in haste to return to Parson's End in the morning?' Charlotte asked, as he escorted her out to the waiting carriage.

'No.' He turned to look at her in the lamp above the door of the hotel. Her eyes sparkled, there was a rosy bloom on her cheeks and she looked ten years younger than she did in that all-enveloping black. 'I am finding the attractions of Ipswich growing more and more inviting every minute.'

She was not sure what to make of that reply, but decided she would be a fool to read more into it than a little mild flirtation. 'You are looking forward to the ball?' she asked. 'It will be nothing like a London ball, you know.'

Jem appeared from nowhere, opened the carriage door and let down the step with a flourish and a grin, then stood back to allow Stacey to hand her in and climb in behind her.

'My beautiful companion will more than make up for that,' he said, settling himself beside her as the carriage moved forward smoothly.

'Sir, I declare you are flirting with me.'

He turned towards her and could not resist reaching out and lifting one of her curls on his finger. It was silky soft. 'Why not?'

'I might object.'

'But you don't, do you?' He spoke softly. 'I speak only the truth. You are beautiful and you will outshine everyone there, blinding me to any deficiencies in my surroundings.'

'La, sir,' she said with a light laugh, proving she had not forgotten how to flirt herself. 'You will put me to the blush.'

'And a very pretty blush it is too.'

The banter set the tone for the whole evening. Each was determined to be light-hearted and not speak of anything contentious and they alighted at the door of the Assembly Rooms and made their way inside, still smiling.

The ballroom was decorated with spring flowers and greenery. Its floor had been lovingly polished and on a dais at one end an orchestra played for dancing, making up in enthusiasm what it lacked in skill. Everyone from the Master of Ceremonies down to the doorman who admitted them was intent on making it a night to remember, but even without that, neither Stacey nor Charlotte were likely to forget it.

They danced quadrilles, country dances, gallops and waltzes, and though he relinquished her to other partners now and again, most of the time they danced with each other, happily ignoring the protocol that decreed that a man who danced more than twice with an unmarried lady was as good as proposing to her. They were both mature and widowed and surely such strictures did not apply to them? As far as Stacey was concerned he meant to propose, just as soon as he found the right moment, but it had to be exactly the right moment because he did not know what he would do if she rejected him.

'People are looking at us,' she said, as they danced a waltz before the supper interval.

'They are looking at the belle of the ball,' he said. 'I am having to fight off the young men who want to take a turn about the room with you.'

She laughed. 'Flummery! I am too old for such nonsense.'

Her laughter pleased him. It was a light merry sound that told him she had at last relaxed. 'Old?' he murmured. 'You are in the prime of life, the best age to be, not silly, not empty-headed, but beautiful and intelligent and wise and I think... No, I know...' He stopped, looking down into her upturned face. 'I love you.'

The shock of hearing the words she had so longed to hear made her stumble. He pulled her closer to steady her. 'My lord—'

'My name is Stacey. I should like to hear you call me by it, at least when we are alone.'

'We are not alone. We are in a room full of people and attracting attention.'

'Then we will go somewhere where we are alone.' He took her hand and started to lead her from the room. She tried to resist, but, aware that they were being watched, could do nothing but go with him.

'They think we are having a lover's tiff,' she said when they found themselves in a deserted corridor.

'We can hardly have that, since we are not lovers.' He drew her into an alcove and turned to face her, taking her shoulders in his hands, feeling the softness of her bare flesh, where her shawl had fallen down about her arms and manfully resisted the urge to put his lips to it. 'Not that I do not wish we were.'

He had introduced a jarring note; he would like her for a lover, a little dalliance, nothing more. Why did that shock her? Had she expected him to be any different from Sir Roland and that odious Augustus

Spike? The answer to that was yes and her disappointment brought the tears welling in her eyes. 'My lord, just because I entered into the spirit of the evening and allowed you to flirt with me a little does not mean you may take liberties.'

'It depends what you mean by liberties,' he said, drawing her close against him and lifting her chin with his forefinger, so that she was looking up into his face. 'Do you mean this?' And before she could utter a sound he had covered her mouth with his own. The kiss began roughly because he was annoyed and frustrated, but when she stopped struggling, he softened the pressure of his lips and gently explored her mouth with his and then moved it down her neck and along her bare shoulder until he felt her shudder and groan low in her throat. It made him suddenly aware of what he was doing, and he lifted his head to look into her face. Even in the poor light from a lantern further along the corridor he could see her eyes were bright with tears.

'Oh, God, I am sorry,' he said, huskily. 'Please forgive me.'

She had nothing to forgive. She could have pushed him away, could have left him and gone back into the bright lights of the ballroom; he had not held her by force. He had been gentle and she wished, oh, how she wished, that it had meant as much to him as it had to her. She could not bring herself to say she was as much to blame as he was, nor could she say she forgave him. She did not need to forgive the man she loved for kissing her, not when her whole body had been longing for it, longing for more than just kisses; she was quivering with suppressed desire. It was many years since she had experienced the physical loving of a man, but only since she had met Stacey Darton had she felt the loss so keenly. If they had been anywhere but in a public place, she would have been lost to all reason and allowed even greater liberties. And that was not his fault.

'Charlotte?' he ventured, when she did not answer.

She swallowed hard to rid herself of the great lump in her throat before she could find her voice and then it came out as a sharp retort. 'Sir, I did not give you permission to address me by my given name.' Why was she so angry? Why was she snapping at him? Her anger was directed against herself for being such a fool. She should have known that flirting was a dangerous pastime and where it could lead.

'Then, my lady, I beg your pardon,' he said stiffly and could have wept.

'I do believe the dance has finished,' she said, as people began streaming into the corridor to go to the supper room. If they noticed the couple standing in the shadow of the alcove, they gave no indication of it.

'Yes, shall we go into supper?' What more could he say? She would not listen and he had lost an opportunity, which just proved his timing was abysmal.

They followed the crowd and he found her a seat and went off to fetch two plates of food, without speaking another word. A waiter came with a tray of glasses filled with a pale wine and he took two of these and set them on the table.

'Thank you,' she said. She could not swallow the food, but she drank the wine and he took her glass to be refilled.

He watched her as she drank it far too quickly and his heart ached for her, for the mess he had made of everything, for wanting her. He did not speak, afraid that whatever he said would exacerbate the situation. When supper was over, he offered her his arm to return to the ballroom. The dancing continued, but this time he did not attempt to fight off those who wanted to stand up with her, but stood leaning against a pillar, watching her as she danced, eyes bright, lips smiling, making light remarks in answer to her partner's comments and never once making a wrong move, even though he knew she was ever so slightly foxed.

The last dance was a waltz and he was determined

to try to mend fences, if only so that they could go back to being to each other what they had before, though he had no idea exactly what that was. Schoolteacher and father of one of her pupils, he supposed, gambler who had been instrumental in salvaging her jewels, protector perhaps. Nothing more. He walked forward as her last partner relinquished her and bowed before her. 'May I have the honour of this dance?' he asked formally and humbly, offering her his hand.

She took it and smiled, the same bright smile with which she had been favouring her other partners, a smile of bravado. Nothing seemed quite real. The people about them were hazy, his face, his dear face was unclear, the expression in his dark eyes unfathomable. It was as if the whole evening had been a dream—from the moment she stripped off her black silk and dressed in the filmy ball gown, she had become someone else, not Charlotte Hobart, respectable widow and mother, though she was very unsure of the woman who had taken her place, a flirt, a wanton. Was that what he wanted? There was no Parson's End and Easterley Manor, no school, no children, no past, no future, there was only a woman in love and a man who tormented.

They danced in perfect unison, her right hand in his left, his right arm at her back, she could feel its warmth and longed to feel closer than the permitted twelve inches, which, she told herself severely, would prove nothing except that she had abandoned all sense of decorum and he was a rake. Neither spoke until the dance ended and he bowed low while she curtsied. 'Thank you, my lady,' he said, offering his hand to raise her.

She smiled wanly and went to the ladies' retiring room to fetch her cloak before joining him in the general exodus towards the door. Jem was waiting with the carriage, one of a long line stretching the length of the street. He jumped down to open the door and let down the step for them to enter, which they did in silence, making him look sideways at his master, but he was met with a frown and not his usual smile.

'My lady,' Stacey began when they had negotiated the traffic and were on their way to the hotel. 'I have apologised. Am I not to be forgiven?'

'You are forgiven. We will put it down to the heat of the moment and say no more about it.'

He wanted to say a great deal more about it, wanted to explain, tell her that he had kissed her because he loved her, but he was sure such a declaration would not be welcome. But he could not stand her silent reproach. Anyone would think he had tried to rape her! 'Could you not sound just a little as though you meant it?' he asked. 'After all, you are not a green girl, you have been kissed before. *I* have kissed you before—' He stopped and began again. 'Until all this is over, we have to deal with each other and it would be better done in a spirit of friendship.'

'All over?' she asked. 'You mean our journey home?'

'Not that, not just that. I meant everything. The free-traders, my problems with Julia, the school, Lord Hobart…'

'Oh, that game of chance. I had hoped, for one evening, you might have managed to forget it.'

'I did,' he protested. 'Not once has it crossed my mind since we left Parson's End. I have had my mind on other things.'

'So I collect.'

'If you have forgiven me, why are you still so up in the boughs?'

'I am not up in the boughs, I am sitting here beside you, perfectly calm.'

He gave a grunt of amusement. Calm she certainly was not. He could feel the tension in her, though they were not touching each other; it was in the air around her, palpable, threatening.

'I see you find me amusing.'

'Vastly,' he said, unable to resist it.

She turned away and looked out of the carriage window, though there was nothing to see but empty, ill-lit streets. How could the evening have gone so wrong? What had she hoped for? What had she expected? He was a man, wasn't he? A virile, lustful man and she should have known better than encourage him if she did not welcome his advances. But she had, she had welcomed them with open arms. Why not admit it? She gave a sudden cracked laugh. 'Your daughter will have no need to rid you of me, you have managed to do that all by yourself.'

'What do you mean by that? What has Julia to do with it?'

'She told us she has her own way of dealing with ladies who aspire to be your wife. I collect something about horse muck…'

He burst out laughing, making her turn towards him. 'Oh, my dear, she did me a favour. The woman was a positive antidote, but that does not mean I will allow Julia to dictate whom I may see. You surely are not influenced by what she says.'

'Whether I am or not is of no significance, since I do not aspire to such giddy heights.'

'Oh.' He held his hat in one hand and stroked it, a habit he had when he was agitated. It gave his hands something to do and stopped him from turning her over his knee and spanking some sense into her. Did she imagine her supposed lower status would weigh with him? And if she did, why did she not tell him the truth? Or was he jumping the gun to think she cared for him?

'And what did you mean by the school being all over?' she demanded suddenly. 'Did you imagine it to be a whim, something to pass my time, which I will discard the moment something more interesting comes along?'

'No, I know it means more to you than that. But I collect the lease is only for a year. You will need somewhere else after that.'

'And I will find it, do not doubt it.'

'I am sure you will.'

The carriage was drawing up outside the hotel and he did not wait for Jem to get down, but jumped down on the road side and walked round to open the door himself, letting down the step and holding out his hand to assist her.

She took his hand and stepped down; for a moment they stood face to face in the street, looking at each other in perplexity, neither able to say what was in their hearts. The silence stretched until she could bear it no longer. 'Good night, my lord,' she said.

He raised her hand to his lips. 'Good night, my lady. I will call for you all at eleven in the morning.

We must not disappoint our daughters, even if we have managed to disappoint each other.'

She was aware as she walked towards the door of the hotel that he was watching her and she managed to keep her back straight and her head up until she was inside and then her whole body sagged. His last words echoed in her head. Yes, she was disappointed and she supposed so was he; the night that had promised so much had ended in disaster. Aware that the night porter was watching her, she pulled herself together and climbed the stairs. How had it happened? How could such a magical evening have taken so wrong a turn? They had battered each other with words, words loaded with hurt and self-righteousness and she was too tired to go over them now, too tired to work out how to resolve the situation, if it could be resolved. She wanted her bed.

Joan Quinn was waiting in her bedchamber to help her undress, a broad smile on her face. 'Did you enjoy yourself, my lady?' she asked, taking Charlotte's cloak and urging her to a seat so that she could remove her shoes.

'Yes, thank you, Quinny, it was a lovely evening.' So it had been until the interval waltz.

'The girls wanted to stay up and see you home, eager to know all about it, but I told them you would be tired and if they did not go to bed, they would not be fit to go out with his lordship tomorrow.'

'Bless you, Quinny. I am exhausted.'

'Did you dance every dance, then?' She was busy removing Charlotte's dress as she spoke.

'Yes, every one.'

'Oh, I am so glad. The Viscount is such a fine gentleman. I didn't think so when he first came to the Manor, but he's not like the others, is he?'

'No, not at all.'

The rest of her clothes came off and her nightgown was slipped over her head. 'There, you have a good sleep, my lady. Tomorrow is another day.'

Yes, she thought as she almost fell into bed and Miss Quinn covered her and left her, tomorrow was another day and so was the day after that and the day after that…

Stacey was at the hotel promptly at eleven the following morning dressed in a brown tailcoat and strapped trousers. He was bright and cheerful and no one would have suspected he had had a sleepless night. He greeted Charlotte politely and easily, pretending there was nothing wrong between them, hoping that she had simply been a little out of sorts the evening before and worried that they might be seen and recognised and his behaviour might cause a scandal.

He had behaved badly, there was no doubt of it, succumbing to a temptation that was too inviting to resist. Stuck in Parson's End, looking after an old man and two little girls, she had been shielded from the more relaxed ways of society and he ought to have realised that and not taken her lack of resistance for acquiescence. Now she was back in her black silk, her hair tucked under a plain black bonnet, looking pale but dignified. He bowed. 'My lady, good morning. I trust you are well.'

'Very well, thank you, my lord.'

He turned to look at the three girls, Charlotte's two were dressed alike in pale blue spotted muslin and Julia in green jaconet. 'My goodness, what a bevy of beauties,' he said. 'I shall be the envy of all.'

They giggled, all except Julia, and he decided he would have to speak to her alone, to try to explain that, no matter what she said or did, he would marry Lady Hobart, though he hoped she would behave herself and love her stepmother because he had no intention of giving her up. How he was going to persuade Charlotte herself of that, he did not yet know.

'Are you ready?' he enquired.

'Oh, yes,' they chorused.

It was a beautiful day for a stroll and he smiled to himself as he led them down Upper Brook Street towards the docks; he felt like a shepherd with a flock of sheep who were intent on straying and he must watch out that they did not wander off or dart into the road. For a man who professed not to like children, he was behaving very oddly. And all in the name of love!

The workman he had spoken to the day before came forward when he saw him bringing the children up to look at the vessel and doffed his hat. 'Would the young ladies like to go aboard?' he asked.

There was a chorus of assent and the man led the way up the gangplank. The children followed eagerly and Stacey turned to take Charlotte's arm to assist her. They were shown round the whole ship—the captain's cabin, the crew's quarters, the galley—and looked aloft at the tall masts with their furled sails, while their guide explained that the ship had been built in the record time of fifteen months and it had taken two thousand loads of Suffolk oak to build her hull.

Having given the man a half-guinea for his trouble, they left to return the hotel thoroughly satisfied with their visit and Stacey's credit was sky high, which gave him an inordinate sense of achievement. Little girls could be quite charming and he wondered how he could ever have thought otherwise. Even Charlotte was smiling at him again.

They were on the quayside when they met Gerard

Topham, who came to a halt in astonishment when he saw the girls. 'Darton,' he said in his booming voice. 'Never took you for a nursemaid.'

Stacey was about to make some rude retort, but thought better of it and grinned instead. He turned to Charlotte, who had been walking beside him but stopped when he did. 'My lady, may I present my good friend and comrade in arms, Captain Gerard Topham. Captain, Lady Hobart of Parson's End.'

'Your obedient.' Captain Topham clicked his heels to attention and bowed his head.

'And this is my daughter, Julia,' Stacey went on, drawing Julia forward. 'And the others are Miss Hobart and Miss Frances Hobart.'

To give Gerard his due, he concealed his amusement very well as he bowed to the young ladies. 'I was on my way to see you,' he said to Stacey when the formalities had been concluded. 'I have news.'

Charlotte looked from one to the other; they both appeared secretive and obviously not prepared to speak in front of her. 'Come, girls,' she said. 'We will walk on and allow Lord Darton to talk to Captain Topham.' And she ushered them out of earshot.

'The vessel is only a few miles off shore,' Gerard said when they had gone. 'We thought it was making for the Kent coast, but a cutter went out to it from Felixstowe and it turned north. It is battling into the wind, but, if you are right about its destination, it should reach Parson's End in the early hours of tomorrow morning.'

'Sunday. Will they unload on a Sunday?'

'Don't see why not. If the wind and tide are right and there's no moon, they wouldn't put it off simply because it was the Sabbath, but they might not arrive in time to have everything off the beach by dawn and will stand off until it's dark again.'

'I must go back and make sure the villagers keep indoors. How many men will you have?'

'Enough.'

'Make sure they keep away from the house on the cliff, will you?'

'They will have their orders.'

'Good. Will you round up the free-traders on the beach or after they have taken the cargo to the Manor?'

'On the beach, I think. I don't want to give them the opportunity to take it anywhere else, I'd have a devil of a job finding it and proving it is contraband if they do. The usual trick is to mix it with legitimate merchandise to be taken inland.'

'Bentwater and Spike may not go down to the beach themselves and, if they are not present, you will have a hard task proving they were involved.'

'Then it is up to you to persuade them their presence is needed on the beach. You can do that, can't you?'

'Yes, if they realise the villagers have not turned out they will want to know why.'

'Good. I will see you then.'

Stacey strode after Charlotte and the girls and carried on laughing and teasing them as if he had nothing else on his mind at all.

Immediately after they had eaten an early dinner at the Great White Horse, Stacey hurried to the inn where he had stayed the night and changed into riding clothes, leaving Jem to oversee the harnessing up of his carriage and saddling of Ivor. In less than an hour they were leaving the town and on their way back to Parson's End, though now Jem was driving the carriage and Stacey was riding beside it on Ivor.

Julia had been overjoyed to see the horse and had patted it and nuzzled up against its neck. 'Oh, please, Papa, could you not send Jem to fetch Ebony, then we could ride together? It must be wonderful to gallop along the beach with the waves pounding on the shore.' He looked from her to Charlotte, the one eager, the other inscrutable. 'Does that mean you are resolved to stay at school?' he had asked.

'If I could have Ebony, I would.'

'That is blackmail.'

'No, no, it is a promise.'

'Perhaps I might allow it after you have finished your month's trial and if Lady Hobart gives me a good report.'

'But that is ages away.'

'Nevertheless it is my decision.' He had turned from her to pay the reckoning at the hotel, which Charlotte had allowed him to do only after a heated argument. Why was he always arguing with her? Why did she have to be so damned independent, and why insist that Sir Grenville had provided her with enough to pay her way and she was no longer impoverished? It was the last straw and made him more determined to have his own way.

It was almost dark by the time they arrived at The Crow's Nest. Jenkins was waiting to help Jem see to the horses and put the carriage away. Stacey accompanied Charlotte and the children into the house where Betsy and Miss Quinn ushered the children up to bed. They were so sleepy they made no protest.

'Thank you for your escort,' Charlotte said to Stacey when they were alone. 'Everyone had a lovely time.'

'Even you?' he asked quietly.

'Especially me. I am sorry I was a cross-patch. It was not fair when you have been so kind.'

Kind, was that all it was? He smiled a little crookedly. 'It was my pleasure, my lady.'

'Captain Topham… He was talking about the smugglers, wasn't he? Have they been? Has it all happened while we have been away?'

'No, according to the Captain, they have been hindered by adverse weather. They may come tonight, perhaps not until tomorrow night. So please, stay indoors and keep the girls in, will you?'

'Of course.' Did he think she was such a ninny as to take the children down to the beach in the middle of the night? 'What are you going to do?'

'I am going to warn the village men that if they value their freedom, they, too, will stay indoors. I only hope they will listen to me.'

'Why not ask the Reverend Fuller to speak to them? They will take notice of him.'

'That's a good idea. I'll go now, before I go back to the Manor.'

'Do you think Cecil knows that you know?'

'Perhaps. I must let him know that I have nothing against free-trading. I might learn a little more.'

'Would you like to go up to the tower and look through Captain MacArthur's telescope?'

He had forgotten all about that telescope. 'Yes, if they are already off shore then they may try landing tonight.'

She conducted him up to the room at the top of the tower and he spent several minutes scanning the sea and the horizon. 'Nothing there yet,' he said. 'I doubt it will be tonight now.'

He preceded her back down the narrow stairs. 'Where are Captain Topham's men?' she asked.

'They are on their way.'

'Then I beg you, try to make sure the village men are not involved. I should feel so guilty…'

They had reached the hall again and he turned towards her. 'Guilty? Why?'

'It started up at the Manor with Cecil and his gambling. I should perhaps have tried to dissuade him.'

He gave a low chuckle. 'You could not stop him, no one could have.'

'But you encourage him.'

'No. The issue is more important than that. You have lost your home because of it.'

'You are doing it for me?' she asked in astonishment.

'Not just for you.' He grinned suddenly. 'For me. One day I will explain, there is no time now. I must go.' He reached forward, took her hand and, turning it over, kissed the palm. The touch of his lips sent shivers right through her body, convincing her, if she needed convincing, that her desire was still alive, still strong, still ready to engulf her. The only way to control it was to stand rigidly and pretend, pretend for all she was worth, that it meant nothing, that he meant nothing, that he was simply trying to rouse her for his own amusement.

He raised his head and looked at her, but she would not meet his gaze; instead she seemed to be concentrating on the pin in his cravat. 'Good night, my lady.' It was said softly, as one would speak to a child one wanted to soothe. 'Tomorrow or the day after, we will have that talk and perhaps learn to understand one another better.' He released her hand, picked up his hat from the table and made for the door.

'My lord,' she said softly as he reached it. 'Be careful, please.'

He turned back to her with a smile that lit his whole face. 'I will, my love, I will. Until tomorrow.'

And then he was gone and she was looking at the closed door, unable to believe she had revealed so much in those few words and he had answered as he had. Surely, surely it meant more than mere flirtation?

Stacey, smiling to himself in the darkness, walked to the village. Ivor was out of condition and had had a long run that day and he decided not to saddle him up again. There was still a light on in the Rectory and he assumed the Reverend Fuller was working on his sermon for the next day. He knocked and was admitted by a maid who conducted him to the parson's study, where he sat at his desk surrounded by books and papers, with a glass of brandy at his elbow.

'I am sorry to interrupt you,' Stacey told him, wondering briefly if the brandy had had its excise duty paid. 'But I need your help.'

He was invited to sit and offered a glass, which he accepted. 'Now, what can I do for you?' the old man asked, sipping his own drink.

'Have you heard anything of smugglers in these parts, Reverend?' Stacey asked.

'Would anyone tell me if they were breaking the law?'

Stacey smiled. 'No, but I am sure you hear things.'

'Sometimes it is better to be a little deaf.'

'Oh, I agree, but unfortunately there is even now a contraband ship approaching Parson's End and the Coast Blockade have been alerted. There could be trouble and I wish to prevent it.'

'And you think I can do that? You must have a great belief in miracles, my lord.'

'Not in miracles, but in your powers of persuasion. I am almost sure the men of the village have been recruited as tub carriers and I hoped you would persuade them it would be a foolish thing to do and they had better stay indoors.'

'The lure of a guinea or two might be stronger than my words, my lord. These are poor people.'

'I know. But I want you to assure them they will be paid whatever they lose by not taking part. I do not want to see the men arrested and their wives and children made destitute. It will ruin all the hard work you and Lady Hobart have put in to help them.'

'Ah, Lady Hobart,' the Reverend said. 'She is a splendid lady, full of compassion.' Then he added with a smile, 'Did you enjoy the ball?'

'Very much.' He wondered if the parson was deliberately trying to change the subject. 'I have asked Lady Hobart to keep the girls indoors until the situation with the free-traders is resolved,' he said, reverting to the reason for his visit. 'I have seen no ship close to the shore so I do not think it will be tonight, which means tomorrow will be a day of waiting. Presumably the village children will be doing whatever they usually do on a Sunday…'

'Playing truant from church if they can get away with it,' the Reverend said drily.

'We must endeavour to keep them from the cliffs and the beach. Their parents too.'

'I will send my manservant with a message to everyone that I want them all in church in the morning, even those who have not set foot in the place for years.' He stopped to chuckle. 'Then I will deliver the longest sermon they have ever listened to in their lives. By the time I have finished, they will be too afraid for their eternal souls to dare lift a tub.'

Stacey smiled. 'I should like to hear it, but unfortunately I must ask to be excused. I shall be otherwise engaged at the Manor.'

'Is that where the goods are to be taken?'

'Yes, which is another reason for wanting it stopped. I know Lady Hobart does not live there now, but it was her home and her name would be connected with the scandal that might ensue. I wish to prevent it.'

'It is a great shame she had to leave the Manor.'

'That is true, but she has shown great fortitude and courage, which is why I would like to see those who used her so ill put behind bars, but not the villagers, whom she loves. You do understand?'

'Oh, I understand perfectly. It is because she cared about the children that she stayed in Parson's End after old Lord Hobart died when she could have gone to her great-uncle.'

'Ah, yes, Lord Falconer. I collect they are estranged.'

'Yes, I am sure he knows nothing of what has been going on. Once or twice I have been burdened with a conscience over it and wondered if I should write and inform him myself, but I knew such interference would not find favour with Lady Hobart and so I did nothing. I was prodigiously relieved when you arrived and seemed to be taking charge.'

Taking charge! Stacey smiled to himself. One thing he was not and that was in charge. Charlotte Hobart would not allow it; they had quarrelled, though for the life of him he could not say exactly what it had been about, except that she had taken exception to being kissed. Was that the aristocratic side of her coming to the fore? Why had she never told him about her mother's family? Was she testing him, trying to find out how he behaved towards anyone who was not highborn? He did not care a groat for that, though undoubtedly it would weigh with his parents and for that reason alone he was glad of her rank. He wondered if Hardacre had written to his lordship as he said he would and what the reply had been. Was she still to be ignored? It made no difference. Apart from Julia and stopping those evil men at the Manor, there was nothing he wanted more than to have that promised talk with Charlotte and to resolve their difficulties.

# Chapter Ten

Charlotte went round the house, checking that everywhere was locked up and all the lamps extinguished and then she went to bed and lay there thinking about Stacey, reliving every word they had said to each other, worrying about the smugglers, or more correctly about the villagers. Unable to sleep, she put on a dressing robe and climbed the stairs of the tower to search the horizon through the telescope. There were a few sails on the horizon, but as none approached land, she had no idea if one could be the contraband ship. She gave up when the pink light of dawn began to lighten the sky and returned to her bed. It was, as Quinny had a habit of pointing out, another day.

She took the girls to church and was astonished to find all the pews packed. It looked as though the whole population of the village was there, except the men from the Manor. Except Stacey. They sang more hymns than they had been used to do and said more prayers, most of which revolved around doing no evil and not assisting others to do evil, and the wages of sin being eternal damnation. The Reverend Fuller was at his tub-thumping best when it came to the sermon and it was then she realised why there were so many in church and why so many of them were fidgeting and looking sheepish. Without actually saying so, he made them aware that he knew what was going on and that he condemned it and, if they persisted, they would be punished. 'And I do not mean in the next world,' he thundered. 'I mean in this. Retribution is at hand, closer than you think.' A concerted gasp went round the church at this. 'Now let us pray for guidance.'

He let them go at last, but he stood at the door and spoke to each of the men and the bigger boys. 'Doing what is right should be its own reward,' he told them severely. 'But in case it is not, whatever your sinful wages would have amounted to will be replaced by honest coin. If you are without guilt and you know what I mean by that, come to me tomorrow afternoon. Now, go home and think about it.'

He smiled at Charlotte as she came out of the

church, ushering the girls along. 'Ah, my lady, a fine day, is it not?'

'Yes, Reverend, very fine.'

'Not so fine one would want to wander too far abroad though. There might be squalls.' His words were loaded with meaning which she had no trouble interpreting.

'There might indeed, but perhaps we are worrying for nothing and the day will pass uneventfully.'

'Let us pray so. And the night too. Shall you open the school tomorrow?'

'Oh, yes, it is important to maintain a routine, do you not agree?'

She took the girls home, wondering if and when Stacey would come, but there was no sign of him. He preferred playing cards to visiting her, even though he had said he would come and they would talk. She concealed her disappointment even from herself and set about trying to amuse the girls. Confined to the house, they were inclined to be fractious and quarrelsome and could not understand why they could not go for a walk when it was such a lovely day.

They played cross-questions, Jackstraws, Speculation and Lottery Tickets with mother-of-pearl fishes, which was very noisy and which Julia won. They had dinner at three and after that

Charlotte had them take it in turns to read aloud from the bible while the others sewed. They were soon bored by that and Julia wanted to know why they could not read *Waverley* instead and Charlotte gave in. Outside the sun still shone and the ill-kept garden, which Jenkins had been trying to restore, looked inviting.

'Why can't we go out, Mama?' Lizzie asked. 'I know it is Sunday, but surely a little walk would not be wrong? We have done it before.'

'Because Viscount Darton asked me to keep you in.'

'But why?'

'No doubt because he is coming to visit and he would not like to find us out.'

'But we have been in all day and he has not come,' Julia said. 'It is always the same with him, he makes promises and does not keep them. No doubt he has found company more to his liking.'

'Oh. Julia, you should not say that about your papa. He always wants to do what is best for you. You had a lovely day yesterday, looking round that ship, didn't you?'

'Oh, he only suggested that because he wanted to meet his friend there.'

'I do not think he expected to see Captain Topham. They both seemed surprised by it. You must have more faith in your papa, Julia.'

'I will when he deserves it. If he fetches Ebony for me to ride, then I will believe what he says. He is not coming today now.' She gave a huge sigh. 'I'll wager he is out on Ivor, galloping along the beach, which is what I should most like to do.'

'You know he is not,' Charlotte said. 'The horse is still in the stable.'

'Could we not play hide and seek?' Fanny, the peacemaker, suggested. 'I am sure we would all enjoy that.'

Fanny was the first to hide and was soon discovered in the pantry; Lizzie, the next, was found under the desk in the library, but when it came to Julia's turn, she could not be found anywhere. Charlotte, worrying that she might have gone outside, searched the garden, coach house and stables, but there was no sign of her. Jem, who was polishing Ivor's saddle, said he had not seen her. Turning to go back, Charlotte glanced upwards just in time to see a flash of light from the window of the tower as the sun caught the glass of the telescope. She ran indoors and up the stairs to find Julia with her eye to the glass.

'Julia, what are you doing? You know you have been forbidden to come up here.'

The girl swivelled the instrument to look up and down the coast. 'I am looking to see if I can see Papa.'

'Oh, Julia, he will come, I am sure.'

'You can see so much through this,' the girl went on as if Charlotte had not spoken. 'All the ships out to sea and the little boats, and even some men on the beach further along.' She sighed. 'But you cannot see what is directly below us. Do you think he might be down there?'

'I do not think so, he would have called on us on his way.' Charlotte wasn't sure of the truth of that, but she was on tenterhooks, having Julia up in the tower where she had no business to be. 'Come away, Julia. I gave my word to Captain MacArthur I would allow no one to come up here. How did you get in? The door is usually locked.'

'It wasn't. It wasn't even shut properly. I was looking for a hiding place and I peeped in. Then I saw this.' She pointed to the telescope. 'I was doing no harm, only looking.'

Charlotte realised she had not locked it after her when she and Stacey had been up there the day before. She could hardly blame the child for her own negligence. 'Leave it, Julia. Come down. It is supper time.'

Reluctantly the girl left the room. Charlotte locked the door and put the key in her skirt pocket, then followed Julia downstairs. She was inclined to agree with the child; Stacey would not come now. She tried to imagine what might be happening up at the Manor. Were they still gambling? Really, the parson would do better to preach his sermon against the evils of the gaming table because that was what had caused all this upheaval.

Stacey was bored and longed to go to The Crow's Nest, but he dare not absent himself from the Manor until he knew exactly what was going on and that he had Sir Roland and Augustus Spike where he wanted them: down on the beach when the contraband came in and Gerard appeared. Although Sir Roland, not one for more exercise than he could help, was in the room, Augustus Spike was out and Stacey assumed he was patrolling the cliff top. He prayed the man would go nowhere near The Crow's Nest.

Had the parson managed to persuade the village men to defect? He had no way of knowing. He played cards for cobnuts again because, unsurprisingly, Cecil did not have the cash to cover the vouchers. 'A slight delay,' he told Stacey, cracking and eating a nut from the pile at his elbow, thus depleting his stake. 'Tomorrow I will have it.'

'Are you going to conjure it up from the air?' Stacey asked him.

'None of your business.'

'A little trading, perhaps, goods sold for cash and a profit made?'

Cecil laughed. 'Of course. What did you think?'

'I think the delay might have something to do with a northerly wind.'

Stacey heard Sir Roland growl angrily and turned to him, smiling easily. 'Did you think I was a cabbage head to be gulled into believing you were staying here for the love of the company?'

Cecil laughed harshly. 'And why did you stay? Or do we need to ask? Though what you see in her I do not know. She hasn't a penny to her name, or pretends she has none.'

How he remained seated Stacey did not know. He felt like giving the man a facer—more than that, battering him to a pulp. 'Nothing to do with the lady,' he said, controlling his voice with an effort. 'Much more to do with a pile of useless vouchers. And unless they are redeemed, I shall shout it from the rooftops that Lord Hobart is a welcher.'

'We made a bargain,' Cecil reminded him. 'Are you going to renege on that?'

'No. I am here, ready and willing. What about you?'

'At your service, but tomorrow it will have to be.'

'Then I assume the merchandise will arrive tonight and be despatched to its buyers by dawn. That's how it works, is it not?'

Sir Roland rose, standing over him, a threat in every gesture as he waved a wine bottle in one hand

and a glass in the other. 'A revenue man! I might have known.'

'Not at all,' Stacey said levelly. 'I have no more liking for excise men than you have. Just rotten bad form not to offer a man a cut, don't you know? Especially when you are in his debt.'

'Never mind that. What have you heard? Who said it?'

'Your friend, Cecil,' he said with a smile. 'He has a very loud voice. When I overheard the words "tub carriers", I knew it could only mean one thing. And tub carriers are usually local men, so I spent some time in the Dog and Fox.'

'Peasants!' The man resumed his seat, to Stacey's immense relief. 'They know nothing, so what can they have told you?'

'Oh, they told me nothing. I deduced it from over-hearing them tell each other how they would spend their sudden windfall.'

'I said we should not have trusted them,' Sir Roland told Cecil. 'No notion of how to keep their tongues between their teeth.'

'Imported men would have cost more and would have drawn attention to themselves,' Cecil retorted.

'It's of no consequence,' Stacey said. 'All you have to do is include me in your plans.'

They looked at one another, mentally sizing up the

consequences of not complying against the cost of allowing him a part of the proceeds. He could almost see their brains at work, wondering how they could pretend to comply and then cheat him. It made him smile.

'How do we know we can trust you?' Sir Roland asked.

He shrugged. 'Does it matter? I am not going anywhere, not tonight anyway, unless I decide to take a stroll down to the beach to see the fun.'

'Well, I am not going down there,' Sir Roland said. 'Someone has to be here when the goods arrive. If you want to be included, Darton, you can go and keep an eye on those tub carriers, make sure they don't purloin any of the cargo.'

'What time are you expecting the vessel to arrive?' Stacey asked.

'As soon as it is dark enough and the tide turns. It's a large cargo and we want it all off the beach and safely stowed in the cellar by dawn.'

'The buyers are coming here for it?'

Cecil gave a cracked cackle. 'I'm giving another house party and they'll all have blunt in their pockets. You will have your game, Cousin Darton, have no fear, though whether you will be the richer at the end of it, I cannot say.'

Stacey laughed. 'That's all I ask. I'll be off now, take a walk, see what's going on.'

'Take the flasher with you.' Sir Roland handed him a pistol without a barrel. 'It will burn a blue light when you pull the trigger. Make sure, before you do, that it's *The Kentish Maid* lying offshore and there's no revenue cutter lying in wait. You won't see another sunrise if you make a mistake over that, I promise you.'

'Do you expect a revenue cutter?'

'No, they are too busy watching the Kent coast.'

Stacey laughed. 'Clever of you.' And with that he went to his room, put on top boots and a black cloak and left the house, carrying the strange pistol in his pocket. If *The Kentish Maid* was there, he would signal it in and then send a message to the Manor that the village men had not arrived and the beach was littered with contraband and no one to shift it. That would bring them down to the shore in a great hurry and Gerry and his men, who were safely hidden, would round them up. And then, his part done, he would go to The Crow's Nest and have that talk with Charlotte. Somehow or other, they had to come to an understanding.

Charlotte was frantic. Julia was not in her bed, had never been to bed by the look of the neat quilt and unmarked pillow. What had made her go into the girl's room to check she was asleep and not reading by candlelight, she did not know, but it was as well she had. A quick search established Julia was not in the house. Where had she gone? The back door, which Charlotte had so carefully locked and bolted, was undone, so it looked as though she had escaped that way. Oh, what a night to run away! It would have been bad on any night, but with a shipload of contraband expected, she could easily run into danger. But perhaps she was hiding in the coach house or the stable.

Slipping her cloak round her shoulders, Charlotte ran to the outhouses; there was no sign of Julia, but Ivor had gone. Surely the child could not ride that great stallion? And there was no lady's saddle, so it must have been Stacey who had come and taken it. Had he taken Julia with him? She dismissed that idea at once; he was too wrapped up with the smugglers and his card game and had left the girl in her care while he resolved whatever it was needed resolving. His daughter did not figure in that. So, where was Julia? She went back indoors and roused Betsy and Miss Quinn.

'You'll have to inform his lordship,' Joan Quinn ventured when the three adults were sitting in the kitchen with the heavy curtains pulled across so that their light did not show. Betsy and Miss Quinn didn't know why that should be important but Charlotte had said they must not show a light out to sea in case the sailors confused it with the light-house. It was the first they had heard of that, but their mistress was obviously too worried to think clearly.

'Let's see if we can find her first,' Charlotte said, looking wildly about her as if the girl would suddenly pop out from a cupboard. 'She surely cannot have gone far. It's dark. She will be frightened.'

'Not that one,' said Miss Quinn. 'Don't know the meaning of the word. Wants her breeches dusting, she does.'

'I'll go and fetch Jenkins and Jem,' Betsy said. 'They will help.'

While she was gone, Charlotte searched the house again, even going up to the tower, but to no avail, and by this time her daughters were wide awake and sitting up in bed demanding to know what was happening. 'Did Julia say she was going out?' she asked them. 'What was she wearing? Do you know where she could have gone?' But they knew nothing. Julia had not said a word to them and had gone to her room when they had, but no doubt had crept out again when the coast was clear. They were round-eyed with a mixture of excitement, envy and fear.

Julia was always boasting she might run away, but they never believed she would.

Jem and Jenkins arrived, carrying storm lanterns that Charlotte, even in the middle of her panic, thought might confuse anyone lying offshore waiting for a signal. 'Ivor has gone from the stables,' she told them. 'Do you think Lord Darton came for him?'

'Could have done,' Jem said. 'But he never said he was going riding. He wanted the horse to have a good rest after yesterday, bein's he's so out of condition.'

'Julia can't ride him, can she?'

'She can ride anything, my lady. Ought to 'ave bin a boy, I've told her so many a time. Her own mount is only a hand or so smaller.'

'And can she saddle him and ride astride? There's no lady's saddle in the stable that I know of.'

'She learned to ride that way, my lady. The Earl bought her a little pony when she was a tiny thing, barely able to walk, and so impatient was she to learn she couldn't wait for a suitable saddle to be found and we put her on an old one the Viscount had when he was a boy. It amused the Earl no end.'

'Then we must conclude she has gone riding. I know she wanted to gallop along the beach. But in the dark!'

'It was likely not dark when she left, my lady.'

'But it's been pitch black for at least an hour.' Charlotte was grabbing her cloak from a hook behind the door as she spoke. 'Come on, we'll go down to the beach and see if we can see her. Betsy, find me another lantern.'

'Don't you think you should fetch his lordship?' Miss Quinn ventured.

'Not unless I have to,' Charlotte said, unwilling to have to confess to Stacey that she had failed in her duty to his daughter. He would be furious and any cordiality they might have restored between them since going to Ipswich would be gone, never to return. And it would certainly not help her school if word went round that she was not to be trusted with anyone's daughters. She had to fetch Julia back herself. Whether she would tell Stacey of it afterwards, she did not know. 'We will try and find her ourselves first. If she's simply riding on the beach, we can bring her back and no harm done.'

She took the lantern Betsy had lit for her. 'You and Betsy stay here and look after the other three. Lock the door behind us.' She hurried from the house, followed by Jem and Jenkins.

'My lady,' Jenkins said. 'You shouldn' be going down to the beach at night, 'specially this night.'

'You mean because of the free-traders? They are not in sight yet. We have time.'

'If they're anchored off shore they will see our lights…'

'Then we had better douse them.'

'And break our necks falling down the cliff? I beg you, my lady, go back, leave this to Jem and me. They won't think nothing of two men on the beach; they would take us for carriers.'

'But we should be able to see the horse from the cliff top, surely? If it's there—' She stopped when the thought struck her that perhaps Julia had been thrown, had fallen down the cliff, horse and all. Would she have tried to go down that steep path with a horse, or would she have had the sense to go by the village where there was a slipway the fishing boats used?

'But perhaps his lordship did take Ivor himself,' Jem put in. 'Just because he wanted to rest him, don't mean he wouldn't take him if he needed to get somewhere quick. Shouldn't we discover that first?'

Charlotte sighed. She was being headstrong and foolish, not exactly good traits in a schoolmistress, and certainly not the best way to find Julia quickly. 'You go on,' she told them. 'See if you can find her. I'll go to the Manor to see if Lord Darton is there. He'll have to be told.'

She left them and set off for the Manor, half-walking, half-running, praying that Stacey would be there and not angry. Oh, but he would be angry. He had expressly told her to keep the girls inside with all the doors and windows bolted and he would not have said that if he did not think there was some danger. And Julia was out in it, probably on the beach, which was worse. Very soon now it would be humming with activity, men from the boats, those dreadful men from the Manor and the revenue men, perhaps even some villagers. And there might be shots fired. Someone— Julia—might be hurt, even killed. That thought set her racing again. She dropped her lantern and though she picked it up again, it had gone out. She threw it down and raced on.

She turned in at the Manor gates and tore up the drive, so breathless she would not have been able to speak if she tried. It was in darkness, not a glimmer of light at the front. Chest heaving, she ran round to the back and in at the kitchen door where a startled Mrs Evans, sitting dozing by the fire, woke suddenly and screamed at the sight of her. 'Oh, my lady, you did give me a turn,' she said.

'I'm sorry, Mrs Evans. Is the Viscount in? I must speak to him urgently.'

'He's not here, my lady. He's been gone an hour or more, saw him go myself.'

'Was he on horseback?'

'No, my lady, walking.'

So they were down on the beach already. And Julia was down there. Unless Jem and Jenkins had found her. 'If he comes in soon, will you ask him to come to The Crow's Nest? Tell him it's important.'

'Yes, my lady. Is there anything I can do to help?'

But Charlotte did not hear her; she was already out of the door. She was in such haste, she hardly noticed the carriage with its four matched bays standing in the lane outside the gates, until its occupant put his head out of the door and hailed her. 'Madam, is this the way to The Crow's Nest?'

She stopped her headlong flight and turned towards him. He was getting out of the vehicle. He was an elderly man and not very tall, she could see that, and he was wearing a tail coat and breeches, but his features were unclear. Was he one of the smugglers or was he a revenue man? And why did he want to go to her house? 'Why do you want to know that?'

'I believe that is my business.' He was standing in front of her now, his dark eyes surveying her from under beetle brows, as if he were not sure if he knew her.

'It is also mine. The Crow's Nest is my home.'

'Then you must be Charlotte.' He made no move to stand aside. 'Elizabeth's child. I might have known. She was always a hoyden and it seems you have inherited that trait. Being married to a re-spectable baronet has not tamed you.'

Anxious as she was, his words caught her attention. 'What do you know of my mother, sir?'

'I know she was a fool and married beneath her. I warned her at the time—'

'Oh. Then you must be Lord Falconer.'

'I am indeed.'

'What are you doing here?'

'I came to see you. Had a letter from the lawyer fellow, told me I was needed.'

'Not now, you are not. Please stand aside, my lord. I am in great haste. I have to find Stacey.'

'Who, may I ask, is Stacey?'

'Viscount Darton. His daughter is staying with me and she has run off, probably taken his horse, and we've got to find her before the smugglers arrive.'

'Smugglers?' He took her by her shoulders and shook her. 'What in damnation is going on here?'

She was a little calmer now, though not much. 'If you take me in your carriage, I will guide you to the house and perhaps Julia will have come back on her own or Stacey will be there…'

'You make very free with his given name,' he commented, though he led the way back to his carriage.

'Do I?' she queried, suddenly realising that was how she thought of him, had been thinking of him along those lines for some time. 'He is a second cousin of Cecil, but not a bit like him. He is…' She stopped as he helped her into the carriage and climbed in beside her.

'Go on.'

'Tell the coachman to take the lane on the left about a hundred yards up the road. It's a bit rough, but if he goes carefully, the carriage will come to no harm. Lord Darton's carriage made it easily enough.'

He gave the coachman his instructions and then sat back. 'Now, out with it? What have you been up to, and why, in all these years, have you never written to me?'

'Why should I? You washed your hands of Mama. She said you told her you never wanted to see her again.'

'So I did,' he said grimly. 'But she should have known I did not mean it and I would certainly want to make the acquaintance of her daughter, especially if she was in trouble. If it had not been for that lawyer fellow writing to me…'

'Mr Hardacre?'

'Yes. Said you had to leave the Manor on account of the new Lord Hobart…'

'Yes. I could not stay. The man is intolerable and his friends are worse. Criminals too.'

'Why did you not come to me?'

'I could not. I had no money, not even enough for the coach fare. Cecil stole it. He is a gambler, you see.'

He was furious with her, though he knew he was being unjust. 'I would have sent you money, had you asked.'

'I didn't know that. I did pen a letter to ask you for help, but then, before I could mail it, out of the blue Mr Hardacre wrote and told me Grenville had left a fund in trust for me and so then I did not need it. I took a lease on The Crow's Nest and moved in with the girls and my pupils.' She smiled wanly. 'You see, now I have a school, only Julia has run off and we must find her before something terrible happens to her.'

'You think she might have eloped?'

She gave a cracked laugh. 'She is only thirteen. If she has eloped, it is with a great white stallion.'

'I am coming to the conclusion you have a fever of the brain,' he said, refusing to allow her obvious agitation to affect his normal calm. The carriage had come to a stop.

'Can't go any further, my lord,' the driver called down. 'Less'n we go over the edge of yon cliff.'

They were outside The Crow's Nest. Without waiting for the carriage door to be opened for her, Charlotte jumped down and ran to the kitchen door. 'Betsy, let me in,' she called, thumping on it.

Bolts were withdrawn and the door flung open and Betsy stood in its frame. 'Have you found her, my lady?' The question made Charlotte's heart sink into her boots; Julia had evidently not come back on her own.

'No, nor the Viscount either. Have Jenkins and Jem returned?'

'No, my lady, aren't they with you?' She peered past Charlotte to the man who stood behind her. 'Who's he?'

She smiled wanly. 'My great-uncle, Lord Falconer,' she said.

He put his hand into the small of her back and propelled her indoors past the startled servant. 'A reviving cup of tea for her ladyship,' he ordered. Then, to Charlotte, 'Which way is the drawing room?'

'I do not have one, only a little parlour,' she answered with a weak smile. 'And if you think I can sit and drink tea at a time like this then you are mistaken, my lord. I have a missing pupil and I cannot rest until she is found. Betsy will find refreshment for you.' And she pulled her cloak about her and slipped past them all before they could stop her and set off for the cliff top.

He stopped only long enough to tell his coachman to look after his horses before following her. By heavens, he would ring a peal over her when this night's work was done. And Stacey Darton too. He had met the Earl of Malcomby once, years ago, but never made the acquaintance of his son. He was a soldier, he recalled, and had a reputation for bravery in action, but if he was a cousin of that scapegrace, Hobart, and colluded with him in turning Charlotte from her home, he would live to regret it.

Was that why Charlotte seemed so afraid of the man's anger? But if that were the case, why did she refer to him by his given name, as if they were close? And why was she so hard up? It was unbelievable that her husband had not provided for her, nor that she could be so foolish as to think she could run a school. Ladies should not indulge in business. He should never have lost touch with her mother and now he had to make amends.

He caught up with her as she stood at the top of the cliff, looking out over the sea. A ship lay at anchor a little way off and there were boats being lowered. 'They're here,' she said. 'They've come.'

'Free-traders. You knew about them? You were expecting them?'

She did not answer, but hurtled down the steep path, so fast she could not stop herself. He scrambled after her.

Stacey was pleasantly surprised at how well his plans had gone so far, though he had not seen Augustus Spike since he left the Manor. He had seen the ship hove to and, with a spyglass which he had brought with him, recognised *The Kentish Maid* simply by the crude flag she was flying atop her mainmast. He had looked towards the lighthouse, hoping Gerard and his men were there, though there was nothing to be seen except the light shining out to sea. He turned from there to look at The Crow's Nest, further along the cliff. The house was in darkness and all he could see was its stark outline against the moonless sky. He breathed a sigh of relief that Charlotte had obeyed him and shut herself in and was showing no light. There was no reason why the free-traders should interest themselves in that house.

He allowed himself to muse a moment on what might be going on there: Charlotte reading, the girls sewing, Betsy making supper and Miss Quinn tidying the girls' clothes—a bit like Susan Handy, he thought, both fussed about a great deal and imagined themselves indispensable. And Julia, would she be behaving herself, coming to like Charlotte? Oh, he had a mountain to climb to persuade his daughter to accept a stepmother, but, if anyone could help him do it, Charlotte could.

He smiled and beckoned to Joe White, young Danny's father. The man emerged from the shadows at the base of the cliffs. 'My lord.'

'You know what to do?' he said.

The man grinned. 'Yes, knock them up at the Manor, tell them the villagers hin't turned up, and I couldn't mek them come and what was I to do? I couldn't shift a boatload all on me own.'

'Good. Tell them the ship's master has come ashore and is demanding to see them. He'll not land the stuff unless they meet him. And he's mighty angry there's no tub carriers. When you are sure they are coming, you get on home and, for all anyone but your wife knows, you've been in your bed all night.'

'Yes, my lord. And thank yer.' He pocketed the two guineas he was given and hurried off. Stacey took the flasher from his pocket and gave the signal. It was answered by three flashes from the ship and then he saw the boats being lowered and grinned in satisfaction, though he hoped Gerard would not reveal himself until Sir Roland and Augustus Spike appeared on the scene. What he would do about Cecil if he came too, he had not quite made up his mind.

He whipped round when he heard loose stones falling down the cliff behind him and saw a figure hurtling down the steep path at such a rate she was in danger of tumbling head over heels. It was a woman, he could see that much; her voluminous cloak billowed out behind her, hampering her. Her hands were held out as if to save herself; her feet scrabbling for a foothold and often slipping. There was no doubt who she was. He ran to catch her just as her feet gave up the struggle to keep up with her body, and she fell the last few yards.

'Charlotte! What in God's name do you think you are about?' It was said roughly, his fear for her safety doing battle with his annoyance that, after all, she had not obeyed him.

For the second time that night, she was too winded to speak. She stood in his encircling arms and laid her head on his shoulder, struggling to regain her breath. 'Are you hurt?' he asked.

'No,' she panted. 'It's Julia…'

'What about Julia? Is she ill? Hurt?' The boats were nearing the shore and he could see other people coming down the cliff path, three dark shapes picking their way carefully over the rough ground, and assumed it was Sir Roland, Augustus Spike and Cecil. He had to get her off the beach. Once the ringleaders arrived he had to signal to Gerard and then all hell would be let loose. And Gerard would not thank him for any delay that resulted in him losing his prize.

'She's disappeared.'

'When? How?' Smugglers were forgotten for the moment. This was far more important.

'She crept out after she was supposed to be in bed. We think she has taken Ivor.'

'Oh, my God! Couldn't you have kept an eye on her? Three women and four children and you couldn't keep one silly girl in. How long has she been gone?'

'We don't know. We've searched everywhere. Jem and Jenkins came down here to look for her because we knew she wanted to ride on the beach. Did you not see them?'

'No. God Almighty, woman, can't I trust you to do anything?' It was his concern, his guilt, perhaps, that he had left her to manage a daughter who was nigh unmanageable that made him speak so brusquely, but he felt her wince and regretted his outburst immediately.

'You will cease to speak in such tones to a lady,' said a cold voice behind him. 'And release her at once.'

He turned. It was not Cecil or Sir Roland, though they hovered in the background, nor was it Augustus Spike. This man was a stranger. Stacey looked seawards. The boats had not yet reached the shore so he could not have come from the ship. 'I shall speak to her as I think fit, sir,' he said angrily. 'She had the care of my daughter and has managed to lose her.'

'And you would do better to go in search of her instead of lining your pockets at the taxpayers' expense. I've a good mind to hand you in.'

Stacey was reminded of Gerard, patiently waiting for his signal that everyone they wanted was assembled. Should he give it? Would it make any difference to Julia's safety or Charlotte's if he did? The girl was on Ivor and there was no sign of the horse on the beach, nor had there been while he had been down here, so she must have ridden elsewhere. He prayed as he had never prayed before that the stallion had not thrown her down the cliffs or into the incoming tide and that, wherever she was, she was safe.

'I do not think I have had the pleasure,' Sir Roland drawled lazily, turning towards Lord Falconer.

'Nor I,' Stacey put in. 'Who are you, sir?'

'He is my great-uncle,' Charlotte said.

'Lord Falconer?' The expression on Stacey's face would have made Charlotte laugh if she had not be so overwrought.

'The same. Now unhand my niece and go and search for your daughter.' He looked at the boats, which were drawing up on the beach and had men tumbling from them, expecting tub carriers to be on hand to take over the cargo, but there appeared to be none. Stacey had to give the signal: it was now or never.

'Stacey,' Charlotte said, looking up into his face. 'We must look for Julia—'

She got no further. The revenue men suddenly

appeared, running along the strand, some making for the boats, others straight for the group under the lee of the cliffs. The boatmen assumed they were the late-arriving tub carriers and did nothing to save themselves. Until they produced pistols, determined that no one should escape. Stacey flung himself in front of Charlotte and Cecil started to run, followed by Sir Roland. Lord Falconer simply stood his ground.

'Halt or we will shoot,' Gerard roared at the retreating backs.

When they did not obey he fired, but only around their feet, bringing them to a sudden halt. Two of the Coast Blockade went and fetched them back, while the others rounded up four seamen who had been too slow getting back to the boats. The rest were rowing away as fast as they could, with bullets spattering in the water round them.

'Do we have them all?' Gerard asked.

'No,' Stacey said. 'Augustus Spike is missing. I haven't seen him all evening.'

'Oh, Stacey,' Charlotte whispered. 'You don't think he's got Julia, do you?'

'My God, if he has, I'll kill him.' He looked wildly about him, but there was no sign of horse or rider. Nor Spike, come to that. 'Go home with Lord Falconer and leave it to me. I'll find her.'

'If you think I am involved in this débâcle, you

are mistaken.' His lordship's angry voice came to them as Lieutenant Tarrent tried to herd him with the other prisoners. He was given another prod before the distracted Charlotte intervened. 'He is my uncle, Lord Falconer,' she told Captain Topham. 'He is visiting me.'

'And why, my lady, were you on the beach at all?' Gerard asked, nodding at the lieutenant to release the irate baron.

'Viscount Darton's daughter is missing. We have been searching for her. Oh, please help us to find her.'

Gerard looked at Stacey, who nodded. 'I'd be grateful for your help, Captain.'

The prisoners were rounded up and hustled up the path to a prison van that waited at the top. It was a closed affair with tiny slits instead of windows and was drawn by four heavy horses. They were bundled in, a guard left on duty and the rest of the men dispersed to look for the missing girl. Stacey went with them, leaving Charlotte and her uncle to return to The Crow's Nest.

And there they were in for another surprise. Stacey's horse stood in the yard, still saddled, his reins trailing, munching the grass beside the path. 'Ivor!' Charlotte cried, starting forward. 'Julia has come back on her own. Oh, thank God!'

She ran to the door, expecting it to be locked, but it swung inwards as soon as she touched it. No sooner had she stepped inside than she was grabbed from behind and a hand was put over her mouth and the door slammed shut. A harsh voice said, 'Not a word if you value your life. I have a gun and I am not afraid to use it.' It was Augustus Spike.

She struggled ineffectually, wondering as she did so why her uncle had not followed her into the house. 'Keep still, my lady, or it will be the worse for you.'

He pushed her into a chair by the table and it was then she noticed Miss Quinn, Betsy and Julia, all white-faced with terror, their eyes telling her not to fight back. 'You can't shoot us all,' she managed to say, though she was as frightened as they were.

'One at a time, then.' He grinned. 'Who'd like to be first?'

'Why shoot us at all? What have we done to harm you?'

'Nothing, except bring the law down on my head. I warned Cecil I'd take you if he tried anything foolish, but it seems he does not value your life as much as I thought he did.'

'What do you want with me?'

'I want a carriage and horses brought to the door. Then we are going for a little ride.'

'We can't harness horses.' She put her hands in the

folds of her skirt to stop him seeing how much she was shaking.

'No, but your men can.'

'They are not here. They are out looking for Miss Darton.'

'That filly?' He grinned at Julia. 'She's a game one, I'll give her that. Fought like a wild cat, she did. And who taught her to ride like that, I wonder?'

'My grandfather, the Earl of Malcomby,' Julia said defiantly. 'And he will have something to say about all this when I tell him. So will my papa.'

'Viscount Darton!' He hawked into the dying embers of the fire. 'That's what I think of that muckworm.' He pointed the gun directly at Julia's head, making the other women gasp. Julia's eyes filled with tears, but she dare not move. 'We shall just have to wait here until he comes and then he'll harness the horses fast enough, don't you think?'

'Then you might have a long wait,' Charlotte said as calmly as she could, wondering as she spoke what had happened to Lord Falconer. Augustus Spike could not have known he was there or he would not have slammed the door almost in his face, but why had he not hammered on it, demanding to be let in? Unless he knew there was something wrong. 'He has no reason to think his daughter is not safe in her bed and he is busy on the beach,

helping the Coast Blockade men round up your confederates. Why would he come back here tonight?'

The man laughed, though he did not take the gun
from Julia's head. 'He won't be able to resist
coming to see his light o' love, all fired up he'll be,
thinking he's got us all nabbed and not expecting
to see me—'

They were startled by a loud knock on the door
and the women looked at each other. Augustus
turned a little, but he still pointed the gun at Julia.
None of the women dared make a move against him
in case it went off. 'Open the door,' he said to
Charlotte. 'And not a word unless you want a bullet
in your back.'

She rose and slipped the catch, easing it back
slowly. It was not Stacey, but her great-uncle who
stood on the step. She could see no one else. 'Let
me in, Charlotte,' he said.

'I can't.'

'Let the man in,' Augustus ordered.

Charlotte threw back the door and his lordship
stepped over the threshold. He did not seem at all
surprised at what he saw, but Augustus Spike was.
He had been expecting Stacey and this man was a
stranger. 'Who are you?' he demanded.

'Lord Falconer,' he said. 'And who are you? What
are you doing in my niece's house?'

'Your niece?' The man laughed raucously and the gun, no longer trained on Julia, was brought to bear on Charlotte. 'If you value her life, you'll do as I say. I want a coach and horses put at my disposal. As you see, I have a pistol and it is loaded and primed.'

'Then may I offer you my carriage? It is at the door.' For an elderly man he was uncommonly calm, Charlotte marvelled. Fleetingly she wondered how he would get his equipage back if Mr Spike used it to escape the law.

'Show me.'

His lordship turned and preceded him to the door. Augustus grabbed him and used him as a shield as he stepped outside and looked around. But the yard was deserted and a fine carriage and four of the best cattle he had seen in a very long time were harnessed to it. Charlotte, who had started after them and been restrained by Miss Quinn, watched with her hand to her mouth as Spike prodded his prisoner with the pistol towards the coach and opened the door with his free hand. 'Get in, you'll do instead of your niece. No one's likely to stop the illustrious Lord Falconer, are they?'

# Chapter Eleven

Charlotte, who had ventured as far as the kitchen door, saw her uncle suddenly duck sideways and a man leaped from the interior of the carriage, bowling Augustus to the ground. It was a mad thing to do with the pistol in the hands of that maniac and Charlotte's heart was in her mouth until she saw the pistol skid away across the yard. Lord Falconer, nimble for his age, picked it up, but he could not use it because the two men, Augustus Spike and Stacey, were struggling together, rolling around in the dirt, first one on top, then the other.

Other men appeared from behind the side of the house and the stables, including Jem and Jenkins, and though they gathered round, ready to intervene should the Viscount need their help, they did nothing but watch. Stacey was incensed and determined to punish his man before the law stepped in. He was battering him for terrifying Julia, for what had been done to Charlotte, his normally calm eyes red with fury. Nor was he having it all his own way; his opponent was not one to give up without a struggle. The noise of neighing horses, of things clattering about the yard and men's voices, brought the other women and Julia running to the door to watch with Charlotte in fascinated horror. At last, with Augustus Spike looking the worse for wear, Stacey broke off the fight and stood up, somewhat unsteadily. 'Take him away,' he said to Gerard, dusting himself down.

Augustus was led away to join his fellow smugglers in the prison van, leaving Stacey to look around for Charlotte and Julia. They were standing side by side in the kitchen doorway. Charlotte had her arm about his daughter, who was clinging to her, pale faced and wide-eyed, though the earlier terror had gone to be replaced by excitement and pride that her father could be so brave.

He held out his arms and she ran into them. 'Oh, Papa! Papa! Are you hurt?'

'No, my sweet, a few bruises, nothing more.'

'He said he would kill me.'

'Well, he can't do it now.' He looked over her head at Charlotte. She was looking at him, unsure of herself, and he remembered the last time he had seen her, down on the beach as the smugglers came ashore, and he had spoken harshly to her. He hadn't meant it, surely she realised that? He smiled and held out his hand to her. 'Charlotte?'

She joined Julia in his encircling arms. He held them both close against him and breathed a deep sigh. They were safe, these two women of his, and if he had his way he would never part from either of them again. 'It's all over,' he said softly. 'You are safe.'

Gerard coughed behind him, reminding him he had an audience, not that he cared about that, but there was still a little unfinished business to see to before he could have that talk with Charlotte. And he supposed that later it would have to include Lord Falconer and Julia. He put them gently from him. 'Time you were in bed, Julia. I will talk to you in the morning.'

'You are not angry with me?'

He was tempted to tell her he had never been so angry in his life, but then he smiled. Somehow or other he would tame her, he and Charlotte between them, and she would grow into a beautiful young woman, to be unselfish and consider others, to feel compassion for those less fortunate, as Charlotte did, but he hoped she would never lose her spirit. 'Do you not think I should be?' he asked mildly.

'Oh, yes, but I am so dreadfully sorry and I promise I will never disobey you again.'

He laughed joyously. 'Do not make promises you cannot keep, sweetheart. Now go indoors and go to bed. I will see you in the morning.'

'It is morning already.' She pointed at the eastern sky where the light of dawn tinged the sea on the distant horizon a coral pink.

'So it is. You have been up all night. Now go and sleep. I will be there when you wake.'

She went reluctantly. He turned to Charlotte. 'You, too, my darling.'

She turned her face up to his. His hair was falling over his eyes, there was a blue-black bruise forming beneath one eye and a small cut on his chin. His knuckles were rapidly turning black and blue. 'And are you still angry with me?'

'I never was.'

'It sounded like anger to me.'

'I am sorry, my love, I was worried and spoke in haste. Please go to bed and try to sleep. You are exhausted and we have a lot to talk about, but that will do after you have rested. I must bid Captain Topham goodbye and talk to his lordship. I am afraid I have not made a very good first impression on him.'

She turned to look at her uncle, who was watching them, a look of bewilderment on his face. There was so much to say, so much to explain, so many questions she wanted to ask— Why he had turned up at that particular time? How they had contrived the trap for Augustus? What had they said to each other? What would happen in the future, to her and her school, to the Manor, to the captured smugglers, Cecil in particular?—but she was so tired they refused to form themselves into words.

Stacey lifted her hand to his lips and turned it over so that he kissed the inside of her wrist. Oh, how bittersweet that was and how it made her long to be in his arms, but there were a dozen men watching her, not to mention Betsy and Miss Quinn, who stood in the kitchen doorway, grinning like a couple of Cheshire cats. 'Goodnight,' she whispered. 'Come soon, won't you?'

'Try keeping me away.'

She turned and went into the kitchen, weariness in every bone of her body, and it was not simply that she had been up all night, but the emotional turmoil she had been through. And it was not over yet. She was in for a quizzing from Lord Falconer and Stacey would still want to know why she had not kept a better watch on his daughter. If she had prevented Julia from going out, then Mr Spike would never have been able to force his way into The Crow's Nest and his lordship and Stacey would not have been put at risk. How could he forgive her for that? How could she forgive herself?'

'Did Julia go to bed?' she asked Joan Quinn.

'Yes, but she swore she would not sleep until you had been up to see her.'

'I'll go now. You both go to bed.'

'My lady, it will not be worth the bother; it will be time to start breakfast in less than an hour,' Betsy said. 'I'd sooner stay awake.'

'Me too,' Miss Quinn said. 'Lizzie and Fanny will be stirring soon. You go up. We'll see to everything.'

'But there is Lord Falconer. He must be accommodated.' She turned to him. He was sitting at the table, eating a cake Betsy had put in front of him. 'My lord, I am sorry to be such a poor hostess.'

'It is of no consequence. Go to bed. We will talk in the morning.'

'Very well.' And to the servants. 'You will call me when Lord Darton comes, won't you?'

They smiled knowingly at each other and assured her they would and she climbed the stairs to Julia's room, fully expecting to find her asleep, but the child was awake and waiting for her. Charlotte sat on the edge of the bed, reaching out to stroke the girl's cheek. 'You must sleep now, Julia. You must be very tired.'

'I couldn't, not until I'd said sorry. I should not have taken Ivor.'

'No, you should not. You gave us all a terrible

fright, you know, but you are safe now and we'll talk about it later, when your papa comes.'

'He will be angry.'

'Perhaps. There were bad men about tonight and that was why he wanted us to stay safely indoors.'

'He was very brave, wasn't he?'

'Yes.'

'I wasn't running away, you know. I only wanted to have a ride. I didn't mean to be gone long, but I couldn't find a way down to the beach. I rode through the wood and into the village and found the place the fishermen use for their boats and I had a lovely gallop along the water's edge.'

'We were looking for you, so why did no one see you?'

'I went the other way. I thought I would be back before you missed me, but it was so good to be on horseback and Ivor was enjoying it so much I stayed too long. And then, when I was nearly home, I heard a commotion on the beach and some shots and that horrible man jumped out at me from the trees and grabbed Ivor's bridle. He pulled me off…'

'Never mind,' Charlotte soothed as the girl showed signs of distress. 'Do not think of it.'

She gave a little giggle. 'He wanted to steal Ivor, but as soon as he climbed on his back Ivor threw him. He won't let anyone ride him but Papa. And me. He knows me.'

Charlotte smiled. 'Animals are often wiser than we are, you know.'

'The man pulled out that pistol and made me lead the horse back to the house. I was very frightened and—'

'You were very brave.'

'I am sorry, truly, I am. I won't do it again, I promise.'

'Good.' Charlotte pulled the covers up to Julia's chin and bent to kiss her forehead. 'Now go to sleep and when you wake, your papa will be here.'

'If he is angry, you will tell him I mean to be good. Tell him I don't want to leave and go to that other horrid school.'

'How do you know it is horrid?'

'Oh, it is bound to be. All the others were. I want to stay with you. I will be good...' Her eyelids drooped and she was asleep before she finished the sentence. Charlotte rose and left to go to her own bed.

In a few hours she would have to face Stacey and explain herself and she wished she could be as sure of forgiveness as Julia. Without it, there was no hope for her with Stacey. But, oh, how wonderful it was to hear him call her his darling. He would not have done that if he meant to ring a peal over her, would he?

Not that she didn't deserve it. She had been very remiss, negligent to the extent she had allowed one of her pupils to run into danger. Even if Stacey forgave her, she could never forgive herself. They had been right, those people who said she was not capable of running a school, and it was conceited of her to think she could. And she could not blame Stacey if he insisted on removing his daughter from her influence. She undressed and climbed into bed, not expecting to be able to sleep, but her weariness overcame her as soon as her head touched the pillow and she sank into oblivion.

She woke later to find the sun streaming through the window and the clock in the hall striking noon and her first waking thought, as it had been the last before she slept, was Stacey. She scrambled from her bed to find Miss Quinn quietly fetching out her clothes for the day. Over her arm she held a gown in dove grey sarcenet, trimmed with blue ruching under the bust and in several rows around the hem. It had a round neck filled with a lace bertha and puffed sleeves. 'Quinny, why have you brought that out? I am in mourning still.'

'No, you are not, my lady, beggin' your pardon. I reckon your mourning is done. You could go into half-mourning, or none at all. His lordship has been gone these three months now and he was not your own father, was he?'

'I loved him.'

'So you did, just as you loved Sir Grenville, but they would both have wanted you to be happy.'

'Is Lord Darton here?'

'He came, but you were asleep and he said not to wake you, he would return later. I think he went into the village with Lord Falconer. I heard tell there's men lining up at the Rectory…'

Charlotte hurried with her toilette and half an hour later was dressed and sitting over a cup of coffee in her little sitting room, having refused breakfast, and it was there Stacey found her. She rose to greet him, suddenly as shy as a young girl. He looked so big and, in spite of that dreadful bruise on his face and the little cut in his chin already healing, so handsome, dressed in a brown frockcoat, nankeen waistcoat and long straight trousers strapped under his shoes, emphasising the length of his legs.

He stood in the doorway, drinking in the sight of her. Her cheeks were pink, her wonderful aquamarine eyes so luminous they seemed to bathe him in their light. Her lips, rosy and inviting, were smiling just a little diffidently. If he had not known otherwise he would have taken her for someone ten years younger than her thirty years. Not that her age made the slightest difference to the way he felt about her. He loved her and would do so until the day he died.

'My lord,' she said, making a wobbly curtsy because all of a sudden her knees felt weak.

'How formal you are, Charlotte,' he said. 'Last night I was Stacey.'

'Last night was different.'

He strode towards her, taking her shoulders in his hands and looking down into her upturned face. 'How, different?'

'I was overwrought.'

'Does that mean you can only call me by my given name when you are upset?'

'No, of course not. Oh, I don't know what I mean. You must be very angry with me and I do not blame you. Why I was so conceited as to imagine I was capable of looking after other people's children, I do not know.'

'Oh, my love, you are a natural mother and you want to mother every child you meet and that is wonderful. And I am not angry. How could I be? I asked too much of you. Julia—'

'Please do not be cross with her. She is very sorry and I do not think she will do anything like that again. She had a nasty fright.'

'And so did you, and so I told her.'

'Oh, you have not scolded her, have you?'

'We had a long talk.'

'When?'

'While you were asleep. And it was not a scolding—well, only a very little one—but a talk about how we are to go on.'

'Oh. And how are we to go on?'

'That depends on you, my love.' He took her hand and led her to the sofa, a solid affair, well upholstered in brown leather, more used to Captain MacArthur's bulk than her slight weight, and pulled her down beside him. 'You are my love, you know that, don't you?'

'Am I?' She said it dreamily as if she were still half-asleep, which she supposed she must be.

'Always. I think I knew it the very first time I saw you, that's why, when I met John Hardacre and he told me about Cecil and those other two, I knew I had to protect you from them. But I was worried about Julia too, so I hit on the idea of bringing her to you, to your school. I did not know anything about the smuggling then.'

'I have not been able to teach her very much.'

'She has learned a very great deal, and so she admits.' He chuckled suddenly. 'And she will not have a word said against you. She begged me not to be angry with you, that it was all her fault, and she wants to stay with you.'

'Here?'

'Wherever you are. You see, I told her that I loved you and I intended to ask you to marry me—'

'Marry me?' She interrupted him. Dare she believe what she was hearing? Did he really love her? 'Do you mean it?'

'I never meant anything more in my whole life.'

'But you can't want to marry me.'

'And why not, pray? I love you. We are both single. Unless the idea is abhorrent to you.'

'Of course it isn't. It's just…'

'Go on.'

'I am too old to give you an heir.'

He put his head back and laughed. 'Is that all?'

'But surely that must weigh with you?'

'No, it does not. You are in your prime, and if we are blessed with children, then I shall be overjoyed, but if not, then I shall lose no sleep over it. I love you and want you for my wife, even if we have no more children. We have three between us already.'

'They are all girls.'

'And delightful they are too. Charlotte, can you not get it into your head that the prospect of a life without you is not to be borne?' He paused to put her hand to his lips and give her time to absorb what he had said. 'But before that can happen, I have a confession to make. Lord Falconer insists I must and I suppose he is right, even though I know you will hate me for it. Except, of course,' he added, 'I know there is no room for hate in your heart.'

'Go on.'

'When I won your jewels from Sir Roland and Augustus Spike, I intended simply to return them to you, but when you said you had to sell them, I decided that I could not allow that. I took the London mail and went to see John Hardacre.' He paused, unsure whether she was listening. She seemed to have a faraway look in her eyes as if she was looking at something he could not see. 'Charlotte, please pay attention.'

'Oh, I am. You went to see Mr Hardacre and suddenly he found money for me he knew nothing about before. I thought it was strange, because Grenville would have told me about it at the time he did it and I would never have said Mr Hardacre was an incompetent lawyer, just the opposite. I know he was worried about me and I thought perhaps he had provided it himself, but then I did not think he was so well up in the stirrups that he could afford to give so much away. Then I thought it might possibly be my great-uncle, but why he would do it after all these years and in secret too I could not fathom. Last night when we were talking it was clear to me he had known nothing of the money because Mr Hardacre had written to tell him I needed help. It was why he came. When I woke up this morning it was as if it had all become clear to me in my sleep. It had to be you.'

'Oh.'

'I'm glad you told me. But why did you do it?'

'Because I knew I loved you, but it was much too soon to tell you that and I wanted you and Julia to become acquainted. How else was I to do it?'

'Oh, Stacey…'

'So I am Stacey again now, am I?'

'Yes. I don't know what to say.'

'Tell me you love me and you will marry me. Everyone else thinks it will be a very good thing.'

'Everyone?'

'Julia and his lordship, though I had a devil of a job persuading him that I was not made in the same mould as Cecil Hobart and his cronies and I was not a gambler—'

'Oh, but, Stacey, you are.' She laughed.

'No, I am not. I learned to play cards in the army and found I was very good at it, but I never gambled more than I could easily afford to lose, I told you that before. And Cecil is too hot tempered to make a good player. I have no need to gamble ever again.'

'What about that game you were going to have with him today? Or was it yesterday? I am losing all track of time.'

'Hobart can't oblige now, can he?' He was doing his very best to be patient with her, but he wished she would stop quizzing him and consent to marry him. He wanted to kiss her, he wanted to kiss her very much, and she must surely know that. 'He is on his way back to India with all his debts paid.'

'How can that be? I heard him say he was dished up.' She paused and gave a tiny chuckle. 'Did you pay them?'

'My darling, how could I when most of his debt was to me?'

'The house!' she exclaimed. 'It was all he had left. Stacey, do you own Easterley Manor now?'

'Yes, my darling. I think, until I come into my inheritance, it will make us a splendid home and you can continue to teach the village children if you wish. It was all you really wanted to do, wasn't it?'

'Oh, Stacey!' Her eyes were alight.

'So will you marry me now?'

'Stacey Darton!' she said sharply. 'Did you think that being able to return to the Manor would make one jot of difference to whether I said yes or no? I love the old house, but I love you more—' She stopped when he gave a delighted chuckle and folded her into his arms to kiss her. He kissed her on the forehead, on each cheek, on her rosy mouth. He ran his lips down her throat and into the cleft of her breasts. He kissed her hands and arms and then his mouth went back to her lips, where it stayed, gently teasing, until they were both too breathless to continue.

'Now, will you say yes?' he demanded.

'Yes, oh, yes, please.' She turned and clung to him, returning his kisses with a fervour that thrilled him. She was the woman he had been seeking all his adult life and he was never going to let her go.

But they had to come back to reality—there were sounds outside the door, people about, voices. Charlotte sat up and tried to straighten her hair as someone knocked. Stacey rose and went to stand by the window as if gazing out towards the cliffs and Charlotte called, 'Come in.'

'Lord Falconer, my lady,' Betsy announced, looking from her mistress, all pink and flustered, with her hair falling down and her lips all swollen, and the Viscount, staring out of the window pretending nonchalance just as if he had been there all the time and not sprawled on the sofa kissing her ladyship.

His lordship passed the maid and strolled into the room, putting his hat, cane and gloves on the table. 'Well?' he demanded. 'Am I to felicitate you?'

'Oh, Uncle, of course,' Charlotte said. 'You shall be the first to know.'

Betsy retreated to pass the news to the rest of the staff, Miss Quinn and Jem, who had recovered from the carpeting he had received from his lordship for letting Miss Julia slip through his fingers and take Ivor, and Jenkins, who had come to help feed the horses and prepare Lord Falconer's carriage for the journey back to Hertfordshire.

'It is all arranged,' Stacey said. 'We are to make our home at Easterley Manor after we are married.'

'Good.' He came and took Charlotte's hands and held her at arm's length to look at her, before bending to kiss her cheek. 'Be happy,' he murmured. 'You have my blessing. And write to me. Often. We have a great deal of catching up to do.'

'Yes, I promise.'

'If you'd been a boy, you'd have been my heir, did you know that?'

'No, my lord, I did not. Have you no family?'

'I had a son, but he died three years ago. It was then I decided that I ought to try to find my niece and heal the breach.'

'Mama has been dead these ten years.'

'I discovered that when I travelled to Portsmouth, her last known direction, and I also learned she had had a daughter, but no one knew what had become of her. It was not until I heard from Mr Hardacre that I knew your married name and where you lived.'

'Now you have found me.' She smiled at him. He was really a very agreeable man, not the ogre she had always imagined him to be. 'And Lizzie and Fanny too.'

'Naturally. And who knows, you might yet produce a male child for me.'

She heard Stacey grunt, but decided not to comment; they had already said what had to be said on that subject. 'My lord, how did you know Mr Spike would want a carriage?'

He chuckled. 'He did not know I was behind you, did he? I thought of knocking and demanding to be let in, but there had been so many strange things happening during the night, I guessed you must have walked into a trap. Thank goodness you did not tell the fellow I was there. I crept round to the window and luckily it was open a little way and I heard everything. Then all I had to do was find the Viscount.'

'And do you approve of him?' It was not said with any seriousness because she knew the answer, but it made Stacey draw in his breath for a moment.

He grinned. 'Does it matter if I do not?'

'Not a bit, but I should like to think we shall all deal well together.'

'I do not doubt it. Now, I am an old man and all

this excitement has knocked me up. I need my own bed, those little sticks of wood you call beds are devilish hard.'

'I am sorry for that. They are meant for children. But you will come back for the wedding?'

'No, I'm not risking those beds again. I expect you to go to your nuptials from Falcon Court, the family home.'

She looked at Stacey, eyebrow raised in a question. 'If that is what you wish, of course, my love,' he said.

'Then, Uncle, I shall let you know just as soon as we have arranged a date.'

'And how soon will that be, my love?' Stacey enquired mildly

'Just as soon as you please,' she replied, her face a picture of happiness; it positively glowed. Stacey, who thought the same thing every day, decided he had never seen her look so lovely.

'If I had my way, it will be tomorrow,' he said, and then added with a sigh, 'But I suppose there will be arrangements to make.'

'But what about this house?' she asked, suddenly remembering her agreement with Captain MacArthur. 'I am supposed to be its caretaker until Captain MacArthur returns.'

'Please do not tell me I am expected to wait another eleven months.'

'Not if I can persuade Jenkins to take on the task on a day-to-day basis. If we are at the Manor, we will not be far away and can keep an eye on it.'

'I have already spoken to him, my love, and he has agreed.'

'Oh, you devil! Can you read my mind?'

'I wish I could,' he said with a sigh. 'So, tell me, when are we to be wed?'

'Six weeks from now. It will give me time to make all the arrangements, and you have to take Julia home and tell the Earl. You do not think he will object, do you?'

'No, he will be delighted.' He felt sure that was true. His father wanted to see him married and he could have no possible objection to the great-niece of Lord Falconer.

Lord Falconer took her shoulders in his hands and looked down into her upturned face. 'Just like your mama,' he said. 'But I loved her, you know.' Then he kissed her on both cheeks, shook hands with Stacey and picked up his gloves, hat and cane. 'I shall expect you at Falcon Court in four weeks' time.'

They accompanied him to the door and watched as he climbed into his carriage and was driven away, then they returned to the parlour to carry on where they left off when he had interrupted them. But not for long. Lizzie, followed by Fanny with Julia bringing up the rear, burst into the room.

'Mama—' Lizzie demanded, stopping short when she saw her mother with Lord Darton's arm about her. She took a deep breath. 'Julia says you are going to marry her papa. Is it true?'

Charlotte looked up at Stacey and smiled, then turned to put her arms about both her daughters. 'Yes, it is. Shall you mind?' She did not know what she would do if there were hostility, but if Julia had been won round, surely her daughters would cause no problems?

'No, I like Lord Darton.'

'So do I,' Fanny echoed.

Stacey threw back his head and laughed. Never in all his adult life had a child ever said that of him, not even his own daughter, and he suddenly realised it pleased him prodigiously. 'And I like you, too, all of you.' He held out his arms and all three girls flew into them.

Charlotte, watching, smiled. 'Whatever gave you the idea you did not like children?' she murmured, but he was too busy answering their questions to hear her.

Six weeks later, Charlotte married Stacey at the little church on the Falconer estate, dressed in a gown of duck-egg-blue satin, attended by three very proud young ladies, dressed alike in pink. It was not a hugely grand affair as neither wanted that, but in spite of that the church was crowded with family and friends, some of whom had made the journey from Parson's End to attend, including the Reverend Fuller who officiated, aided by Lord Falconer's own chaplain.

Lord Falconer, who had been alone ever since his wife and son died, was delighted to find himself the patriarch of a ready-made family, even if they were all girls. There would be others and, with luck, one might be a boy, and what a legacy he would have! He had missed Charlotte's growing up and he regretted his stubbornness, but he meant to make up for it. For the moment she did not need him. Her happiness shone from her eyes, as she looked at her new husband and hugged her daughters, all three of them, for Julia, who had never known a mother, was thrilled that at last she had someone to call Mama.

The girls were to return with the Earl and Countess to stay at Malcomby Hall while Stacey and Charlotte took a short wedding trip to London to catch the end of the Season. He was looking forward to showing her off on his arm and taking her to another ball. And this time it would not end in tears.

'Oh, Stacey, I am so happy,' she said, as their carriage bore them away, followed by the cries of their well-wishers who stood on the gravel outside his lordship's palatial home to wave them off.

'And I, my love.' He put his arm about her shoulders and drew her towards him, knocking off her new bonnet as he did so, but neither noticed as he kissed her.

Up on the box, Jem grinned. It was going to be like that all the way to London, he supposed.

* * * * *

# HISTORICAL ROMANCE™

LARGE PRINT

## THE BRIDE'S SEDUCTION
### *Louise Allen*

Miss Marina Winslow assumed she would never marry. Then, Justin Ransome, Earl of Mortenhoe, proposed a sensible, practical, *passionless* match. Marina knew it was madness to accept his bargain when she had tumbled head over heels in love with him, but his honesty touched her. Perhaps she could risk her heart…

## A SCANDALOUS SITUATION
### *Patricia Frances Rowell*

Her past was a dark country and Iantha Kethley was trapped at its borders – until the day she held Lord Duncan at gunpoint, and he offered her a future she had never dared imagine! He recognised the effort it took Iantha to maintain her control, but he was sure he could help her – if she would let him close enough. Yet even while she began to heal, danger pursued Iantha…

## THE WARLORD'S MISTRESS
### *Juliet Landon*

Powerful warlord Fabian Cornelius Peregrinus must quell the rebellious hill tribes at this northern outpost of the Roman Empire. From the precision of their raids on Hadrian's Wall, he knows someone has inside information. Dania Rhiannon has kept her true origins hidden. Wealthy officers are drawn to her House of Women by night. Is Fabian truly attracted – or does he suspect what lies beneath her mantle of respectability?

MILLS & BOON®

Live the emotion

HIST0107 L

# HISTORICAL ROMANCE™

LARGE PRINT

## MISTAKEN MISTRESS
### *Margaret McPhee*

To her spiteful aunt, Kathryn Marchant is little more than a servant. That's about to change, when Kathryn falls into the arms of the most notorious rake of them all. Lord Ravensmede draws the line at seducing virgins, although once he has tasted the lips of the delectable Miss Marchant, he wants her! Could her temptation prove just too sweet to resist…?

## THE INCONVENIENT DUCHESS
### *Christine Merrill*

Compromised and wedded on the same day, Lady Miranda was fast finding married life not to her taste. A decaying manor and a secretive husband were hardly the stuff of girlish dreams. Yet every time she looked at dark, brooding Marcus Radwell, Duke of Haughleigh, she felt inexplicably compelled – and determined – to make their marriage real!

## FALCON'S DESIRE
### *Denise Lynn*

Emboldened by grief, she had ensnared the infamous Rhys, Lord of Faucon. Now, imprisoned in her castle, Faucon posed an even greater threat – not to her defences, but to her heart. They established an uneasy truce. But would that be destroyed when she learned a new-found alliance bound her to him as his bride?

MILLS & BOON®
Live the emotion

HIST0207 LP

# HISTORICAL ROMANCE™

LARGE PRINT

## A LADY OF RARE QUALITY
### *Anne Ashley*

They have never seen Viscount Greythorpe listen so intently when a lady speaks. To have caught the eye of this esteemed gentleman, Miss Annis Milbank must be a lady of rare quality indeed. Innocent to the world, the question of who the beautiful Annis will marry has never been foremost in her mind… However, Viscount Greythorpe is confident she will soon be his…

## THE NORMAN'S BRIDE
### *Terri Brisbin*

Recalling nothing of her own identity, Isabel was sure her rescuer, Royce, had once been a knight, for he expressed a chivalry that his simple way of life could not hide. William Royce de Severin could not quell his desire for this intriguing woman. Unbroken in spirit, she made him hunger for the impossible – a life free of dark secrets, with Isabel by his side.

## TALK OF THE TON
### *Mary Nichols*

Her name was on everyone's lips. They were agog to find out what Miss Elizabeth Harley had been doing down at the docks. And in such shocking apparel! Elizabeth had not meant to sully her good name. All she had craved was a chance to travel. Andrew Melhurst had come to her rescue when she needed him most, but should she consider marrying him to save her reputation?

MILLS & BOON®

Live the emotion

HIST0307 I

# HISTORICAL ROMANCE™

## LARGE PRINT

## AN IMPROPER COMPANION
### *Anne Herries*

Daniel, Earl of Cavendish, finds the frivolity of the *ton* dull after serving in the Peninsula War. Boredom disappears when he is drawn into the mystery surrounding the abduction of gently bred girls. His investigation endangers his mother's companion, Miss Elizabeth Travers. Tainted by scandal, her cool response commands Daniel's respect – while her beauty demands so much more…

## THE VISCOUNT
### *Lyn Stone*

The young man who appears late at night at Viscount Duquesne's door is not all he seems. Dressed as a boy to escape the hellhole in which she has been imprisoned, Lady Lily Bradshaw must throw herself on the mercy of a ruthless rake. Viscount Duquesne soon finds himself captivated by this bold lady – and he can't resist her audacious request for a helping hand…in marriage!

## THE VAGABOND DUCHESS
### *Claire Thornton*

He had promised to return – but Jack Bow was dead. And Temperance Challinor's life was changed for ever. She must protect her unborn child – by pretending to be Jack's widow. A foolproof plan. Until she arrives at Jack's home…and the counterfeit widow of a vagabond becomes the real wife of a very much alive *duke*!

MILLS & BOON®

*Live the emotion*

HIST0407 LP

# HISTORICAL ROMANCE™

## LARGE PRINT

## NOT QUITE A LADY
### *Louise Allen*

Miss Lily France has launched herself upon the Marriage Mart in style! The wealthy and beautiful heiress is determined to honour her much-loved father's last wish – and trade her vulgar new money for marriage to a man with an ancient and respected title. Then she meets untitled, irresistible and very unsuitable Jack Lovell – but he is the one man she cannot buy!

## THE DEFIANT DEBUTANTE
### *Helen Dickson*

Eligible, attractive, Alex Montgomery, Earl of Arlington, is adored by society ladies and a string of mistresses warm his bed. He's yet to meet a woman who could refuse him… Then he is introduced to the strikingly unconventional Miss Angelina Hamilton, and Alex makes up his mind to tame this headstrong girl!  But Miss Hamilton has plans of her own – and they don't include marriage to a rake!

## A NOBLE CAPTIVE
### *Michelle Styles*

Strong, proud and honourable – soldier Marcus Livius Tullio embodied the values of Rome. Captured and brought to the Temple of Kybele, he was drawn towards the woman who gave him refuge. Fierce, beautiful and determined – pagan priestess Helena despised all that Rome stood for. She knew she must not be tempted by this handsome soldier, because to succumb to her desires would be to betray all her people…

MILLS & BOON®

Live the emotion

HIST0507